Justin Myers is a writer and editor from Shipley, Yorkshire, who now lives in London. After years working in journalism, he began his popular, anonymous dating blog The Guyliner in 2010, spent five years as dating and advice columnist in *Gay Times* and is now a weekly columnist at British *GQ*. His work has appeared in a number of publications including the *Guardian*, *BuzzFeed* and the *Irish Times*, and his first novel *The Last Romeo* was published in 2018.

Follow Justin online:
@theguyliner
www.theguyliner.com

THE
LAST
ROMEO

Justin Myers

piatkus

PIATKUS

First published in Great Britain as a paperback original in 2018 by Piatkus

1 3 5 7 9 10 8 6 4 2

A CIP catalogue record for this book
is available from the British Library.

ISBN 978-0-349-41691-5

Typeset in Caslon by M Rules
Printed and bound in Great Britain
by Clays Ltd, St Ives plc

Papers used by Piatkus are from well-managed forests
and other responsible sources.

MIX
Paper from
responsible sources
FSC® C104740

Piatkus
An imprint of
Little, Brown Book Group
Carmelite House
50 Victoria Embankment
London EC4Y 0DZ

An Hachette UK Company
www.hachette.co.uk

www.littlebrown.co.uk

*To Mum, for everything, especially
her resolute belief in me.*

*And to Dad, for his unwavering
pride and encouragement.*

'No one cared who I was until
I put on the mask.'

—Bane, *The Dark Knight Rises*

One More Romeo:
a manifesto

Hello! Well.

As my last ever headteacher told me, while they held out their hand in anticipation of my spitting chewing gum into it, 'rules are rules'. They're important. Call it your set of commandments, a motto, a mission statement, a manifesto, what*ever* – it's important to know what you're doing, why you're doing it and where the hell you're going.

So welcome to **One More Romeo,** my blog. And I am your Romeo. The name seemed like a good idea at the time and that time is now. It's called that because I'm looking for another Romeo – I am gay, you see, so I'm afraid there's no room for Juliet in this tragedy – and I'm hoping there'll always be one more around the corner until ... well, until I need to stop looking altogether. But I'll come to that.

This is how it works: I'm on a dating site, packed with fantastic single men and also *other* single men. I arrange dates with these men – my Romeos, are you still with me? – and if there's anything worth saying, I blog about the evening we spend together. Anonymously.

I can feel you clenching now. Not another one. There's a lot of them about, I know. Dating blogs. I've seen them. They're all great in their own way, of course, but I think there's room for something a little bit different. Dare I say, something with heart? Someone. Maybe it's shallow to score men out of 10 for their behaviour on one night out with a stranger but **newsflash** we're judged and graded every second we walk the earth for much more superficial reasons.

Dating is weird and awkward and uncomfortable and the way we behave when we're swirling a mangy old slice of lime around a badly made gin and tonic in a (horrible) pub *they* chose tells us a lot about ourselves and the world. Sometimes it's funny, sometimes it's excruciating, sometimes it's outrageous and, often, it's a little dull.

So, the rules:

1. I only ever write about a Romeo I'm absolutely sure I'll never see again. If I started blogging about a guy I liked and was hoping to get into something with, that would be pretty awkward. So, if he gets blogged, I'm afraid that means – for whatever reason – it didn't work out. I know, I'm sad for me too.

2. To spare a few blushes, I always change a few details so the Romeo can't be identified. Although if he can't recognise *himself* then, wow, some self-awareness for table 5, please – but the hope is he won't because that wouldn't be nice. And I don't

make the dates up. I don't need to: people really *are* that fucking strange. I'm an unreliable narrator but I'm all you've got. I'll be as truthful as I dare.

3. I'm never horrible about a Romeo for no reason. I'll be nice about them unless they start being dicks to me and, guess what, quite a lot of guys need no provocation whatsoever to start behaving like a huge asshole, so buckle in for that one.

4. I spent the last six years with a guy who broke my heart every day and either never noticed or didn't care, so I will not break someone's heart, spirit, or trust for the sake of a blog post. Never. It's not in my nature. But I'm not going to be a doormat, either.

5. If a date goes badly and it's my fault, I'll never lie to make myself sound good and the Romeo sound bad. I'm not here to make myself sound amazing. If I wanted you to fall in love with me, I'd just show you my face and cook you breakfast because my eyes and my eggs are to die for, babycakes. Yes.

6. No shaming. If someone's not for me, they're not for me. I won't ever criticise anybody's looks unless they go in for me first. And well they might, because I look like the dish that ran away with the spoon. See? I told you I was an unreliable narrator.

7. I'm not going to date anyone just so I can fill space in my blog. Anyone I date I want to feel a *connection* with. I'm not sure I believe in 'the one' anymore, because of that guy I was telling you about who took a sledgehammer to my heart, but I do believe in the 'next one' and that will have to do for now.

8. Yes, the picture at the top of the blog and in my Twitter avatar really is a close-up of my lips. A friend told me I had great lips and I was, like, OK, and I couldn't think of another pic to use that wouldn't get me sued by a photographer. Other options included abstract snapshots of my arse, my hair and my right eye but none of them had the pulling power my lips do. And I'm going to be using those a LOT, if things go well.

9. Whether it takes five weeks, five months, or five years I will NOT stop until I meet someone who I think is worth giving it all up for. I'm thirty-four and the thought of still doing this when I'm nearly forty does kind of make me want to take a really long drink of something poisonous tbh but I have *integrity* and if this train stops, it has to stop for a reason. And when I meet him, you'll know – because I'll call him the **Last Romeo.** Weird thing is, I'm in no hurry whatsoever, yet I can't wait to meet him.

10. Don't ask who I am, don't ask what I do, or why. Just two months ago I was someone else. None of it matters other than the fact this is who I am now. And this is where we are.

I'm tired of calling up to the balcony in vain. Let's do this.

1.

Two Months Earlier

I felt disoriented, and a bit peaky. How was it possible I was here, right now, like this? That weird feeling when you arrive somewhere on holiday after a long flight, and are unpacking and you suddenly realise only this morning you were standing in your dingy kitchen in west London worrying about the taxi being late and now, here you are, thousands of miles away in a hotel room, realising your phone charger is ... back in that dingy kitchen. Unsettled, displaced, exposed – yet superhuman, because however you got there, you made it happen yourself. In an unfamiliar lounge of an unfamiliar flat, surrounded by boxes and bags containing the life of the stranger I was ten minutes ago, listening to the sound of the supposed love of my life plodding down the six flights of stairs that would take him outside and away from me, for ever, my life began.

Breaking up with Adam would've been easier if it had been over something headline-grabbing and dramatic. But he'd never played away from home, wasn't embezzling my savings account and never laid a finger on me. Adam's crimes were stealthy, his talent was wrong-footing me, or trying to fix me up to be less of an inconvenience. His love for me felt like a series of favours, with the repayment on each one becoming harder and harder to meet every time.

I had it all worked out, the day I finally made up my mind. Many a time, after an argument about money or his insistence I order something different from him in a restaurant, I'd fantasised about what I'd say if I ever decided to leave. Great long speeches, full of adjectives I never got to use in everyday life, to explain why I couldn't do it anymore. Tears, perhaps, or crockery shattering against a wall. I considered a trip to Ikea to make sure we had plenty to spare. He would beg my forgiveness, I decided, cling to my ankles as I strode majestically out of the flat. He would implore me to reconsider, tell me he'd change, and I'd half-smile, put my index finger to his lips, bid him hush, and say, evenly, 'Go fuck yourself, Adam.' The reality was different.

It was Tuesday. He clattered in, late, from his gym class and kicked off his shoes, slumping into a chair. Usually Adam didn't talk after he'd been to the gym; he liked to eat whatever I cooked in silence, either with headphones in or glued to his laptop. The dead hour, I called it, when I'd sit and wait for him to come round and notice me again, like a coquettish maid trying to catch her master's eye, and not a thirty-four-year-old man who'd been in this relationship for six long years. Too long. Jupiter years. But tonight there'd be no dead hour. It would live. He would hear me.

I remember the words coming out of my mouth and being disappointed at how badly they scanned. It wasn't poetic – I stammered like an adolescent giving a presentation in sex education, reddening and nervously scratching my chest, as I usually did whenever a video camera was pointing at me. Adam sat, his eyes bulging, not saying a word until I got to what I thought was my masterpiece.

'It's just ... we're not going anywhere. We go to the same

places, do the same things.' Would it be bad form to pour myself a glass of wine before I went on? Probably. 'And I wanna go to other places. I wanna ... you know, try different things, walk down streets I've never walked down before.'

I saw a vein throb in his head. 'Streets?'

It sounded amazing in my head – brave and powerful – but now it seemed crass and melodramatic.

'By "streets you haven't walked down before", do you mean ...' He bristled. 'Are you seeing someone else?'

'No!'

It was the last cruel trick of our relationship that I couldn't tell him why I really wanted it to end. He wouldn't understand; it would sound even more foolish. How do you tell someone that despite paying the rent, turning up to weddings beside you, tilting their head just-so in your couples selfies and being to all intents and purposes a great boyfriend, that they actually *weren't*? His knack for filling me with self-doubt at every turn with just one look or a carefully chosen word, his dismissiveness of my career, disdain for anything I liked to do, gearing our social life toward his own interests, the ceaseless commentary on what I assumed were my little quirks or harmless faults but were, to Adam, behavioural abnormalities that must be curbed. Nothing went unchecked, ever. How do you explain to someone that you feel owned, insignificant, without making them feel terrible? I knew, then, as I watched Adam slowly pour himself a glass of wine – none for me, eternally the Gretchen Wieners – that the easiest way to do this would be to make him think the fault was all mine. Because I didn't actually *want* Adam to have an epiphany, or beg me for forgiveness, or clutch my ankles. I wanted him to let me go. For all his outward calm, I could tell he was shocked, because he downed the wine immediately – 'James, you're supposed to sip it, not throw it back like you're on an all-inclusive to Magaluf' was always a favourite line of his – and poured another. His eyes were moist but he didn't look sad. I realised these were tears of anger.

'Well,' he said, finally, after another glass of wine was down the hatch and I was done stumbling through my apologies. 'You'd better move into the spare room.'

I wasn't expecting him to suggest we flat-shared, so I asked him what he meant.

'You've got a month, Jim. More than kind under the circumstances.' He unbuttoned his shirt and started to walk out of the room. 'From now on, you're a lodger. Four weeks today, I want you gone. If it's over, it's over.' I heard the bathroom door slam and the shower jerk into life.

Lodger. Wow. This was cold, even for him. How could he be so calculated, so *transactional* already? And then it dawned on me. Adam obviously thought he'd be the one to end it. He was the catch, he had the cash. He was tall, loaded, handsome and popular, with a huge circle of friends who adored him – his friends had become mine, while I had few of my own – and a great future ahead of him. Everybody brushed his faults aside because the idea of him was so attractive. But I rejected it. And I was probably the first person ever to do so.

My phone rang, echoing against the bare white walls of my new flat. Someone calling?! My phone was strictly for messaging, tweeting and occasionally writing out panicked articles or correcting mistakes in ones I'd just published, before the boss saw – everyone knew that. It was my best friend, Bella; I wouldn't answer for many, but for her I did.

'Well?' She sounded breathless, nervous.

'He's just left, actually.'

'You in the new flat?'

'Yes.'

We were silent for a few seconds.

'It's fine.' I sniffed loudly as my eyes began to water.

'Oh, Jim.' Bella's voice faltered. 'Was he a dick about it? Do you want me to come and stroke your hair and tell you everything's going to be all right?'

'No, I don't,' I whimpered. 'But I've got a duty-free bottle of Patrón crying out to be poured down my throat by a willing volunteer, while Céline Dion plays very loudly in the background.'

Bella laughed. 'Queen Céline, count me in. I've had a shit day and work can go fuck itself tomorrow.'

'You're an icon.'

'I know. Do you want me to bring pyjamas and stay over, or are you being a special brave boy who can totally do this on your own?'

I looked around. I listened to the din of the traffic outside. It was starting to get dark.

'I *can* do it alone,' I said. 'But, well, bring pyjamas. Just in case.'

I dug into a box that looked like it might have shot glasses and tumblers in it to prepare for Bella's arrival, unearthing all kinds of treasures and artefacts that I'd hurriedly packed. I remembered when I had decided I couldn't go on, just twenty-nine days earlier. Monday morning. Singing in the shower, the most ridiculous of things. I was just croaking my way through the chorus of 'Into the Groove' – the only song I ever sing in the shower – and soaping what I will call an intimate area, when the door flew open and Adam appeared at the frosted screen, his face angry and contorted like a gargoyle.

'Are you ever going to get to the middle-eight?' he spat. 'I'm late for work.'

I looked down at my crotch. 'I'm washing my dick, Boo.' Our cutesy pet name for one another, derived of about a hundred previous bastardisations neither of us could remember. We often

9

used it to disarm a potentially explosive situation but recently it seemed more flammable than ever. 'I didn't know my singing bothered you. You used to like it.'

I sensed he was about to say something noxious, but the sight of me naked and pathetic as water bounced off my shoulders stopped him. He took a breath. 'You sing the same bit over and over. It's fucking annoying, especially when I need to be in here.' When Adam wanted the bathroom, he 'needed' it – my own ablutions were nothing but inconvenient whimsy. If I got to the bathroom before him – even if I was doing an early shift – I'd emerge to find him pacing outside like a bad-tempered tiger, waiting to rip my head off.

It looked like my turn on the karaoke would have to wait. Without taking my eyes off him, I slowly turned the tap until the water stopped, and with a sponge covering my party zone, I climbed out of the tub, suds drifting to the floor and onto his pyjamas. I didn't reach for my towel, just stalked out of the bathroom in a rush of steam, leaving only wet footprints behind me, my head throbbing with helplessness. And that's when I absolutely knew. Adam had taken my voice away one time too often. I never complained, never explained. I just accepted, smiling beatifically by his side while the world gazed on adoringly. I'd let it happen over six years, and that was my own fault, but no more. I couldn't love a man who wouldn't let me sing.

'How was it?' Bella took off her coat and pulled an Edvard Munch face in anticipation of my reply. She'd always liked Adam but harboured suspicions. Whenever I hinted all was not well in the plush, perfect Brodie–Nardini household, paid for with Adam's crazy salary, she would narrow her eyes and tell me, 'The trouble with Adam is he's too good-looking. Society tells hot people they never have to try, that we're lucky to have them. And you' – here she would prod me in the chest or, if it were after midnight, brandish a cocktail glass in my face – 'you let him get away with it, because you believe it, too.'

I handed Bella a crisp packet. Empty. She looked at it like it was a used condom. 'Is this symbolism?' she asked. 'We're not back in English Lit with Mrs Ramsbottom, are we? Fucking hell, Jim. We don't have time for that.'

I'd known Bella since we were teenagers. A mutual roll of the eyes across a boring French class soon made us firm friends. Through my coming-out, our boyfriends, moving houses and even escaping to different cities, one thing remained: our friendship. It never faltered, and despite terrible taste in men, we had excellent taste in each other. We shared various dives together for years until she met a man who made her ring-finger itchy. Dear Drew. We congratulated ourselves on how grown up we'd become, cooed over interiors magazines picking out expensive drinks cabinets we'd never buy, and met for boozy brunches, telling ourselves we were being ironic. Drew and Bella lived together for years until, one day, Bella took off her engagement ring to wash up and never put it back on, experiencing a revelation amid the bubbles. After being part of our lives, birthday gatherings and Facebook photos for so long, Drew was gone, almost overnight, and Bella spent two weeks in our spare room while I continually, dutifully, agreed she'd done the right thing. She'd been happily single and turning up to lunch in various states of hungover ever since. She understood. We were bonded by our secrets. She was the only person I wanted near me in the post-Adam fallout – which was lucky, as many of our 'mutual' friends were not returning my calls.

'I cried over that sodding crisp packet earlier,' I sighed. 'It was Adam's.'

Bella stared at it. 'Monster Munch, really? Mr Eat Clean? Adam, we barely knew thee. Why the fuck were you crying over it?'

'Because I feel like I've done something terrible. Ruined his life. His face when he left.'

Bella sat on the battered red sofa that had followed me from flat to flat and Adam had tried to get rid of at least a hundred times, and patted the seat next to her, elbowing papers and blankets out of the way. I sat.

'Fuck his face. You haven't ruined Adam's life. You've saved your own.'

I laughed at the melodrama. 'I swear you should be the journalist, not me. That is incredible.'

She didn't laugh in return. 'I'm serious, Jim. You weren't happy. And you don't realise it now because there are boxes everywhere and everything is scary and this flat smells fucking *weird*, but you will be absolutely fine. You can be yourself again.'

I swallowed hard. 'Why did you say it was scary? It isn't. I'm not scared.'

Bella peered at me. 'Aren't you? Oh. You should be. It's terrifying out there.'

'How was I not myself before? Why didn't you say?'

Bella shifted in her seat. 'It's not the kind of thing you bring up. I didn't want to upset you. You'd only deny it.' She chewed her nails. 'It was like a light was dimming.' She looked away from me for a moment before immediately brightening. 'Anyway, Adam is what we call *histoire* and the future is fucking blinding so let's start it now.'

'You sound like Geri Halliwell.'

'Biggest compliment you've ever paid me. Get me the Patrón and rig up those speakers. It is time for Céline.'

Once my pity party was over and Bella had departed, lugging an entire week's worth of empty pizza boxes down to the recycling, it was time to give reality a try. And nothing could be realer than going back to work.

You know those people who post on social media about how much they love their job and wouldn't change it for the world? Do they *mean* it? Don't they have days when they'd rather stay under the duvet getting intimate with a packet of biscuits and back-to-back episodes of *Seinfeld*? They must. No, mine wasn't the *worst* job in the world and plenty of people would kill to park their arse in my swivel chair, but three years hadn't done much to dull the sinking feeling I got as I stepped out of the lift and onto the seventh floor and the funsponge of entertainment news that was *Snap!*

If you've never heard of or read *Snap!* you'll know someone who has – although they'll also pretend they've either never heard of it or wouldn't dare demean their precious brain cells with it. That was pretty much the thing to do whenever it came up in conversation. *Snap!* was a celebrity gossip magazine, owned by a newspaper with a decreasing appetite for morals yet a ravenous hunger for eyeballs on the page. While print sales were dwindling – good news for trees, bad news for staff with mouths to feed – the online version was thriving. Gossip was still huge, but nobody wanted a permanent relationship with it, and a magazine felt too much like commitment. What people really wanted was to see at least one huge picture with every scroll of their finger and reasonably amusing or informative words around it to explain what the hell was going on. My job was to guide readers into the abyss by crafting copy around these forgettable snaps to make it look like a real news story and not a desperate attempt to wring some scandal out of fairly tame pictures. And you know, while I was sick of hearing people who'd never picked up a paper in their lives call my job 'lazy journalism', I was bloody good at it. I think.

I walked across the vast open-plan floor and nodded hellos at people in other teams and departments. Every month or so, a face would disappear or there'd be some crafty desk rearrangement to disguise that a whole pod had disappeared. Times were tougher than we were allowed to know, but at least they were still paying *me*. I arrived at my own pod – now just eight desks – to find a half-eaten bacon roll on my keyboard. Hurley.

Sometimes you get those people who, for whatever reason, rub you up the wrong way inexplicably and immediately, and sometimes you are that person for somebody else – Hurley had been waiting his whole life for a nemesis. The battle lines were drawn when he discovered my habit of sneaking into his articles and changing words around. It was like an illness: I couldn't let an errant semicolon or a poorly constructed sentence go unchecked. The trouble was, once I was in there, I couldn't help myself, and when Hurley discovered I'd practically rewritten an entire piece about one of his favourite reality stars, the shit hit the fan.

'I thought it could do with touching up, that's all.'

Hurley's face scrunched up. 'Touch up your own shit. Don't change my words. They're in my *style*.'

He had a point. But seriously. 'It's about the reader, not our egos. It reads better now.'

Hurley was loud, and that voice of his carried. At least five teams' worth of people – desks away from our tiny corner – turned to stare. 'You'd be majorly pissed if I did this to your work.'

I saw my moment. 'You wouldn't *need* to do it to my work, Hurley.' There was a ripple of laughter. Our relationship was dead on arrival.

'Oh, Antiques Roadshow, you're baaaaack,' he drawled, slinking over to my desk like a marionette that had fallen face-first into a jumble sale, covered in superglue. All hair, cheekbones and youthful nonchalance. 'I thought the cold weather might have claimed you.'

'Hello, Hurley.' Our emotional reunions were always epic. 'Is this your sandwich?'

I pointed at the roll. Hurley vaguely looked through it. 'Oh. Yeah. I'm back on carbs. Long story.' He gestured at my chair. 'That thing is shit, by the way. Ouch. You should get one with proper support at your time of life.'

Hurley was twenty-three, on his first job out of university and channelling all his boundless energy into doing as little as possible, except for queuing outside pop-up T-shirt boutiques in Soho and getting his hair cut into weird shapes by men called Dambo. As he often told me while plonking begrudgingly made cups of tea in front of me, 'I just can't believe someone as old as *you* still works at a place like *this*. Like, shouldn't you at least be editor of *something* now?'

Hurley's ambition was to be 'editor of something'; it didn't matter what. Although I never corrected his words again – there wasn't enough time in the day – whenever I offered advice, or suggested ways of phrasing things differently, he'd throw his head back in incredulous laughter. 'Here we go with the grey-splaining.'

If I knew anything about journalism and the gay scene, it was that Hurley would go a long way.

His entire raison d'être was to make me feel ancient, but thank heavens, then, for Alicha, who divided her precious time between writing stories, composing perfect, zinging tweets and designing memes. While, at twenty-four, she also made me feel old, she was at least affectionate with it, keeping me up-to-date with the latest celebrity feuds and hookups, and saving my hide when I drew a blank. Around once a week I'd ask her a question about something and she'd shriek: 'You wrote about that last week; can't you remember?! Oh my Gaaaaaawd Jim, you are so unashamedly laaaaaaame, I love it.' Once a story was posted out to the world, I tended to forget it existed. It wasn't that I thought

I was above it – it kept me in cappuccinos and Converse, after all, and sometimes I genuinely got my hands on an exclusive – but I knew it wasn't for me. Alicha, however, lived and breathed it. Her very existence made me feel less a miserable huckster and more like I was actually here for a reason. And what Alicha didn't know about the celebrity circuit wasn't worth knowing. She had every B-lister on speed dial and they all called her Auntie Alicha.

Once Hurley had sashayed off, Alicha wheeled over to my desk, phone in hand, and put her head on my shoulder.

'Hun,' she said, in the kind of tone you would use at a funeral when trying to comfort a widow. 'Are you OK?'

I laughed. 'Oh you. Honestly, I'm fine.'

Alicha tapped at her screen. 'I made you this.' She played me a video which was a collage made of my and Adam's faces, with a tiny space invader shooting out all the Adams until only I was left, with hearts exploding out of my eyes. I felt a lump in my throat. It was the most beautiful, yet ugly, gesture I'd ever seen.

Alicha stared at me like I was a kitten. 'Aw, baaaaabes, are you gonna cry? Shit, should I have done a reaction video?'

I was about to answer when Roland, our boss, summoned me to his lair in the corner. Roland's ever-shrinking kingdom wasn't up to much – its sole concession to interior design being a pathetic-looking pot-plant and an ancient coffee-stained coaster that said, *I rode the Pepsi Max Big One at Blackpool Pleasure Beach!* As bosses went, Roland wasn't exactly a supervillain, but he would ingratiate himself with just about anyone if there was a perk or a free cracker involved. He was the scourge of every canapé-carrying waiter and goody bag attendant in central London, but he shouted at me the least of all the team and that was good enough for me.

'How is – uh – everything? You, um, moved house, didn't you?' The office was like a village and boredom thresholds were low; gossip was seized upon immediately. I knew he knew.

I steeled myself in case a pep talk was coming. Instead: 'I just wanted to remind you that as you're a freelancer, who does his own tax, those days off won't be paid.'

Gee. Thanks, you bastard. 'I know, Ro.'

'If you want more time off, I need plenty of notice so I can arrange cover. I mean, you have more holidays than a Kardashian.'

I'd have preferred Joan Collins as a reference point, but fine.

Roland tapped his pen on his desk. 'You know how pushed we are.'

'Maybe get Hurley to put down his phone for half an hour and actually *write* instead of tweeting his breakfast.'

Roland groaned. We had this discussion a lot. 'Hurley has a huge social following. It brings traffic to the site.'

I'd had the displeasure of sitting through Hurley's dreary vlogs, in which he forensically analysed everything from Beyoncé's eyeliner to old pairs of trainers he'd once loved.

Roland was fond of telling me Hurley was the future, but really I was envious I'd never thought to film *myself* talking non-sense years ago. Mind you, I knew nobody would watch – unless I put a bag over my head. And set it on fire.

A while ago, I asked Roland if he'd considered trying deeper analysis into celebrity culture, something readers could get their teeth into. Go behind the scenes more, be fun instead of bitchy. He quickly dismissed it, saying our readers' teeth would fall out if forced to sink them into anything other than a gallery of nose jobs gone wrong.

'Long reads? Nobody cares. You want to wax lyrical, get a blog, James. It's what everyone else does.'

I gave a long sigh and looked out at the newsroom in time to see Hurley standing on my chair, photographing his shoes. Roland followed my gaze.

'I'll talk to Hurley.'

'I think you're better off tweeting him,' I snarked, and left him to it.

I moved my keyboard into position before turning to Alicha, but she was busy zooming in on a zit on an A-list actor's face so she could draw the 'hoop of horror' around it – our regular tool for directing readers to particularly embarrassing flaws in paparazzi shots of their usually immaculate idols.

I started to wonder if I'd ditched the right relationship. Perhaps it was time to walk away from everything.

Suddenly, Roland shouted from behind his partition.

'Jim! Pics just coming in of Julianne Moore carrying something in a bag. The bag is green. That's all. Can you work some magic?'

'Sure, Roland; live in ten.'

Five Tuesdays ago my life had been so different – somebody else's. Where the hell would I be in another five?

2.

Even as I was telling Adam it was over, I wasn't thinking about what would come next. We'd moved in together after just a year of going out, more from convenience than any desperate need to be together at all times, I now realised. I'd never lived by myself, with nobody telling me what to do, no dinner to have on the table, nobody about to barge through the door and moan that they'd had a bad day. Being a novice, I embraced what I imagined was true bachelorhood and practised the most basic hedonism I could stand. Sleeping naked. Scratching my balls at will. Eating nothing but ham sandwiches, on WHITE bread – take that, vague intolerance to gluten – and having huge bags of roasted peanuts for pudding. I swilled around in beer like it was bathwater and idly watched porn while waiting for the kettle to boil. As long as I was holed up in my strange little cocoon, I was fine. Reality came in the shape of curt messages from friends I'd shared with Adam – in short: 'oh darling yes isn't it terrible you two were perfect for each other please don't call us or it would be awkward' – or emoji-laden texts from the few pals of my own I'd hung on to. Being alone was weird.

The key to enjoying being alone, according to Alicha, was not to spend too much time in my own head. One evening, as I was switching off my computer and pretending not to notice Hurley changing all the captions on one of my articles, Alicha wandered over, wearing her best concerned face. 'What is it tonight then, Bridget Jones? Takeaway in front of the telly and early night in your fleecy nightie?'

I had actually been planning to get two-for-one pizza and eat until I was at the point of explosion, but I kept quiet.

Alicha perched on my desk and fiddled with her phone. 'Come out with me, if you like. I'm meeting the girls in Dalston.'

'It's Wednesday!'

Alicha roared with laughter, 'Baaaaaabe, you're single now. Wednesday's a state of mind; every night of the week is a Friday!'

I politely refused, but Alicha wasn't having it. She'd heard of a new app, she said, and I should be on it. Dating! Wasn't it a bit too soon? And as for apps . . . weren't they just for shagging?

'I don't want a boyfriend, I just got rid of one.'

Alicha showed me her phone. A grid of photos stared back, row upon row of men of all ages, each flashing their best 'trust me I'm a serial killer' smiles.

'There are loads of apps to hook you up with guys just like you.'

'I don't want to meet anyone who's just like me.'

'This is MadgeMatch!' she whooped. 'It's amazing. Basically you find your perfect guy based on what Madonna songs he likes. What's yours again?'

I remembered that fateful chorus-that-never-was of 'Into the Groove'. '"Angel".'

Alicha nodded, either impressed or totally oblivious but playing along. 'Hmmmm. Digging out the deep cuts. Nice.' She tapped her screen a few times, nails clacking in staccato efficiency.

'What would I say to a man I've never met before?'

Alicha flashed the phone at me. 'Jimmy baby. Are you kidding? Me and you chat shit all day! Pretend it's me. Give him your best zingers. Get drunk, talk about Madonna all night. Then shag him. Vogue on his dick! If there were one of these apps for Beyoncé, I'd be on dates every night of the week.'

'There is,' I deadpanned. 'It's called Twitter.'

'Whaddya think?'

I looked at the screen.

> HI! I'm Mike, I'm 32, and a shameless sapiosexual. My favourite Madonna song is 'Hung Up', but her best album, for me, is *Ray of Light*.

Alicha screwed up her face. 'What the fuck is a sapiosexual?'

'They *claim* to find intellect much sexier than looks.'

'Seriously?'

'Yeah. Basically, they wank with one hand and turn the pages of *War and Peace* with the other.'

'Ugh, yuk. He's right about "Hung Up", though. Banger.'

'A bit basic.'

Alicha socked my arm. 'Basic is good. Keep it light for your first time. Come on, download it, let's do this.'

I don't know how I'd pictured my first date – if that's what this was. I'd never been on one before. I met Adam in a bar and went home with him, and his predecessors were the same – onenighters that lingered like summer colds. Arranging a date, and a fairly blind one at that, was a new concept. I was wearing too much fragrance, had overdone the hair wax and was running low on hope. Mike was late. Like, very late. When he arrived, he didn't look like the cheery, down-to-earth Madge fanatic who signed off each of his texts with a different lyric from 'Hung Up' (I know). Instead, he was a slurring, quivering mess who plonked

21

himself on the chair beside me and planted a huge wet kiss on my cheek. He was drunk. Plus, it seemed, he was not alone.

'Who's your friend?' I asked, aching with rictus, nodding at the tall, dour guy he'd walked in with, who was now standing at the end of the table like a pallbearer waiting for a coffin to drop onto his shoulder.

'That,' exclaimed Mike theatrically, 'is Gabriel. Just ignore him.'

I'd heard about dating disasters before. Wrecked cars, embarrassing tampon malfunctions, being mistaken for a shoplifter and arrested when nipping out for a packet of cigarettes, but nothing prepared me for two excruciating hours in the company of a man determined to pretend he wasn't drunk and his perma-silent bodyguard, whose angelic name I assumed was ironic – he looked like one of Beelzebub's finest had come up for a recce. But it was a Thursday night and only my pile of washing up was waiting for me at home, so I endured it.

It turned out, after some light questioning, Mike wasn't a Madonna fan at all – he'd had to Google the lyrics. 'I'm really into trying all the different apps,' he slurred. 'You meet so many different people. I'm lapsed Catholic but I'm on two Jewish apps, which doesn't bother me because I don't think I'd miss bacon that much, and I'm a premium member of Men911.'

'What's that?' I asked, praying I'd die before finding out.

'Everyone on it works for the emergency services.' It took him three attempts to get to the end of 'emergency services' with all the letters in the right order.

'It's not all sexy firemen though, mainly just a few guys who bought clinical scrubs off the internet but really work in KFC. But I don't mind. I just really love people, don't I, Gabriel?'

When Mike finally decided to make more room in his bladder for the pints of Stella he was chucking down his neck, I asked Gabriel if he normally played chaperone to his drunk mates.

22

He eyeballed me wearily and sipped his mojito. 'Mike is my *boyfriend* and we're working through some problems right now. He'll try to kiss you when we leave.' I gulped. Gabriel shrugged. 'To be honest, it's best if you let him. It'll save me an argument on the bus home.'

I watched them both drink two more rounds before excusing myself to go to the bar and slipping out into the cold night, wrapping my scarf round my head as I crept past the window where Mike and Gabriel sat, looking about fifteen seconds away from a cataclysmic row.

I ordered my pizza from the comfort of the bus – my pepperoni-stacked amour was waiting for me at the front door.

'I think you might need a bit more time,' said Alicha the next day, as she helped me delete my MadgeMatch profile. 'Maybe get to know yourself a bit first.'

'Look, I love you but we've FaceTimed every night this week, and you're not going to get any sex from me, so you need to make *arrangements*.'

Bella came over with a dusty bottle of something she vaguely remembered being given three Christmases ago and told me I couldn't be holed up in this flat any longer. It was time, she said. But I wasn't ready for proper *dating*, and I wasn't 'holed up' anywhere – I'd been living alone for precisely four weeks. She scoffed when I told her about my nightmare night out with not-so-magic Mike.

'He is one arsehole among a cast of thousands. I can't promise he'll be the last you'll meet, but at least you'll be ready.'

'It's too soon.'

Bella stood up and walked over to my chaotic bookshelves. 'Where's your laptop? Let's log you on.' She liberated my battered MacBook from within a pile of ancient magazines.

'Internet dating?' I spluttered.

Bella sat back down, opened my MacBook, and berated me for my filthy screen. 'You're being a pissbaby about the apps, too in-your-face for our little prince. So it's either online, or speed-dating, or shitty singles nights. Is that what you want?'

I didn't. I'd tried speed-dating before, years before, when it was first huge. Greeted by a perma-smiling, harassed-looking drone in Patrick Cox loafers brandishing a clipboard at the door of a bar decked out in neon lights and flyers for long-dead tribute acts, handed a glass of complimentary 'fizz' – flatter than the school choir's high notes – and relayed a list of rules that made the Riot Act look like the limerick in a Christmas cracker.

'OK, first things first,' he trilled. 'No, you can't ask me on a date.' Good to know.

Every three minutes for an hour and a half, someone would ring a bell to get us to change partners, and the first five times I made jokes about 'for whom the bell tolls' or something Quasimodo-related, and each time the guy would look at me like a rat peering through jelly, or like he was trying to read an optician's chart over my left shoulder. The night ended as any normal night would've done. All the beautiful ones congregated at one end of the bar getting off with each other, while me and the other miseries sat chatting to the event organiser, who reassured us with aphoristic throwaways about the 'right person' being 'out there somewhere'. At the end of the night, as bartenders mopped the floor and the pong of bleach assaulted our eyeballs, he asked for my number. I pointed at his clipboard, his list of rules now curling at the edges and filled with doodles, and shook my head.

Bella noisily typed in my password – see, no secrets. Subscription-free sites were dismissed by my matchmaker. 'On a dating site like Soulseekers,' she gestured at the screen, 'these studs are paying a monthly fee. Less bullshit, no murderers, no dick pics . . .'

I looked at the models posing on the homepage. Studs?! One of them was wearing a burnt-orange cardigan. With a button missing. 'Would dick pics be so bad?'

Bella laughed. 'Oh it's too *soon*,' she whined, mimicking my earlier protestations. 'We need to give you a username, something that describes you in a couple of words. Like your own personal billboard, or a sign above a shop.' Bella scanned the existing members in a separate window. '"Desperate" doesn't seem to have been taken yet.'

I tutted my disapproval. 'Ooh. What about something literary? You know, show my creative side. Like Maxim de Winter or, uh, Romeo? Too cheesy?'

Bella grimaced. 'Hmmm, a bit specific, and both with quite grim backstories. What about something more generic to tell your story?'

What did every story have at its heart? 'What about Our Hero?'

Bella gave a thumbs up. 'Perfect. Right, let's crunch the numbers and do the old show-and-tell.' It was time to lay it bare. Vital statistics, hopes, dreams. Nothing major. Bella kept control of the keyboard, barking questions like sadistic airport security.

'Are you sure you're five eleven?'

'The *doctor* measured me.'

'Were you wearing your hiking socks? I'd say five ten. Maybe and a half.'

'Do you want me to get the sodding tape measure?'

My hair.

'Option here for "greying" – shall I tick that?'

'My hair is brown with *one* or *two* flecks of grey. Greying makes me sound old.'

Bella warned me it was important to be honest.

'Fuck you, it's brown. Put brown.'

My eyes.

'Green? We've known each other twenty years, Bella. They're blue.'

Bella regarded me anew. 'Oh, yeah, I'd never really looked before.'

I fixed them on her furiously. 'I will always treasure these final moments of our friendship.'

I'd never deconstructed myself so forensically before, or thought about things like my 'build' – slim, we decided. Now here was the tough part: personality.

'Why don't you put the truth – wildly neurotic and prone to random existential crises – and watch the offers come flying in?'

'You are literally neither of those things. Enthusiastic? Kind? Spontaneous? Reliable? Trustworthy? All good. All true.'

'Let's not get hysterical.'

I was suddenly, acutely, aware of all my competition. What if all the other men on the dating site were better than me? Eyes bluer? Taller, perhaps? More enthusiastic and spontaneous? The unseen enemy.

'Look,' said Bella impatiently. 'This isn't going to work if you're going to be so down on yourself.'

'It's hard not to be.'

Bella tapped the side of the laptop. 'I know. But you have so much going for you – we don't actually *have* to lie.'

'I have no money, a tiny flat, no prospects and zero security.'

Bella waved dismissively. 'Boring. They're just stuff. *Stats.* Look at what you *do* have. I don't know anyone as dependable as you. As level-headed. Someone who always knows the right thing to say.'

'I'm not sure Adam would agree with you there.'

'Adam is not our target audience here. You're bright, know how to keep a conversation going, kind. Your friends made you godfather twice, for heaven's sake.'

I glanced over at photos of my friends Nicole and Richie's two sons. 'Only because they knew I'd make an effort and wear a nice suit to the christening.'

Bella jabbed the air forcefully. 'Bingo. And that's it, Jim. You make an effort. So many people ... just *don't*. Dumping Adam is the first selfish thing you've ever done. And I see it more as self-care, to be honest.'

I sat up straight and pushed my shoulders back, finally feeling I'd earned the right not to slouch and be miserable.

'What are we saying for hobbies?' I poked my nose over Bella's shoulder. 'Activities and stuff?'

Bella turned to face me. '*Activities*?'

'Yes. I want to say that I go running.'

Bella choked mid-swig of the very, very awful wine. She eventually composed herself. 'You don't run!'

'I'm going to start. Tick it.' Adam had always berated me for having no fitness routine whatsoever, and I kept slim by saying no to pudding and pure nervous energy, but if I was going to compete with the broad-shouldered, lantern-jawed blokes on Soulseekers – or so I assumed, before I actually saw them – I needed to step things up.

Bella swept her hand over my body as if trying to magic up some muscles for me. 'If you finally make use of one of those gym memberships you haven't bothered cancelling, you'll soon notice a difference.'

I looked down at my torso. It wasn't that bad, actually. I used to run years ago, before I met Adam, but once I had 'my man' I guess the need for self-improvement faded away. I brought my hands up to my chin and felt around, hunting for my jawline. 'Yeah, maybe,' I said, 'but there's no gym for the face.'

Bella brought her face level to mine. 'Jim, I'm not one for compliments, but you are reasonably good-looking.'

The 'reasonably' burned but I let her carry on. 'People look at you in the street. *Women.* I've seen them.'

'How old are these women? Are there cataracts involved? Are they senile and mistaking me for their dead, brave, war-hero husband?'

'They're *all* ages. And let me tell you, we don't just look at any old bloke like gay guys do.'

I elbowed her playfully. 'Errrr, that is homophobia at its finest.'

'I'm serious, though. We don't. You've got *something*; it's a case of making it work.'

I laughed. '*Something.* OK, I can live with that.'

It was photo-shoot time.

'If you look twenty-five in all your photos and turn up look-ing . . . ' she paused here, presumably thinking better of the killer barb she was about to unleash, 'well, looking *not* twenty-five, it can be damaging, make you seem like you can't be trusted, so we have to take new ones.' She suggested poses, giving instant feedback, most of it brutal. A 'big nose situation' on one, 'dimple issues' on another.

After half an hour of being told my eyes looked dead, I'd had enough. We picked two selfies, dug out a picture of me trying to squish Big Ben and one lit by candlelight – Adam took that one, ouch – and then I was ready to upload.

Was Adam on a dating site right now? Fucking hell – I'd never thought of that! Would he be on *this* dating site?! I hoped even-tually there wouldn't be space in my head to relate everything I did back to Adam, that one day he would inhabit a different compartment, along with old family holidays, songs I used to like or once-favourite foods now banished from my palate because of some 'incident' or another. I couldn't decide whether I was dreading that time or willing it to come all the quicker.

'Hand me your card, I'm signing you up for a year.'

Twelve miserable months of 'What's your name and where do

you come from?' A year of saying all the stupid things you say to get people to fancy you, hiding the craziness? It occurred to me I hadn't kissed anybody but Adam in six long years and my blood ran cold.

'A year is a long time. I might meet someone tomorrow.'

Bella laughed and slipped me the side-eye. 'You won't.'

'How do you know?'

She tutted. 'I just *know*. And why would you want to meet someone tomorrow? This isn't about "the one". Just . . . the next one. Card. Now.'

I handed it over. 'Now then,' she said brightly, like a children's TV presenter, tapping in the details. 'Our lucky winner today is James Brodie, of delightful Camberwell, and he's going to press our big red button for us.' She turned to me and grinned widely, motioning at the screen. 'Push it, Jim.'

My finger hovered over the button and I was trying to work out if clicking it would cause disaster. Just like being at work, then, except usually the button was 'Publish' and my panic was the fear of being sued for libel. Today, however, the button was even more menacing – this would put me right back out there. Dating. A million more Mikes at my disposal.

Click.

No flashes of light, glitter cannons did not explode – but I did feel strangely different, lighter, maybe. Excitement. Nerves. The sense of an ending.

'OK, Our Hero, you're on – let's see who's waiting for you.'

3.

'Our Hero?!? Right. OK. Well . . . You're certainly *my* hero today, Jim. Those two were doing my head in,' Nicole chirped as she watched her husband Richie heave a huge bag of shopping out of the boot and her sons tumble out of the car and into their house. Once a month was Sunday Club – a huge roast dinner round at theirs, where we'd reminisce about all the hangovers we'd had at university and embarrass the children by getting drunk and doing 'sexy dancing' to student disco classics. It usually kicked off in the supermarket, emptying the shelves into a trolley but today, sensing my friends were about to have some kind of temporary breakdown, I had dragged my rambunctious godsons off to the gaming shop to hammer each other to bits in virtual reality, while their parents shopped.

Nicole strode off into the house swinging her handbag, preparing to do battle, while I took pity on Richie and relieved him of one of the bags.

'Nah, it's all right,' he protested. 'Leave it to the men. You're going to need all your strength anyway, aren't you? All those new internet dating blokes you'll be tossing off.'

I gasped in mock indignation, although I was well used to

Richie's affectionate jibes. 'I am not going to be tossing anybody off, Rich.'

Richie looked aghast. 'What? Not even *one*? What's the point in being gay then?!'

When you think of straight allies, heterosexuals – usually men – who fight gay guys' corners and are willing to talk about gay issues openly and honestly, you might think of metrosexual pretty boys stripping for charity calendars or Hollywood actors with one eye on LGBT rights and the other on a bright shiny Oscar. Richie was a different proposition: married, a plumber, Londoner born and bred, and descended from a long line of manly men. Whether it was a youth spent hugging strangers in clubs, the worldliness honed from growing up in London, or years spent married to one of my best friends, Richie was more than a straight ally – he was practically an enthusiast. There weren't many aspects of gay life that didn't fascinate him, from the music and the saunas to a supposed keen eye for fashion. He would always proudly show off his new outfits and, if I was wearing something he didn't recognise from a previous visit, tell me his opinion and, the bit I loved best of all, ask me 'Is it from this season?'

You never knew how it was going to turn out when your gal pals coupled up. In the past, I'd gently removed myself from friendships with women whose partners couldn't handle a gay man being around, because it affronted their dreary masculinity. With Richie, though, Nicole and I had struck gold. He was interested, sympathetic and genuinely enthralled by it – he just wanted to know more about the world around him, and if some of it was absolute filth, then even better.

Richie put the kettle on and lit a cigarette. 'The trouble with Adam was that he wasn't . . . nice.'

Nicole nodded.

This surprised me. Nicole and Richie had always got on really well with him on the few occasions he'd joined the group.

'That time he stormed off to that wedding without you because you were running late,' offered Nicole. When I couldn't find my shoes, Adam had lost his temper and screamed he was going without me, speeding off in a cab to the station. I didn't have the address and was reluctant to text any of his friends in case they realised we'd been arguing. I left messages all afternoon, and stayed at home, in my wedding clothes, just in case he calmed down and texted me the address, but he didn't. When his friends asked why I wasn't there, he said I'd refused to come.

Even now I made excuses. 'Adam was always very kind. He supported me when work was tough. Still paid the bulk of the bills.'

Nicole and Richie exchanged a look. 'Yeah,' said Nic. 'He liked you relying on him. It was like he owned you.'

Richie took a deep drag. 'He wasn't *nice*, Jim. Not to you, anyway. Perfectly polite, a stand-up guy, a good laugh, actually. But not nice.'

Nicole handed me a cup of tea. 'I've known you a long time. You basically fed me all through college, made sure I got to lectures, would do anything for anyone, independent, in charge. But that's not how you were with Adam. You see that, don't you?'

Nicole was one of the first friends I'd made at university and had witnessed each of my evolutions, be they sexual or cultural, without comment or judgement – which is exactly why we'd stayed close for sixteen years. If I needed help or advice, she'd have it, but was very good at waiting to be asked.

After we'd graduated, she zipped off to London on the next train in search of a career in TV. While she'd found it almost immediately, working for an intimidating presenter famous for grilling politicians so hard they left the set weeping, she also found herself pregnant to Richie fairly quickly. And I'd spent the last two hours successfully preventing her twelve-year-old son

Sid leathering the hell out of the result of the next pregnancy four years later, Haydn.

The Sunday lunches were a sanctuary for me when I first started having wobbles about Adam. He never came with me because he couldn't stand children. 'They've always got dirty hands,' he'd complain, subconsciously stroking his pristine white T-shirt at the thought of it being sullied by a kid's paw print.

Nicole looked at me across the kitchen counter. I could sense a mother-hen inquiry coming on.

'You've lost weight, by the way. Are you eating?'

It looked like my early attempts at running were paying off.

'Adam isn't worth starving yourself over, you know.'

'Nic! God. I swear I will eat at least triple my usual serving of roasties today. I'm all right.'

The doorbell went and our final guest arrived. Silvie, another of our university mates, lived round the corner. She kissed me on both cheeks. 'You look awful. Heartbreak diet?'

So good to be among friends.

Silvie was very happily single and our standard Sunday was to listen rapt as she regaled us with tales of all the unsuitable men fate had thrown at her. Now it seemed I'd be joining her.

'OK, so we can get to all your miserable breakup emotions later,' shouted Richie. 'Tell us about this date you had the other night. Did you get any cock?'

When Jack, thirty-five, 'Irish, living in west London', got in touch with me, I was delighted. This was it! It was happening! I couldn't tell much from his photos except he was fond of checked shirts and taking selfies in front of Ikea shelving. He was almost monosyllabic, complimented my smile in my photo and, to my surprise, within three messages, asked me out. So *this* was how you did it when you weren't drunk in a bar or relying on the peach and aubergine emojis to make your point in an app. All I had to do was turn up. OK, I could do this. Turning up was my speciality.

I showered an extra five minutes and washed everywhere twice. I tried on all number of outfits – ending up wearing the very first one – and agonised over shoes. 'Men on dating sites expect a bit more,' Bella warned me. 'It's not like an app where you just rock up with your fly open. This is old-school.'

It quickly became clear that not one of Jack's photos had been taken within the last five years, but he was good-looking. And, while his messages might have been stilted, boy, could he talk in person. He must've been saving it up for me. Not a single part of his relatively short time on Earth was left a mystery. I got the lot. School days. University woes. Dating history. Every flat he'd lived in, including an intricate account of his current pad's plumbing woes – 'I have to flush twice if it's a number two.' I could have compiled a successful pub quiz on his life so far, but get me to name one thing about him that was interesting, or that I liked, and I was drawing blanks. It wasn't amazing, and it wasn't terrible – it was just *happening*.

Keen to avoid a repeat of the Mike disaster, I'd done some research before I set off. I was determined to do this right. First off, I was drinking pints. According to a popular blog I found, *Date Me Daddy* (seriously), this made me look 'butch' – apparently of great importance on a date. If you were going to get a gay man to fancy you, you had to be masculine, apparently. I had worried about this on and off over the years – my voice, my clothes, my hair, were my wrists limp? It never quite reached the point of obsession and since school bullies stopped being a daily fixture in my life, it hadn't caused too many problems. But *Date Me Daddy* said I had to embrace 'the cult of masculinity' if I wasn't going to spend the rest of my life alone. I considered the idea it might be better to spend the rest of your life alone than pretend to be someone else – wasn't that why I left Adam in the first place? – but I had to give it a go. I toyed with the idea of speaking in a deeper voice or perhaps grabbing my testicles every few minutes, but *Date Me Daddy* seemed to think blurting out the score of a famous World Cup fixture every half-hour and throwing back pints would be man enough.

And I certainly *was* knocking them back while Jack yammered on and on – I was on my third and dying for the loo before I realised he hadn't asked me a single question. I felt redundant, brought here under false pretences, like a call-girl humouring a client who 'just wants to talk'. Perhaps sensing my discomfort, and definitely noticing my drinking speed, he laid his hand on mine and whispered, 'Hey, James, don't be nervous, you're doing great.' And then I was immediately one hundred times more nervous. Jack had done this before, you see, many times. 'I wouldn't call myself a serial dater,' he guffawed, 'but let's just say I've seen more than a few souls on Soulseekers.'

I made the mistake of telling him he was, pretty much, my first. 'Oh woooooow,' he exclaimed, his eyes like saucers. 'So I popped your cherry. We must try and pop it even more another time.'

I laughed as heartily as possible to hide my nerves and ended up spitting beer down into my crotch. Jack's gaze followed it.

I imagine he was just about to say something irrevocably awful, when I heard my name called out from across the bar. Loudly.

'James Brodie! Jimmy Bee! J-Bro! It can't be! I've never seen you in here in my life. Are you lost?' No way. Hurtling toward me at a million miles an hour with his arms outstretched – drink in one hand, free magazine in the other – was Curtis Jacobs.

I'd known Curtis for years, on and off; we'd sat beside each other in scores of editorial teams waiting to get laid off. He was larger than life and knew everything about everyone. He was more lovable than he pretended, but he was also the very definition of an acquired taste. An olive or anchovy in human form, spending someone else's bar tab. We'd lost touch a little over the years – when I met Adam I stopped going out so much, and he got married to a shy American called Parker. 'It's always the same,' Curtis used to say. 'The party boys get dick-no-tised and before you know it they're at home playing househusband.' I was mortified to be caught out on my very first date, but also over-whelmingly relieved to be rescued from Jack's boring chatter. I had no idea what Curtis was going to say next – nobody ever did, and it had cost him a lot of jobs, friends and out-of-court settlements over the years – but he was never, ever dull.

Curtis hugged me warmly and pulled a chair across from another table. When the table's occupants claimed the seat was taken, Curtis pretended to inspect it closely, bellowing, 'By whom? An *ant*? I can't see anyone on there.'

'Jack, this is Curtis.' I gestured at each of them like an air hostess pointing out the emergency exits. 'And Curtis, this is Jack.'

Curtis regarded Jack over the top of his specs. 'Is it, indeed?' He turned back to me. 'James. It's lovely to see you. It's been far too long. What are you doing in this dump? I'm *this* close to calling the vice squad and having it closed down for ever. What happened to Adam, then?'

I paused for the breath Curtis himself hadn't bothered taking. 'Um . . . We broke up.'

'Oh did you?' Curtis sipped his drink. '*Good*. The great big lumbering Welsh buzzkill. No wonder you look so happy and are actually *outside* for once. What happened? Did he leave you for someone younger?'

I laughed a little too loudly. Jack shifted uncomfortably in his seat. 'He was Scottish, Curtis. And, no, actually, *I* broke it off.'

Curtis gasped. 'Did you? He was a Debbie downer but at least he was hot. A hunk, even. Yes, a hunk. *Why* did you? So you could go on dates with *Jack* here? How nice.'

Curtis claimed he only had two minutes – 'I'm off to a *thing*' – so we filled each other in as fast as we could. He was still married to Parker – 'the sex hasn't dropped off yet, which is nice, but he's stopped paying for the Ocado order and leaves more towels on the floor than before' – and was now writing about showbiz for a tabloid. 'What about you? You're not still at *Snap!* are you? Are they managing to keep that cradle of filth going? Last time I read the magazine, it looked like it was being knocked up in someone's garage on a second-hand photocopier. You deserve better.'

After a round of air kisses and promises to grab a coffee 'as soon as the stars of reality television will allow', he was gone, like a freak storm.

Jack and I both sat in silence for a few seconds, shell-shocked.

'He seemed . . . interesting.' Jack grimaced. I smiled weakly. Curtis's three-minute interruption had been the most fun part of the whole night – mainly because Curtis was an adorable force of nature, but partly because Jack hadn't said a word throughout. 'Do you want to go on somewhere?' he asked now.

I suddenly felt very vulnerable. I was Granny peering over her bed jacket at a suspiciously wolf-shaped shadow at the window. I squeaked out some excuse about having work to finish at home.

'I'll walk you to the tube.'

As we walked through Soho in silence, all the pubs started to tip out for closing time. Watching friends laugh, joke and smoke and scream brought home to me just how awkward this was. My pocket buzzed. A message, from Curtis.

> Your date looks like Big Bird from *Sesame Street*.
> DITCH DITCH DITCH. Going to an afterparty later if you
> can stand it. Call. xoxox

We trundled the wrong way round Piccadilly Circus station until we reached the barrier. I thanked him for a lovely evening – a lie – and I thought he was about to lean in for a kiss. Instead he put his hand firmly in the crotch of my jeans, licked his lips and murmured, 'It's still wet.' In the absence of a clue how to deal with this, I pretended it wasn't happening, faked a coughing fit, patted him on the back like I was winding a baby and skipped through the ticket gate, hollering over my shoulder insincere promises to call him.

Richie flicked his apple core into the bin across the kitchen. 'He sounded great. What were you being such a pansy for? Why didn't you take him home?'

'He sexually assaulted me in a train station. I nearly puked when I got home. I wanted chemistry. Fireworks.'

Richie hooted with laughter. 'Fireworks! Friday night; what else were you doing?'

Nicole gave Richie a light switch of her oven glove. 'Not all men are obsessed with getting their end away, you know.'

Richie lit a cigarette and laughed once again. 'Bollocks they aren't. Of all the things I had you down for, Jim, I never thought you'd be frigid.'

Silvie turned to me and winked. 'It'll get better, Jim. Someone will break the spell.'

Nicole handed me a potato peeler. Time to get busy. 'You're allowed to be picky, by the way. Have some fun. You deserve it.'

'Do I?'

Richie threw his head back as if baying at the moon. 'The next time somebody grabs your cock, grab theirs back. For God's sake go out there and get it over with, or I'm not letting you in next month.'

Once home, I traipsed through to the lounge in the dark. I still wasn't accustomed to the layout and stumbled over an unpacked box, steadying myself against the worktop and looking out of the window at the busy road below. The thought of all the Jacks out there waiting to disappoint me made me feel heavy and tired. No more. As soon as I got up the next day, I was going to delete my dating profile. It was the first time Bella and I had been single at the same time for the best part of a decade! We should be out there! In all the bars! Why pretend I was above all that 'straight girl and her gay best friend hit the town' stuff? It was her birthday the following week – I'd pull off one of my usual specials. Get her favourite champagne, Veuve Rosé, and book a spendy meal somewhere. I went online and booked cocktails at one of her favourite haunts, that impossibly dark and opulent bar in the Savoy. The men on Soulseekers could wait . . . for ever if necessary. My plans in place, I went to bed relieved, almost excited about the future.

And then she told me she was leaving.

Russia. I was losing her to Russia. Not to a so-far imaginary husband who didn't like me, as I'd been expecting one day, but an entire country.

Shimmering in special birthday make-up, Bella lined up a martini each as she broke the news. 'Thirty-four today. I'm going nowhere here. I'm over my job, tired of dating and, if I'm honest, sick of not having enough money.'

And so she was off to Moscow to be a nanny, like an improbable soap-opera plot – except this was *actually* happening.

Bella was half-Russian and had aced her Russian language A-level at just sixteen, but she'd never expressed an interest in her heritage beyond a fondness for pelmeni and borscht. She certainly didn't fancy Russian men – 'potatoes each and every one' – and hated the cold. She'd wear a jumper in a sauna. But there was money to be made and oligarchs queueing to pay you to do something for them.

This was not the birthday blowout I'd been aiming for. 'I know it sounds selfish, but what about me?'

'Aw, Jim, you'll be fine. You've earned the right to be selfish. I'm not going for ever, couple of years, tops.'

She'd been planning it for ages, even before I left Adam, which she now confessed she hadn't thought I'd ever do.

'I kind of assumed you two would be OK for a bit and you'd struggle on. I knew you'd find the strength one day, but I didn't know it would be so soon. Let's face it, you procrastinate, take a while to convince yourself. That job, for example.'

I couldn't have a careers chat now, not tonight. 'What about it?'

'You hate it. Despise it. And yet you're still there.'

'Nobody else is interested.'

'You don't know that.'

'I have *tried*. Nobody wants to read my writing.'

I was pushing the self-pity. Always my last-gasp tactic if a conversation wasn't going my way. But it was kind of true. Nobody wanted to pay writers when there were interns or bloggers on hand who could do it for free. The last job interview I'd had went so badly I faked stomach cramps to get out early.

Bella bristled. 'You tried *once*, and gave up when it didn't work out. It takes perseverance. It's the same with dating; you can't give up now. And I don't want to think of you all on your own. Promise me you'll keep going with it.'

I wiped a tear from my eye. 'A load of random men can't replace you.'

Bella laughed. 'I am a hole that can never be filled, it's true. But we can Skype or FaceTime.' Bella suddenly had a lightbulb moment. 'Or email me. I used to love your funny emails when you were away at uni. Yes, write to me about all your dates – that'll be even better.'

Well if nobody else wanted to read my writing, at least Bella did. I smiled and said I would, of course I would. But it'd never be the same as having her right there.

00.59 [compose new message]

Hello, my name is James. Am I supposed to tell you my name? For security reasons maybe I shouldn't. I'm not sure. You can't be too careful, can you? Well, you can be *too* careful – driving overly slowly, for example, is very dangerous.

Erm. Well it's not like I'm sending you my PIN number, is it? Sorry I mean PIN – no need to add 'number' as my ex was always telling me. OK so I definitely shouldn't be mentioning my ex. Adam. We parted amicably. Well, I was amicable. Him not so much.

OK. Right. Well what I wanted to say was that I liked your profile. I mean, you know this, because I clicked 'like'. Well not 'like', I clicked the ♥ thing. Faved you? Hearted you? LOVED you? Too soon? Yes. Too soon. Anyway I HEARTED your profile and the things you said and I can see that in some ways you are a bit like me. Whether this is a good thing or not I can only guess. To sum up:

1. I too enjoy long walks. Longer the better. If I could walk while FAST ASLEEP I would do this. I've considered investing in robot legs to allow me to do just that. Just saving up for a sat nav system and autopilot so that I don't walk into the sea and then achieving my dream of existing in a permanent state of perambulation.

2. Great to see that you love both staying in AND going out. Quite handy because – and please stand by because I am about to deploy the word 'literally' in its proper sense – one's entire life is *literally* spent doing one or the other of those two things. You are either IN or you are OUT, so to like BOTH, well, I mean you're off to the races with that one straight away, aren't you? And so hard to choose between them.

Like, staying in, with all its home comforts, such as the TV – do you watch TV? I'm willing to pretend I don't if it gives me more intellectual points – and the fridge, where wine lives. For a brief period, anyway. And also a toilet that you absolutely know the identity of everyone who has sat on it before you. Unless you live in a shared house, in which case this is something of a lottery unless you have a camera trained on the bathroom door to monitor all the comings and goings. I don't. Live in a shared house, I mean. And nor do I have a camera rigged up to the toilet. Nope. I live by myself. In Camberwell. In the biggest flat I can afford which, in a nutshell, is not very. In fact it really is a nutshell. Perhaps I am the nut. It's basically a box of Milk Tray with a slot for posting utility bills through, and a bed. I probably shouldn't say I live alone in case men take advantage of me. But maybe that's what I want. Not that I'm a slut or anything. Unless you find that empowering. Do you? I am joking I am joking I am joking.

3. Italian food! Brilliant. So nice to find someone still unapologetically eating carbohydrates in the 21st century, and one of the least Instagrammable cuisines in the world to boot. You can photograph a plate of meatballs and linguine all you want – it's never gonna beat sushi, is it? I like sushi too but I can see from your profile that you don't mention sushi at all, so either you *don't* like it, or have no strong feelings either way. I don't think sushi is worth having particularly strong feelings over, tbh. Meat and potato pie, yes. Steak tartare, for sure. Sushi, nah.

You'll notice I used 'gonna' there, a couple of lines up. I wouldn't usually, as I'm a journalist, but I think it makes me sound quite relaxed and cool and willing not to take myself too seriously. Casual, y'know. A little bit, heeeeeeey. Kind of, would smoke a joint at a party and not throw up until I got home sort of thing. And also a slang-reliant philistine. No but seriously.

Is this working? Have I worked my magic enough? Charmed you? Cast my spell? Have a look at my profile too, maybe – that's bound to sway you one way or the other. If the words aren't doing it for you maybe the face will. All photos are NEW apart from the one of me on the London Eye looking nervous. That's a year old. I look nervous because I *am* nervous. I don't like heights. If you're a rock climber or live on top of a very large tree, please do *not* get back in touch.

But I hope you do. Because if I like you and you like me, we should probably do something about that, shouldn't we? Like, as soon as we can. Before we irreversibly age. Not that there's any other way to age. Yes, I *did* only get a D in science at school – why do you ask?

Call me! Well, I can't give you my number until you reply because SECURITY but 'message me back!!' sounds so desperate and I am anything but desperate. That's not to say I could have my pick of the men on Soulseekers or anything. But you know. I'm just a boy standing (sitting) in front of, uh, a laptop screen (or phone if I'm on the go and can get the app to work, which I never can) asking you to love me. Well, ♥ me. My profile anyway. Yes? Cooooool.

James. x

(The kiss is just to be polite; it doesn't mean I'm in love with you. I sign everything off with a kiss unless it's a business email. And this is definitely not business. It's pleasure. I think. OK I'm really going now.)

[send?]

Sigh.

I ... no. Sleep.

[save as draft]

08:47 [compose new message]

Hello. I'm James. I really liked your profile (and your pics too!) and I hope you like mine. If you do, and want to grab a drink sometime, let me know.

J.

[send?]

[message sent]

4.

Oh, Ignacio. It started so well. Too well. Ignacio – and that sodding bike of his – changed my life for ever.

I don't know why I'd agonised over making my dating profile perfect – nobody else seemed to be making the effort. Imagine taking the opportunity to dress your windows with inanities like 'I like going out and staying in'. At the same time? How? Did they spend entire evenings with one leg out of the front door and the other firmly plonked in their hallway?

So many clichés: long walks; I enjoy a pint or two; sick of Soho; looking for a partner in crime; tired of the same old same old; missing that spark. No attempt to woo me, just a 'like' – maybe a 'hey how r u' if he was really feeling amorous. Passive attentiveness at best. I didn't reply to a single one. I started to feel lost.

And then I saw Ignacio and I felt those fireworks so lacking in Jack. I knew I had to change tack, take control. I couldn't wait for anyone to come to me – I had to get the ball rolling. And I had to act fast; men who looked like Ignacio didn't stay on the shelf for long.

I rambled heavily in my introductory message, and must've

deleted and started again a thousand times. Was I too twee? Too funny? Did my personality shine through? Would it all go over his head and land somewhere in the Thames a mile away? Whatever I said, it did the trick – before I knew it, we'd arranged to meet. He was from Costa Rica, which was wildly exotic to me, having barely ventured beyond a series of backyards or package-holiday beaches for much of my life. It always seemed unfair to me that I wasn't exotic. 'Oh yeah, my mum is French and my dad is from Vladivostok' people at school would say. It was always the middle-class ones who could afford violin lessons and had a vegan in the family. But I was resolutely, boringly, inescapably English. I had an Irish nana who refused to play up its exoticness – 'the fact I left Ireland to come *here* should tell you all you need to know about where I came from' – and my paternal great-great-grandmother was from Kilmarnock. But that was IT. Nothing else. I had no fascinating roots or cool familial histories to share. We never killed anybody. We didn't escape any revolutions. We were just born, worked, paid the rent and then died.

Ignacio was incredibly handsome, totally at ease with himself and, as our first date progressed, evidently interested in me. He was attentive, looked at me with what I cautiously hoped was appreciation, and when I got back from the loo about an hour in, he was updating his Twitter. Now, ordinarily, this might have seemed odd, but to have a perfect stranger willing to tell a bunch of other strangers he was having a good time made me feel incredible. Validation at last. It didn't matter that he had only 207 followers (I spent an hour wildly searching for his account later), he was having a good time.

One *small* problem: he had brought his bike with him and he seemed like a sensible person. If he was going to get home in one piece, he'd have to stay sober and respectable so he could ride it. Like meeting your new boyfriend's rancid children for the first time, I pretended to be fascinated by his bike to avoid putting him off. As we moved from the pub to another, he wheeled it alongside us and each time, thankfully, it stayed outside. Inside, magic happened and spells were indeed broken; I felt the taste of someone else on my lips and was weirdly hypnotised by it.

Which is why, a mere five weeks later, I was doubled up on my little red sofa, clutching my stomach in agony and disbelief. No, not gastric flu, but dumpitis. A text. Ignacio didn't want to see me anymore.

Clearing the plates at Sunday Club, Nicole paused at mine, seeing I hadn't eaten anything.

'Where do you think it went wrong?'

'I fucked it up, ran before I could walk. I acted like we'd been going out years.'

'What, you stopped having sex and started arguing over council tax?'

I slumped down further in my chair. 'I nagged, I ... I even gave him a pet name.'

'You rushed it, then,' she said. 'It happens. Can't you just try being alone for a while?!'

'He said I was like his very own Tom Hiddleston, in the text,' I half-smiled at the thought. 'But he said he couldn't be himself with me. I crowded him.'

Nicole sat down next to me as I stared blankly ahead. 'Were you in love with Ignacio? Or,' she paused to fork some chicken into Haydn's mouth as he zoomed past with a toy aeroplane, 'did you just *think* you were?'

I tried to hold back the tears I knew Ignacio didn't deserve. 'I thought I could make it work. I don't think I'll ever be able to get anyone like that again.'

'Look, I reckon this is all the feelings from Adam coming

47

out. You spent so long wrapped up in that toxic relationship you think you can't make it by yourself. You panicked.'

'We only went out for five weeks. Why am I so upset? I feel like I'm going to die.'

Nicole gave up trying to feed her son and ate the chicken herself. 'I'm telling you, this is leftover fucked-up-ness from Adam. You were allowed to be upset then, and you are now. OK?'

Nicole rose from the table and started to clear the rest of the plates. 'The last thing you need is another relationship already, anyway, for fuck's sake. You'll meet loads of other men. Have fun. It doesn't sound like you were having much fun with Ignacio.'

I wasn't. I'd never met someone who didn't text back straight away before, or was vague about meeting up, or would change plans at the last minute. It's the kind of thing romantics would say 'keeps you on your own toes', but so do hot coals or floors covered in glass. It was torture. I couldn't control him, and wasn't it kind of weird that I'd tried? Who wanted to skip the romantic beginnings, excitement and passion, literally the only time in a relationship when mild self-doubt can be exhilarating and adventurous?

And that was before we even got started on the bike. He'd bought a new one just that morning, a gleaming, demonic beast with more gears than I had hairs on my head, and shinier than a sack of baubles. It looked terrifying, but he was thrilled with it; he stroked it like it was a cat. He gave me a guided tour of it outside his flat on that freezing Sunday morning, clenching the brakes and spinning the pedals backward while they whirred in pleasure at his touch. It was both gorgeous and ugly. I stood impassively, like I was being introduced to my ex's new husband – which, in a way, I was – and casually asked what he was doing with his old one.

He scratched his head and considered me. 'Hey! Why don't we go for a ride today? You can use my old one!'

This was the thing about cyclists – they were evangelical. Militant missionaries. You had to be one to fuck one. He described a route, and I mapped it in my head, inwardly freaking out at the thought of the busy dual carriageways, treacherous towpaths and vertiginous hills ahead of me if I said yes. I hadn't been on a bike for years, and saw enough floral tributes and cycles spray-painted white at the roadside to know getting on one could be disastrous for a klutz like me. I made the mistake of telling him this but he laughed it off.

I grasped for excuses. 'The seat's too high.'

'It isn't. Try.'

Try. Years and years of failing in PE lessons at school rang in my ears. My sadistic teacher trying to teach me a gate-vault. 'Just try, James. Try.'

It *was* too high.

Ignacio watched me struggle to mount the bike for five full minutes. Eventually he muttered something under his breath and held it while I hoisted myself up onto it, pushing down on his taut shoulder, digging into him with my fingers for what turned out to be the last time. He released me and I set off, wobbling and juddering, looking for brakes, before realising I was on a racing bike and, oh, the brakes weren't where I expected and, hello, that was a lamppost I was careering toward. There was a pathetic scrape as I pranged Ignacio's faithful old servant, and the pitiful whine of the brake as I finally found it.

The bike we'd drunkenly, amorously wheeled home after our first kiss was now in a very sorry state. As I inelegantly hopped off, the bike took its final act of revenge, the seat suddenly upturning and jabbing me in the arse, before it crashed to the ground.

Ignacio silently, deftly lifted the bike and put it back in the shed. As I went to kiss him goodbye, he still smiled and even gently puckered his mouth to receive me, but I'd be lying if I said I hadn't wondered, while I walked away, how quickly a dumping text would come. But it still stung.

'Onwards and upwards and all that,' said the disembodied voice of Bella over the buzzing and crackling of a dreadful connection, all the way from Moscow. 'As much as I loved your emails about Ignacio, there'll be others.' She made a sizzling sound. 'Mind you, that one about your first date ... I came over all unnecessary when I read it, you saucy sex pig.'

Penning long, descriptive emails to Bella had been a strange kind of therapy. It made a change from theorising about Madonna's favourite pizza topping at work, and I knew I could say anything to Bella and she wouldn't think I was being silly or over the top, even if I knew I was. In turn, she said they helped with her homesickness. While the family she worked for were perfectly nice and, according to Bella, 'richer than every Premier League footballer who ever existed, all put together and multiplied by five', they weren't *home*. They weren't my battered couch, unpacked boxes (still three to go!) or chipped coffee mugs.

'Why don't you write about your dates properly instead of sending me the horny details? Get them published. Ask Roland, maybe?'

'He wouldn't be into them. Doesn't like long reads. Anyway, I'd be too embarrassed.'

'Embarrassed by what? It's the best stuff you've ever done! Do it anonymously, then. Blog, maybe. *The dating adventures of Our Hero.* James Brodie in disguise.'

The chance to be someone else did appeal. I was a fantastic liar as a child. Now you'd call it creativity or an active imagination, but back then it was what it was – lying. My own life seemed so boring compared with everyone else's. No siblings to fight with, no rich grandparents to die and leave me everything, not even a redhead in the family.

'I reckon a secret identity would really suit you. You're a master assimilator.'

Was I?

'You probably never noticed, did you?' Bella's voice was suddenly strong and clear. I winced and turned down the volume. 'Your accent?'

'My accent?'

'Yeah. You definitely picked up a twang from Adam. Rolling your Rs like a plastic Scotsman. But you don't do it anymore. Barely at all. You're back to yourself again. Nearly.'

I felt weirdly uncomfortable. I pressed on. 'But nobody really reads blogs, do they?' Anyway, there was something spiteful about the idea of reviewing oblivious guys under a pseudonym. Undercover. Creepy.

Bella was insistent. 'A blog isn't doing it for money. It's not exploiting them. And these are your experiences. And you're not *like* the others. They're shit. I've seen them. *Date Me Daddy*, for God's sake. What a self-loathing prick he is.'

'*I'm* a self-loathing prick.'

Bella hissed away the beginnings of self-pity. 'You are not. You won't be mean, you won't do anything to make yourself look good. You literally don't know how to be nice to *yourself* – but you're not a bad person. You don't want to settle down, so why not give it all a different purpose? It could take you somewhere.'

'I can't use Our Hero again. What would I even call myself?'

'Then be someone else – a rose by any other name and all that. You'll soon think of one! Wherefore art thou Romeo?'

Bingo.

Romeo Numero Uno

pre-date rating: 8/10 – nice face, good profile blurb, no signs of serial murder
age: 29
stats: 5′9″ (he says); brown hair (shiny, clean, present); brown eyes (small, kind)
where: Royal Oak, Columbia Rd, E1

Sometimes when you don't know where to start, the best thing to do is just get going and hope it all works itself out. It usually does. I have been chatting to a man over email and text. We met on a dating website, because this is how I talk to men now that a boyfriend no longer walks through my door at 7 p.m. demanding his dinner. I'm single, of my own volition, and using the internet and my typing fingers – arthritic, gnarled, but quick – to woo a stranger. To my surprise, it is working. He seems very sweet and really quite keen. So there we go: a start.

We have a lot in common, or so we say, and he seems genuinely interested in me. I refuse to get my hopes up, however; while I am optimistic, it's probably no spoiler to say, just one post in, that he very likely won't be the last. Otherwise we wouldn't be sitting here at all. But let's pretend it is then, and we are who we were then.

There's something I can't quite explain about this man. A good feeling. Romeo texts on the way: he's going to be late. Lateness really annoys me. I am never late, like hardly ever. Only being stopped in the street by a talking dog who wants to tell your fortune would be a decent excuse, but it's Friday night – maybe he had to work late. I give him the benefit of the doubt. I arrive and am about to order a G&T when I change my mind and get a beer. I'm so nervous and excited that if I were to open my mouth right now I'd scream.

It isn't busy. I pick a corner seat – two chairs and a small table between. Intimate, I decide.

Another text: he's on his bike and lost; he'll be a little while longer.

A bike. Oh. I am disappointed. Even though I haven't met him yet, a bike means no matter how well I get to know him during the date, at the end of the night he'll be hopping on his iron-skeletoned other woman and disappearing into the dark. The bike – any bike – is, I must confess, my no. 1 sex nemesis, ever since I accepted a drunken ride on the back of a racing bike from the most handsome man at university, fell off and grazed my scrotum – thereby putting paid to anything else grazing it that night.

Finally, a full twenty-five minutes late, he's there. He saunters. I pretend not to see him, because I imagine this is sexier than an expectant or overly eager face, and only look up when I know for sure he's seen me.

He's whip-thin and toned, like, properly, like a famous person, and wearing a leather jacket and jeans and other stuff, probably – I can barely see, I'm so nervous. He has a cycle helmet in his hand. I don't know much about *coup de foudre* or an instant animal magnetism or whatever but I feel heat. Real heat.

We brush cheeks in greeting. He smells absolutely beautiful. I surprise myself at how much I fancy him, like, straight away. I do that, of course, but only from afar, gazing across at beautiful men and separated by crowds, or cars, or smoothie stands. But this one is right in front of me and – well, what do you know – his eyes gleam and he clearly feels the same. I feel famous. But I mustn't get ahead of myself. I go get him a beer so he can look at my arse. I absolutely want him to look. He does. Ha!

When I return, his jacket's off. He is remarkably handsome, with a slightly squished nose and a lovely full mouth. His teeth are like porcelain. I cannot stop looking at his mouth. I don't want that mouth to leave without me. His eyes are dark brown, but they glint. My own mottled blues are no doubt swallowed up by my dilated pupils.

He's attentive, and his eyes flick from my face to the rest of me, and for most of the date he wears a wry smile. Like he knows something. Or is imagining something. Whatever it is, he doesn't let me in on it. He's erring on the shy side, probably because he thinks it's sexy. And you know what? It totally is.

He too recently ended a relationship and, like me, has occasional, skewering pangs of guilt about it.

He's tactile too. When I make him laugh, he touches my leg. He has a great laugh. We're getting on so well I can feel myself looking out for the catch, the drawback. What's wrong with him? Is he an escaped convict? I've been on dates, but not like this. It's not supposed to go this well, with fire and music and lights; I'm supposed to kiss lots of frogs before I meet my prince, right?

After a few drinks, we move on. He trundles his bike alongside him and we stroll down Columbia Road, feeling slightly merry – high, maybe, on a strange, exhilarating connection – and immune to the evening's chill.

Despite my burgeoning euphoria, I feel strange, awkward and shy, like a schoolboy, and he has an expression on his face I can't quite read.

The next pub is packed to the rafters with all manner of gay guys: fat ones, thin ones, hairy ones, trendy ones, topless ones, hot ones, ugly ones – lots of ugly ones. We get drinks. As we're jostled in the throng, we move closer and closer together. We dance a little. Badly. The sense of anticipation is so strong it could power a jet engine. I can't let this opportunity pass me by. But I need to pee.

'I'm going to the toilet,' I say, keeping my voice as level as possible. 'And when I get back,' I lean in closer, 'I'm going to kiss you. Is that OK?'

He smiles. Nods. Shit, did he understand me? I go to the bathroom, shaking like a leaf as I try to pee as quickly as possible, in case it's all a dream and he's gone when I get back. But as I stride back out, shaking the excess water off my hands, he's in exactly the same spot, still smiling.

'Hey,' he says as I take my place in front of him.

I take a swig of my beer and move closer. We tilt

our heads that way and this, deciding which way to go in. And then we kiss. It seems to last centuries. I hold onto his ear as we kiss and he grabs the waist of my jeans and pulls it tight.

When we break for air, everyone in our eyeline is staring, hissing 'get a room' or rolling their eyes skyward. We must've been really going for it. I don't care: I've just been kissing a very, very hot man. The rest of the room can go fuck itself. I go in for more. And more.

After an hour or so, we've outstayed our welcome and the nudges in our sides are becoming sharper.

The place could be on fire and we wouldn't even notice. We're looking at each other and grinning. Time to go. There's a light, envious ripple of applause as we stumble out, our fingers interlocked. I look back and smile at my audience, wearing triumph like a crown.

My Romeo is too drunk to ride his bike. He lives about twenty minutes' walk away, he says. I insist he pushes the bike and that I'll walk him home. He protests he doesn't want me to go to any trouble. I assure him it's no trouble at all. None.

On the way, the bike falls over and catches my leg. It will leave a scar. We stop and get soft drinks. We laugh a lot. The inevitable arrival back at his place hangs over us. We just want the magic back. Our moment. Twenty minutes is forever.

Arriving back at his house, he asks if I want to come in for tea. He parks his bike in the hall and I go through to the kitchen. I stand against the sink watching every move, more alert than ever.

He half-heartedly places two cups on the worktop but does not turn the kettle on. He runs the back of his hand down my face and moves closer. I bite my lip. He grabs my hips. We kiss lightly. Then not so lightly. Closer into me. We stop. I look down at the floor. We both take a deep breath.

'Do you want to, uh, go upstairs?' he asks. I look back up. That wry smile again. Now I know what that means.

'Yes,' I say. 'Let's.'

So we do.

post-date rating: It's a 10.

5.

'OK, OK, indulge me. Read the last bit again. What does he say?' Bella sat applying a face pack, her eyes peering wonkily just off to the left of the camera as she used the grainy picture of herself as a guide.

I looked again at my phone. 'It says, "you're just what we've been waiting for" – for the third time.' As embarrassed as I was, I couldn't help but beam.

'Fucking hell, Jim, you have got a fan. An actual superfan. How does it feel?'

How did it feel? I couldn't really say. It had all just kind of happened. I had settled on a name, *One More Romeo* – because I really liked the idea of calling myself Romeo and sounding all sexy and mysterious even though I knew the truth was somewhat different – chose an avatar and posted my first blog. And then another one. And another, with each one, if I do say so myself, getting better every time. I didn't expect that much at first, maybe the odd like or two and a random 'well done' here or there but, to my surprise, I'd managed to build up a small, loyal following.

My manifesto was simple: I wouldn't stop until I'd found a

Romeo of my own – yes, it did quickly become complicated being called Romeo and also looking for a Romeo but they do say all gay men ending up dating themselves eventually – and when I *did* meet the one I called my Last Romeo, it would all be over. I pretended that Romeo's profile picture, and his avatar on Twitter – a close-up of my mouth – was to add extra mystique, but in fact it was born of desperation. Nobody trusted a blank avatar and I didn't want to get sued for using someone else's photo. Richie had approved.

'You've got a nice mouth and I suppose for a gay bloke, a picture of a mouth is like me looking at a picture of a pair of tits.'

Nicole was aghast. 'When have *you* looked at a picture of a pair of tits recently?'

Richie looked down at his own wife's chest like a cartoon bulldog with its nose pressed up against a butcher's shop window. 'Feel free to send me one, princess.'

It was like being a character in a movie, albeit a really boring one where the leading man looks like the 'before' picture on a botox clinic brochure. I set the dates up, tweeted a bit of build-up – the followers were growing slowly – and went on the date. If there was anything to report, I'd come home and write it all down. More often than not, my little missives went out into the ether and attracted no feedback. And then along came Luca.

In the short time we'd 'known' each other, Luca, a perfect stranger, had become both my most enthusiastic supporter and my moral compass. Stumbling across my blog on Twitter, Luca liked what he'd read and got in touch to tell me. His intentions were honourable as far as I could see – he had a boyfriend of his own and said his life was complicated enough without falling in love with faceless bloggers – and he was very sweet. If he saw me tweeting that I'd been on a date, he always messaged me to see how it went. It got to the point where, as soon as I'd published a new post, I'd be looking out for a message from Luca, like a cat bringing in a frog from the garden and expecting wild praise. And sure enough he'd be there, more enthusiastic every time. For the first time in a while, I felt I was doing something right, something useful.

> I know I say it every time but that was the best one yet.

> > Hey! Oh, thank you. And yes you do say that every time! But it's still good to hear.

> Do you ever worry one of them will see it?

> > No, not really. Enough details are changed for there to be a little bit of doubt.

But this wasn't strictly true. At first, I hadn't really given it much thought – nobody was seeing it at all, so the chances of one of my victims – hang on, *Romeos* – discovering it were pretty slim. And if they did spot themselves, what were they going to do about it? Unmask themselves? Highly unlikely. So I shrugged it off whenever I spoke to Luca about it – it didn't do to reveal weakness or self-doubt to a stranger, let alone one who seemed to adore you – but I did wonder which of those first posts would be the one to get me into trouble.

'Look, I wouldn't worry about it,' slurred Bella, through the side of her mouth to preserve her masque. 'It's the internet. You can always take it down. And if this Luca guy is anything to go by, you're really resonating.'

Dreary bores, flirtatious heartbreakers or passionate snoggers the wrong side of midnight, it didn't matter – my readers wanted more, and so did their friends, once they'd told them about it.

Luca, especially, was an effective honeybee when it came to pollinating the wider consciousness. There were a lot of men like me out there who, in absence of one of their own, needed a fairytale. And I'd had plenty of frogs to kiss.

Russell owned 'about 250 band T-shirts', played 'MarioKart to relax after a day at work' and thought that the lottery was a 'tax on stupidity'. I'd never seen eyes so green, though – they were kind of enchanting – so I overlooked it and stayed out way past my bedtime. As I bored him half to death about my running routines with the confidence only drinking neat whisky at 1 a.m. can give you, Russell leaned over the table in the Queen's Head, stuck his tongue in my ear and asked, 'Have you ever wanked into your running shorts? Can *I*, maybe?' I declined to answer, parted with him chastely at the taxi rank, and rushed home to give *One More Romeo* its most successful blogpost yet.

Then there was Connor, who took me to a health spa where we lounged around, bitching about how awful London was – but also how we'd rather die than live anywhere else. We were massaged mere inches from one another, before being scrubbed down very hard, yet barely touched throughout, even as we showered together after. On paper, he was annoyingly perfect and aesthetically everything aligned pretty well. Another date looked imminent. And then . . . I thought of Romeo, and started looking for problems. I didn't have to hunt too far – a quick peek down at his feet did the trick. Oh man. Long and bony toes like spokes on a cartwheel and an almost post-mortem lack of flesh on the rest. I ached to have him hold me just once, but Romeo quickly blogged about imagining Connor warming those knobbly tootsies on me in the depths of winter and I decided I wouldn't be seeing him again.

Anwar, the handsome doctor, was like a dream. Never asked to share my nachos, told me if my turn-ups needed adjusting, and had the good grace to look away at the moment of climax.

Both times. I saw rainbows, heard birds tweeting (as opposed to the rest of my timeline) and nervously imagined crowning him the Last Romeo. Already! And then, one morning in bed, he gave Romeo just the excuse he'd been looking for. As we set aside the breakfast things, brushed the croissant crumbs from each other's mouths to make room for one another, and things were hotting up – there was a rush of air against my leg and he grabbed my head and shoved it under the covers. My beautiful bed linen, my euphoric morning ruined. It was too good an opportunity to miss. It went into the blog and Anwar was struck off my list.

If I went on a date that went well, pretty quickly, my followers were excited that this could be 'the one' – even though I'd said I wasn't necessarily looking for Mr Right.

> So what do you reckon @OneMoreRomeo?! Was he the #LastRomeo?!? He sounded amazing!!

> what a loser definitely not yr #lastromeo why not take me on a date instead lol!!!

Yes, there was a hashtag.

'I can't believe it,' I gushed. 'I didn't think anyone would be interested.'

'I told you you could do it. Just don't forget me when you're famous.' Bella craned her neck to the sky. 'Gotta run, the heir to the throne is crying.'

I didn't want her to go, but I grinned brightly so she wouldn't see. 'OK! I sent off your care package by the way. Jelly babies, Yorkshire Tea and a bar of Dairy Milk should be with you sooooon!'

Bella winked and waved. 'You're a dream. Thank you! Love ya.'

The room suddenly felt very empty when the screen went blank. I checked my Soulseekers inbox. No messages tonight. My finger hovered over the icon for Seizer, the, uh, less formal 'dating' app. I'd created an account at least seven times, chickening out and deleting on each occasion. No. I wanted a friend, not feeling up. There must be someone out there who didn't live miles away in Russia, wasn't busy being a parent or, well, didn't hate me. What about Seonaid? She was one of Adam's oldest friends and, along with her girlfriend Carrie, had always been very welcoming to me. Seonaid and Carrie had been together years and had that comfortable, totally-at-ease couple thing that it's impossible to fake.

'We've always agreed that in public, we look out for each other, and are kind,' Seonaid told me once. 'If we're pissed off about something, it waits until we get home. It's easier. You two should bloody try it.'

As the years trundled by, we became quite close, and Seonaid and Carrie were two of the few pals from Adam's coterie I would actually meet on my own for a drink. Figuring it was a relationship worth hanging on to, I texted Seonaid – Carrie never turned on her phone – half-expecting the polite 'Oh gosh yes soooooooooon' I'd got from the rest of Adam's friends. Her reply came quickly, suggesting we meet for a bottle of wine in a park, 'but glamorous, not like winos'.

She was already waiting on a tartan blanket pouring booze into plastic tumblers as I tootled toward our agreed meeting point. I felt a brief tingle of nerves. She stood up and threw an arm around my shoulder, stretching out the other to balance herself in her bare feet, still waving the prosecco. 'Jim, darling, hello. Is it me or is it ever so *slightly* too cold to be doing this?' She stepped back to take me in fully, and smiled brightly. 'It's been ages.'

I sat on the edge of the blanket. 'Yes, it has.'

Seonaid brushed her shiny brown hair out of her eyes and peered over the top of her sunglasses, registering the frostiness of my reply. 'I know. I'm really sorry, it's just . . .'

I shrugged. 'It's OK, I get it. I did the dumping, so I lost the friends.'

Seonaid handed me a tumbler. 'That's not it at all. You haven't lost anyone. We all love you. But Adam needed us to pull tight, and we did.'

I couldn't really imagine Adam being one for emotional support – he'd always dismissed my pleas to talk things over as 'best left to daytime television and shrinks who buy degrees off the internet' – but perhaps he'd changed. I certainly hoped I had.

'And to be honest,' she took a big gulp of wine here, 'I didn't want to be in the middle. Carrying tales. But I *did* want to see you.'

We danced around the subject for most of the first bottle, deconstructing news and politics, or Carrie's latest attempt to make Seonaid go vegan, until we could ignore it no longer.

Seonaid breathed out and shifted herself to lie on her tummy. She held her tumbler up to the light between her fingers.

'He's met someone else, you know. I wasn't going to say, but I thought I should.'

Whoa. Why did that floor me so much? Had I expected him to stay by himself? Even after six years, I wasn't such a hard act to follow.

Seonaid read my reaction. 'I don't think you have a right to be upset about that. He was *gutted*, Jim. You crushed him. Ended it for no reason. As far as he's concerned it came out of the blue.'

No right to be upset? Adam, crushed? No reason?! This didn't sound right. What the fuck was he telling everyone?

'It certainly didn't come out of nowhere for *me*, Sho.' I felt my face begin to burn. 'Every day I felt I wasn't good enough. For years. I thought the day would never come at all.'

Seonaid winced and grabbed the next bottle. This was making her uncomfortable. I wonder how much she really knew about our relationship. She filled my tumbler and looked like she was cooking something up.

'Look, if Adam's moving on, finally, it's time you were brought back in from the cold. We all miss you.'

She had a plan. Her birthday was coming up in a couple of weeks. A few drinks at her flat. People we knew.

'Are you sure? I don't want to create a scene.'

Seonaid whooped as she overfilled her glass and prosecco went everywhere. 'Honestly! You *boys*! You're not *that* fascinating. There'll be no scene, no *drama*. It's my birthday. Everyone will behave themselves.'

I held out my glass for a refill. 'No drama? Why am I even coming?'

'You are coming, then?'

I lay back on the blanket and shut my eyes against the sun. Closure. No hiding, let's do it. He couldn't hurt me anymore. 'Yeah. I'm coming.'

'Attaboy.'

If I was going to come face to face with Adam, I had to do some moving on of my own. Next up was Barry, a friendly Welsh guy who was perfect – despite a strange, incomprehensible confession that he 'only had 30 per cent control of his limbs' before he lunged at me at Norman's Coach and Horses in Soho. A second date went swimmingly and I kind of wondered if Romeo's days were already over (again) and the prophetic hashtag would be fulfilled, but luckily – sorry, I mean, *sadly* – he suddenly went back to his ex-boyfriend. Romeo, of course, was thrilled at this stay of execution, and wrote a searing takedown of men who, at the first sign of loneliness, went crawling back to their former flames. If what

Seonaid said was true, I certainly wouldn't be going back to mine. I wished I felt better about it than I did.

On the day of Seonaid's party, I had an even more important celebration to attend – Haydn's ninth birthday. I stayed up way past my bedtime, sober, the night before trying to get to grips with making his birthday cake, ignoring all my messages. Godson before guys, and all that, and I had to be up early as I'd promised to take Haydn for a birthday swim. I'd ended up being the one to teach him to swim when he was younger, quite by chance, so we'd gone regularly ever since. An hour in the pool and a bacon sandwich on the way home had become our regular thing.

After giving my fingers a quick sniff for traces of chlorine, I took the cake out of the tin and proudly placed it at the centre of the table in Nicole's conservatory, already filled with all Haydn's favourite sandwiches – strawberry jam and lemon curd – and prayed my hair didn't look too bad after an entire morning spent under a swimming cap. God knows what he was doing at a children's party, but Nicole's hot colleague Devon was in the garden swigging beer and doing keepy-uppies to a fascinated crowd of nine-year-olds.

Nicole grabbed some tiny candles out of a drawer and got busy. 'The cake looks brilliant! Thank you so much. I know this isn't your ideal way to spend a Saturday afternoon.'

'Don't be silly. I wanted to come. It's nice to feel useful.' Having only myself to think about wasn't always as liberating as I'd imagined.

Nicole handed me a cup of tea and chuckled as she caught me looking at Devon. 'He's single now, you know. Want me to put a word in?'

I wrinkled my nose. 'Is that why he's here? I think he's out of my league, anyway.'

Nicole huffed dismissively. 'Pah! Surely you have all manner of gorgeous guys at your disposal on Soulseekers? How's work going? You still coping?'

I grimaced. Hurley had just been promoted to being in charge of breaking news – he was the only one of us who could touch type – and had been even more unbearable since. Every time a new story came in, no matter how small, he'd shout over to me and Alicha: 'Sorry to piss in your prosecco you pair of basics but this exclusive is *mine*!'

Nicole laughed. 'Well at least you've got Romeo to keep you busy. How *is* the secret diary of Gaydrian Mole going?'

I had debated whether to let anyone other than Bella into my secret. But I couldn't turn up to Sunday Club without gossip and I knew I could count on Richie, Nicole and Silvie to keep my confidence. Who would they tell, anyway? There was no love lost between them and Adam.

Nevertheless, I blushed at the mention. 'Don't believe everything you read.'

'How many dates have you been on this week?'

'Only two! It was four last week.' Nicole raised her eyebrows. 'Well what else am I doing? That's why I'm glad you asked me to do the cake. I've nothing to be in for, nobody to make dinner for.' My stomach somersaulted at the thought of seeing Adam in a few hours' time, and the memory of those silent meals we used to eat.

Silvie wandered in from the garden and lit a cigarette right over a plate of quiche I'd just laid out. 'Bloody kids! I just tipped every bag of Skittles I could find into that massive bowl and legged it.'

'Can't wait for the sugar crash in about two hours.' I saw Nicole wink. 'Jim was just telling me about the blog, Silv. How many followers you got again?'

I got my phone out to check.

'Lookit, pretending he doesn't know *exactly* how many!'

67

Silvie squealed. 'You gonna be packing out Wembley Stadium soon then, Jim?'

Nicole burst out laughing. 'I think we'd probably be OK shoving a few extra chairs and a camping stool in the conservatory, to be honest.'

I could count on my friends to keep me grounded.

Nicole composed herself. 'Aw, no, but . . . look. You're enjoying it, right? Even the howlers?'

'Yes!' I said brightly, and meaning it. 'They make it fun.'

'They're not getting you down?'

'No, honest. Once I write it all down, it doesn't seem real anymore. When it stops being fun, I'll stop doing it. Promise.'

Nicole's eldest, Sid, strolled past en route to the kitchen, wearing the kind of clothes that make you age twenty years as soon as you look at them in shops, and huge headphones that almost covered his entire head.

'Is there any, like *hashtag-snacks* I can eat that aren't for Haydn's *baby shower*?' he groaned, staring into the open fridge. I'd never been the kind of twelve-year-old who brimmed with self-confidence and now, at thirty-four, I was still amazed that someone as cool as Sid not only wanted to talk to me, but liked me.

'People do NOT say that, Sid!' I laughed. 'Even I know not to say *hashtag* out loud.'

Sid came back over to me and held out a fist so we could bump knuckles. It was his thing. 'I was being ironic, uncle J. You still out there breaking hearts, yeah?'

Sid ignored his mother's protests that one smoothie at a time was more than enough and moonwalked his exit with an armful, winking at me as he went.

Nicole was just telling me about the aggressive soccer mums she had to deal with at the boys' inescapable extracurricular activities, and I was promising to come with her next time and feed her some pithy putdowns, when we heard the front door swing open. Richie was in the building. On seeing me, he pointed an accusing finger and roared with laughter. 'So what's this I was reading today about you wanking off some rent boy in the bath when you was hungover? I couldn't believe my fucking eyes. Finally, some action!'

I cringed at the memory. Now *this* was the trouble with letting friends in on the secret – they actually read the blog, and Richie loved to go over it in forensic detail. '*Not* a rent boy. Just a guy I met. And it was pretty grim, to be honest. All I had to show for it were goose pimples and a ring around the bathtub.'

Richie threw his head back. 'Bollocks, you loved it.' He gave my shoulder a blokey punch. 'Are we gonna start having proper banter now that you're a total lad who bones randoms in the bath or whatever? Roooooomeo.' I still couldn't believe I'd done it. I wouldn't have said boo to a goose a few weeks ago; now I was getting goosed in the bathtub. Everyone laughed, but I shivered, remembering how terrified I was opening the door to a stranger, saying things that felt straight out of the script of a bad movie so I wouldn't betray my nerves. But I did it.

'I'm ... er ... just feeling a bit more confident, I think,' I stammered. 'Either that or this is the beginning of my downward spiral.'

Nicole smiled at me. 'Well I think it's great. Having some fun at last. Sure, I'd love a bath with a stranger.' For once, Richie was silent.

As we headed outside to feed the children, I told them about Seonaid's party. Devon finally tired of being an unpaid children's entertainer and joined us.

'Aw, imagine, right,' Richie was excited, 'if you and Adam had a big fucking catfight or something. Now that you've got all this new *confidence*.' He waggled his eyebrows at me while

Devon looked on, perplexed. 'You know, like, ripping each other's hair out and rolling over the floor calling each other bitches and sluts.'

'Oh, I think I met your boyfriend once,' said Devon. 'At Nicole's barbecue last summer. Are you not together anymore, then?'

I couldn't speak. A direct question. From another gay man. No dating profile. No preamble over text. No awkward hello in a pub. I was out of my depth. How fortunate, then, that Richie was talking enough for the both of us.

'Not with Adam? You're joking, aren't you? Adam's about the only one he's *not* with.'

I saw Nicole's face twitch and Silvie took a really long, tense drag of her cigarette.

'In fact,' Richie took a cigarette from behind his ear, 'you're a gay bloke, aren't you? Do you know who Romeo is?'

Just as my heartbeat reached critical point, Nicole decided enough was enough and launched her drink over Richie to shut him up, some of it splashing Devon's ridiculously low-necked T-shirt. We watched as rivulets of cranberry juice gathered in Devon's chest. We watched a little too long, in fact.

Richie leapt back in disbelief. 'What the fuck?!'

Nicole's eyes flicked to her husband. 'I thought I saw a wasp,' she said, before leaning over and smacking him on the forearm, hard. 'And there was another one.'

Richie pulled at his sodden T-shirt, exposing his furry midriff. He looked at me and Devon.

'Yeah, I guess this is probably turning you two on.' He smoothed it back down. 'You should take a date to the party, Jim, really get things going.' He looked pointedly at Devon, who began to look very uncomfortable.

'I'm just going to dry off,' he said, leaving us to it.

'I don't think that would go down very well,' I sighed, still

70

composing myself after the near-miss, my gaze following Devon's retreating backside.

'I'm free tonight! Take me!' squealed Silvie. 'Adam knows me, so I'm no threat.'

'What if it goes to shit?'

'Then I'll kick his head in for you.'

It was an offer I couldn't refuse.

The Romeo in the Bathtub

pre-date rating: 8/10, for his chit-chat
age: 35
stats: 5'11"; green eyes; mousey hair
where: My bath – yes, that's right

When you think of a first date, you think of awkward conversation in a bar or gentle flirting over an American Hot – hopefully with a hot American – in Pizza Express. I've been wooed in pubs, parks, terraces, diners and more, but no date location has ever been quite so odd, and yet so humdrum and familiar to me, as this one. In my flat – my bathroom, to be precise.

These days, I'm a big believer in doing things you wouldn't normally do. Saying yes when you'd usually say no, agreeing when your instinct is to differ. And nothing encourages my impulsive spirit more than a hangover. There's something about lying prostrate on a red sofa in the middle of the day in a post-booze stupor that brings out the daredevil in me. And my enabler is right here in my hand. No, silly, not *that* – my iPhone.

Within seconds I'm on Seizer ~talking~ to a man who has the misfortune to have the same name as my ex – but the similarities end there. He tells me I'm 'cute' – a word best reserved for puppies and pinafore dresses, but OK – and that we should hook up. So I do what any sane person would do when they want someone to want them even more, and tell him I'm not remotely interested in sex with random strangers, so I'll have to pass.

Yes. Like a charm.

'Can't we just meet for coffee?' he pleads. 'What are you doing right now?' A final gust of alcoholic confidence hits my sails.

'Well, I'm about to have a bath, I'm afraid.'

'Shame,' he replies, and I feel the charge between us begin to drain, much like my phone battery was.

'Unless . . . ' My hand twitches. Go on. Do it. 'Unless you want to join me?'

'Are you serious?'

'Deadly. I almost never joke about anything. The hot tap is on. Here's my address.'

Life comes at you fast, especially when you force your own hand.

My flat looks like a garbage truck crashed into it only seconds ago, but he's coming to scrub my back, not critique my housekeeping, so I do some rudimentary tidying, chuck some bleach down the loo and rinse out the bath. A quick peek in the mirror reveals my hungover look wouldn't win any beauty contests, but I'm sure a guy who agrees to take a bath with a stranger has had doors opened to him by far uglier brutes.

After half an hour the bath is ready and I am sitting

up straight in a clean white T-shirt and two short sprays of Chanel – if I am to be murdered in my own flat, I at least want to smell good as I heave my last breath – and waiting for the buzzer to go.

He certainly isn't a professional selfie-taker – his photos were badly lit and unforgiving – but he is surprisingly beautiful. His online bravado disintegrates as he sits in the chair opposite me, balancing a bottle of water on his knee, which I am delighted to see is trembling slightly.

'I don't normally do this kind of thing.'

If I had half a mind to care about putting him at ease I would admit this too, but his confession empowers me. I listen to the edited highlights of his life story for twenty minutes before setting down my own glass of water and gently turning my head to the bathroom.

'We getting in then?'

'Sure.'

'Excellent. I'll just top up the hot water.'

He follows me through and we watch the tub fill as the steam rises. I probably should've scrubbed the grouting before he arrived. Never mind. I mask my mild panic with a beatific smile which makes me look like I'm smacked out on tranquillisers.

'Well,' I say. 'Are we ready?'

Undressing each other would probably be sexier, but we instinctively begin to take off our own clothes. It's all hysterically shy and proper, like we're two children trying to change into swimming costumes on a crowded beach. We peek at each other as we go, both expressionless. Usually, I'm very self-conscious when exposing my rack to the world, but that hangover is working wonders for my bravado, plus I'm on home territory. His body is good. Wiry, toned. His thighs are strong. His timidity is all for show.

Finally we are naked.

'Which end?' My voice is suddenly loud and charmless as it echoes around the room.

'Huh?'

'Of the bath? I'm happy to take one for the team and sit against the taps.'

He very gallantly says he will instead and gamely plonks one foot in the bath – before instantly retracting it with a piercing scream, like he's been bitten by a shark. I'd forgotten to do the elbow test. His foot is very red.

'I don't think it's fatal.' I turn on the cold tap and watch the gushing, icy water flatten my beautiful bubbles.

We pass a few awkward minutes – still stark-bollock naked, remember – waiting to try again. This time, no shrieks. We both stand up in the bath and lower ourselves slowly into the water at opposing ends with eerie synchronicity, our eyes fixed on each other. There is some shuffling and bafflement at where to put feet, but soon we're settled in the warm suds.

He absentmindedly strokes my leg and I do the same to his as we continue our conversation, like we'd never got up from the sofa. After a while, he tries to sit up so he can approach me to kiss, but his elbow slips and slams into my various potions and lotions, sending them careering into the bath.

I sit up on my knees and steady myself. 'Oh come here.' I grab him and pull him close until our chests, tummies, everything, are flat together and our lips can finally lock. It is wet, and a little amateurish, but not unpleasant.

We shift about in the tub, and pools of water splash onto the floor tiles as it overflows, but we don't stop. His gasps echo heavily against my tiled walls. Once it's over, we retreat back to our respective ends of the bath. I watch him flinch as the plughole makes contact with his balls. I move to get comfortable and inadvertently kick him right up the arse.

He yelps and scowls at me. 'Your nails need a trim.' I smile my apologies and brush my sodden hair out of my eyes.

'Um ... ' he sounds more sheepish. 'I kind of need the loo.'

'Well, uh, why don't you just pop out and have a tinkle and I'll avert my gaze and put my fingers in my ears.'

He looks down at his chest. 'It's ... erm ... it's not a tinkle.'

I pull a face like Margo from *The Good Life* working her way through a bag of Tangfastics. The ends of my fingers are starting to crease. My enthusiasm subsides.

'I'm getting out,' I say, and reach for the nearest towel. 'Knock yourself out.'

I close the door behind me and hear him rip out an absolutely massive fart in the bath, before the rush of water in the drain indicates he's got out.

I wait in the lounge, still only in my towel in an effort to appear alluring, but I'm not one of those people who looks good when they're wet, and he's taking ages in there, so eventually I dry myself off and get dressed.

Once he's fully cleaned out his cage – my throat tightens in displeasure as I hear him go wild with the air freshener – he reappears, his skin now dulled, hair a fluffy mess. It's like waking up on Christmas morning to find the snowman you excitedly built the night before is half-melted and yellow with the piss of every dog in the neighbourhood.

'We should do this again sometime,' he chuckles as I brave the synthetically fragranced fug of the bathroom and squirt moisturiser into my hand.

'Of course.' I begin to apply the cream to my dried-out face.

He puts his hand on my shoulder and I stop, thinking we are about to share a tender moment.

'Don't put the cream on like that,' he says, roughly rubbing his face to exaggeratedly mimic what I'd done seconds before. 'You need to be gentle. Be kind to that face of yours. Look after it better.'

Slobbery kisses, farting in my bath, and destroying my toilet I can just about handle – but no man gets to tell me what to do, even if it is in the guise of friendly advice.

I say his name for the first time, feeling the shadow of my ex across my face, and follow it with goodbye. He slams the door behind him. I reach for the bleach.

post-date rating: 7. Marked down for becoming a little *too* comfortable in my bathroom, not to mention his unwelcome beauty tips.

6.

'I'm so glad you came!' enthused Seonaid as she opened the door. Carrie hovered behind her holding a tray filled with glasses of champagne.

'I can't kiss you on the cheek in case I drop all this booze, but I will later.'

I reintroduced Silvie to the pair of them, and they went through the usual corroborating of where they'd met before. We plonked our bottles of supermarket vodka – which were disguised in Harvey Nichols carrier bags and we had zero intention of seeing ever again – on the kitchen table and took a glass of fizz each from Carrie, before Seonaid showed us into her lounge, where our audience awaited.

On the tube on the way over, Silvie had given me a pep talk as she touched up her mascara, and warned me 'not to rise to Adam's bait'. The last thing I was going to do was cause a scene; I wanted to fade into the background altogether. I couldn't shake the thought that this was a bad idea. Silvie reminded me these had been my friends once. 'Not one of them called you. Why should you hide away? The shame is on them, not you.'

I was struggling with the idea I wasn't a bad person, and the chat with Seonaid had got me worrying about how Adam had chosen to spin the breakup.

'You are a *good* person. Good people end relationships too. Adam was *not* a good person. These are the kind of guys who *should* be dumped.'

'He was everything to me for six years.'

Silvie glanced away from her mirror. 'And you know what? To a casual observer, by which I mean me, he treated *you* like you were absolutely nothing to him.' She winked and put her compact away. 'Just remember I'm there for you. But you have to be there for yourself, too. Stand your ground. Be proud. And if it all goes really badly wrong, just tell him how much sex you've been having!'

We were early, so it was easy to take everyone in. Friendly nods from people who'd been mates not that long ago. Half-smiles from people who'd been tagged alongside me in Facebook photos over the last few years. Nobody came over. I looked back at Silvie and saw she'd already drained her prosecco.

'Well,' she whispered exaggeratedly, 'nobody has murdered you yet, so that's a good sign.'

Suddenly, I heard the squelch of a kiss at my ear and smelled a cloud of Creed.

'Curtis!'

'Hello James, darling. Hello delightful female friend of James I've never met before with cracking knockers.' He gave Silvie an affectionate squeeze on the arm. I never really understood why people found his rampant sexism charming, but somehow he managed to win everyone over.

'I didn't know you knew Seonaid and Carrie.'

Curtis tried to talk and drink at the same time. 'I used to work with Carrie, bumped into her last week at a thing' – Curtis was always at a thing – 'and it was like we'd never been apart. It was just a relief to see she hadn't been sent to the glue factory like everyone else we used to work with.'

Silvie was agog. If I didn't move her away from Curtis very soon she was going to profess her undying love for him, I could feel it. Curtis had that effect on straight women.

'Anywaaaaay,' sighed Curtis. 'Here we all are, as yet unglued.'

Silvie managed to compose herself and nudged me. 'Adam's over there, by the way – seven o'clock.'

I looked behind me. Nothing.

Silvie peered at her watch. 'Oh, I mean ten o'clock. Bollocks. Ten. Ten!'

Curtis spun round for a better view. 'Oh, yes, the king of the fun-sponges, there he is.'

I recognised his entourage – an old university pal and her dreary husband. We'd been at their wedding. She had told me how perfect Adam and I were together. I wondered what she was telling him now. We stood pretending not to stare at them for quite a while, before Silvie decided enough was enough and shouted Adam's name at decibels that would've cut through an open-air reggae concert. He looked up with a self-satisfied smile. He had been briefed about my attendance.

Curtis pushed Silvie and me over toward Adam. 'I'm going to sit this one out, James. I never was one to gawp at a catfight in a lily pond. Good luck. And don't forget we need to go for that coffee.' He pouted exaggeratedly. 'If you survive ...'

I stumbled a little, but Silvie said an awestruck goodbye to Curtis and dragged me over to Adam by my elbow. Adam's face suddenly changed – a wounded look I'd never seen before. He nodded at me and I back.

Then nothing. All five of us looking at each other. Adam's friend, Penny, smiled too widely and broke the silence by telling me I was looking well. Perfect.

Silvie sensed health and fitness was a safer subject than any-thing else, and pointed out Adam had dropped a few pounds.

'Lovesick,' he said lifelessly, forcing a smile before flicking his eyes to me. This just didn't ring true at all – the only time Adam had been sick over anyone was after having four espresso martinis at his work Christmas party.

Silvie either missed Adam's mournful tone or chose to ignore it. 'Jim's been running, haven't you?' Silvie nudged me.

'I have.'

Adam looked me up and down but said nothing.

Suddenly, a small guy with a beer can, horn-rimmed specs and a winning smile squeezed past me and wriggled in next to Adam, snaking his arm round his waist. Oh. Hello.

From his startled, yet mildly contemptuous expression, I saw my reputation preceded me.

'You must be James.' He held out his hand. I shook it.

Adam didn't take his eyes off me for a second. 'This is Charlie.'

Charlie. He looked a tad nervous. I looked at him, back to Adam, and then at Charlie again, like a tennis umpire. I tried to imagine the pair of them having sex, but all I could visualise was two John Lewis gift cards sliding around on top of one another.

Nobody said anything.

Charlie glanced about the room like a meerkat and pretended to spot someone he wanted to talk to, made his excuses and scampered off. I could feel Silvie dying of terminal awkward-ness so I suggested she go off to find more drinks. Penny and husband saw this as their escape route and were only too happy to assist. Adam and I were alone for the first time since that last time. The day I moved. That Tuesday.

He dropped the act and was back to his old self.

'*Running?* It was all I could do to persuade you to get off the bus one stop early. I imagined you'd be the size of a house by now, comfort eating.'

'You sound disappointed. I like running. Clears the head.'

Desperate for normality, I asked him about his family, and friends, all the storylines that are a constant thread through your life when you're together, but suddenly come to a halt when it's over.

Adam cocked his head to one side and took a swig of wine. 'What the fuck do *you* care?'

Somewhere behind me I heard Silvie and Curtis cackling like two drunk drag queens. Silvie wasn't coming back, was she?

I reached for something else. 'Charlie seems nice.'

Adam smirked slightly at the bland pleasantry. 'He is.' He was determined to make this hard for me. I decided to go for it.

'I've been dating.' A twist of the breadknife in his colon. 'Nothing serious, though.'

Adam fixed me another glacial stare. 'I know you have. I *saw*.'

Did he? *Had* he? How? He only used his phone to monitor his daily steps and upload his food intake to *MyCalorieSergeant*. Had he read *One More Romeo*? My chest tightened.

'You saw?' I held my breath. I waited.

'Hmmm.' He ran his tongue over his teeth slowly, like he was checking them for carrion. 'Saw you on Soulseekers. "I like crumpets" – I mean wow, James. Basic.'

'You saw me on Soulseekers?'

He nodded. He'd met Charlie on there. 'I was quite surprised to see you but I guess those streets you want to walk down won't come out of thin air, will they?'

I wanted to be brave, and give one of those dramatic, empowering speeches like you saw at the movies – I'd been dying to all those years. The time he flirted with a waiter and shushed me in a restaurant, on my birthday. The barbecue where he'd flicked his wine glass at me in front of workmates, because I was telling a funny story and getting the attention he always craved so much. The surprise party I'd organised for him, where I pretended I had a upset stomach so I could go and sit in the toilet and cry after I overheard him say that the decorations were tacky and it was fortunate my fellatio was better than my party planning. But movies are movies and this was real life, so I smiled into the distance as the ensuing silence wrapped itself around my throat.

I wasn't afraid of a bit of hush among friends. There was good silence and bad silence, of course. Good: sitting on a veranda in the countryside staring out into the lush green next to someone at least three handsomeness levels above you; the peace and quiet twenty-five minutes after a toddler has given in to sleep; comfortable silence when people-watching in a hotel bar with a strong gin and tonic, and the knowledge you'll be at it like rabbits within ten minutes of getting home.

Bad: someone tells you his style icon is Willy Wonka and you don't know what to say; you just broke a priceless heirloom in a museum; you're stuck in a lift and have a desperate urge to pee. This was a bad silence.

'Well,' I said brightly, finally, determined to be the bigger man. 'Good to see you're moving on. And happy.'

He narrowed his eyes and nodded down at my glass. 'You look a bit thirsty, James.' His mouth crept into the slightest and cruellest of smiles. 'The gin's in the kitchen. I brought your favourite, actually. Why don't you fuck off out there with all the dirty plates and bin bags – make yourself at home?'

I didn't need telling twice.

I spent the next two hours in the kitchen, emboldened enough by the gin – Adam had indeed brought along a bottle of Plymouth, my favourite, and I was determined to drain it – to hopelessly flirt with an impossibly beautiful man at least 1,000 years my junior. We drank together conspiratorially, our measures of gin getting larger and larger, and our sniggering all the more obvious every time someone else came in to replenish their drinks.

I quickly realised that Finn – 'it's short for something you probably wouldn't be able to pronounce' – was the first man I'd met in a 'normal' way since Adam. Dates followed a set pattern of introductions, job titles, favourite films, the dating scene in London, how expensive everything was, before the awkward last hour where we tried to work out if we fancied each other enough to make a pass. This was different. There was, of course, the inevitable 'What do you do for a living?', whereupon he told me he worked in what he called 'content consultancy'. In my experience this could mean anything from writing captions for videos on YouTube to producing and launching an entire magazine on your own, for no pay. He also designed T-shirts in his spare time. Of course he did. Nobody just worked in a factory or cleaned toilets, did they? Not at parties like this. Everyone was a 'creative'. I'd maybe have rolled my eyes at this on a date, but with Finn I found it charming, because *he* was so charming. Adam's sniping became little more than a vague ribbon of a memory.

I leaned back on the counter and looked up into his eyes. I decided now was not a good time to reveal my ex was in the next room.

The only downside came in human form – his boyfriend. I quickly recognised him as Antony, one of my least favourite of Seonaid's friends who had, several years earlier, made an awkward play for Adam's affections. He was in and out several times, trying to drag Finn back into the main room to subject him to his very mediocre dance moves, but Finn didn't budge.

In the end, Antony said he wanted to leave. Finn looked bereft – well, it was only about 11 p.m. after all – but agreed.

Antony went off to say his goodbyes and Finn and I exchanged the usual pleasantries between strangers who bond at parties. Then he asked me for my number, saying we should meet up.

I felt a little breathless as I found myself saying, 'I don't think Antony would like that.' I pretty much passed out when Finn licked his lips and replied, 'I don't care. I'm not going to tell him. Quick. Give it to me.'

I read it out to him and looked up to see Adam standing in the doorway holding two glasses, and it brought me slamming down to earth immediately, so I shook Finn's hand and went in for a light hug. Then I drained the last of my gin and watched him walk off toward Antony, who had at least one more night of Finn all to himself.

Adam shuffled up to the counter and held up the almost obliterated bottle of Plymouth, before pouring the remainder into the glasses.

'You enjoying yourself are you, Jim?'

I smiled brightly, anxious to keep things civil. 'Sure.'

'Drinking in the kitchen with another man's fella, eh?'

Oh, fuck this. No more self-flagellation. All I did was break up with him. I didn't kill anybody.

'You know me, I've always got something to say, and I'll talk to anyone.'

Adam leaned in, his face petulant and mean. He was drunk on gin and acrimony. 'What a shame nobody wants to talk back.'

I wasn't having this. 'Plenty of people want to talk to me, Adam.'

Adam snorted. 'What, you mean sad Silvie and that great big glittery grape Curtis? Pah! Remember how you always used to moan that you never had any gay friends? No men?'

I did. It made me paranoid, wonder if I wasn't the kind of guy other gay men liked. Some revelled in it, but I didn't want to be

85

an outsider all my life, especially not in the very community I'd spent so many years desperate to join.

Adam looked down into his wine glass. 'It's because you think you're better than everyone else. You always have. But here you are, standing on your own in a kitchen at a party you were only invited to out of sympathy.'

I swallowed hard. 'With you.'

Adam half stuck out his tongue in disgust. 'Not anymore. Go home. And stay the fuck away from my friends.' He walked away, glasses tinkling in his hand with each step until they became lost in the music.

Suddenly exhausted, I wandered back into the lounge to find Silvie. She was out on the balcony with Curtis, both laughing politely at the terrible jokes of a man young enough to serve them in McDonald's.

'Where the hell have you been?'

'Talking to the man of my dreams in the kitchen. And now I'm off.'

'And are you off *with* the man of your dreams? Who is he?' I jerked my head in Finn and Antony's direction. Silvie scanned the room. 'Tall dark guy or the pale puffed-up potato with his hand down his trousers?'

'Not the potato. And no, I'm not.'

'He's gorgeous, you can't go without him.' I shrugged and asked her if she fancied a hot date with me and a bag of chips on the night bus, but she was staying, she said, to get inconclusive proof all men were idiots. 'I've decided it's going to be my life's work,' she chuckled.

Once I got home, I stared right into my laptop screen, but the words wouldn't come. Sometimes there wasn't anything to say. It was too late to call Bella. Nobody wanted to read about how I took hours to get to sleep listening to all the traffic, all the people, all the life outside and feeling a million miles away from it all. Nobody would be interested to know Seonaid's party was my last planned social engagement for weeks, that my diary was blanker than a blow-up doll's stare for the rest of the summer. To fill it, then. I was about to check my Soulseekers inbox when Luca popped up on chat.

> Romeo! You're up late! I've just finished watching an old episode of *Dynasty*. Alexis went to prison for crimes against hairspray. What are you doing?

> I'm just about to check my messages and pick my next date. Wanna help?

> HELL YES!

I scrolled through the messages, trying to see which thumbnail pic looked the most promising.

> OK, we've got The_Dalston_Prince here. He says 'hey like ur profile'. Groundbreaking, truly.

I nosed around a bit. He'd been a member of Soulseekers for eight months. Profile pics updated a month ago. He'd obviously met someone, got involved and it had come crashing down, so he'd come back onto the site to try his luck.

> He reeks of rebound. No thanks.

> Delete!

> Seatchanger1987 is next. I assume
> his best friend wasn't on hand when
> he was picking that moniker.

> You need to ask why he's changing seats.
> Has he wet himself?

Pictures. Hmmm. Apologetic. Cute. Kind of translucent and posh-looking. Real name, it turned out, was Oliver. Boys who'd grown up eating fish fingers for tea did not wear knitwear like that.

> He looks like he might be the kind of guy
> who'd do dry January for a New Year's
> resolution but spend the entire month
> glugging from a hip flask behind your back.

> So what's the verdict?

> He's a maybe.

> Your standards are slipping. Any more?

Just one. Another revolutionary opening message: 'I like your pics and you seem a cool guy.'

RegentsParkGuy. Why Regent's Park? Did he live there? A zillionaire with a huge house on the Marylebone edge of the park, or a flatshare in a grotty wreck on the Camden side? But he'd opened with a compliment and I was as vain as the next man – as long as the next man was Warren Beatty going as Beau Brummell to a costume party.

Luca was suspicious.

Maybe he hangs around the park at night.

And why doesn't he have any pictures?

He's online. I'll ask him for one.

The result was low resolution and fairly boring. He said his name was Tom. I sensed a dating newbie. He was going to have to step it up – no blurry jpegs allowed. We needed hi-res, filtered, super-primped pictures of him in multiple poses and locations. This was online dating, the butcher's shop window of the internet – that meat needed to be a prime cut.

I began to type out as detailed a description as I could for Luca but saw he'd signed off – I'd spent too long scrutinising Tom's photo to notice.

I looked at my watch. It was now officially Sunday morning and I was alone in my flat, scouring Soulseekers for dates and talking to strangers. I gave a record-breaking sigh, filed Tom under 'maybe' and closed my laptop, the snapping of the lid echoing round the flat to remind me, yet again, there was nobody else in it. The draining board full of dirty cups jiggled slightly. I thought again of Finn, leaning against the kitchen counter, laughing naturally as he poured tonic into my glass. An opportunity missed. But it didn't have to be.

I opened the laptop again. Bed could wait.

Somebody Else's Romeo

pre-date rating: None!
age: No idea!
stats: Tall; brown eyes; black hair
where: The kitchen, among the gin

It's a cliché, but you'll always find me in the kitchen at parties. Conversations can't be drowned out by music, you're not subjected to the horrendous dancing of lounge revellers and, more importantly, you're closer to the booze. Plus, you always find the most interesting men in there. Even if they do, sometimes, belong to another.

I'm at a party where silences are thick and heavy and friends are thin on the ground, so I escape to find somewhere to text and tweet in peace, among the white goods, toast crumbs and gleaming carving knives.

I pour as much gin as decency allows into the nearest clean glass, before peeking around the kitchen, like a street urchin, on the hunt for tonic. I am not alone. There is another guy in there, and he has what I want, in more ways than one. He is tall, athletic and

Hollywood handsome — and he's sloshing tonic into two glasses. Seeing I want the tonic too, he smiles and waves the bottle at me, holding it out for my glass.

'Wow, I like your measures.' He grins. 'I bet Christmas Day is a riot when you're in charge of the drinks cabinet.'

I am instantly at ease with this delectable deity and so move a little closer, scooting along the worktop to stand next to him.

'If everyone can still see straight by the Queen's speech, I obviously haven't been doing my job right,' I giggle, and we clink glasses conspiratorially. He looks over his shoulder but obviously doesn't find what he's looking for, so we talk more and fix another round of drinks with equally dangerous measures.

Just as we're laughing too loudly over a stupid, unfunny joke, another, slightly older guy comes along and snakes his arm between us. He isn't moving in for a bear hug, however; he's come to retrieve his drink. I quickly recognise him as someone I've locked swords with before. The second G&T my Romeo was making — it felt hours ago, and the gin now looks stagnant — is for him.

The newcomer doesn't stop to chat, just gives me a cursory glance, a flicker of recognition tinged with venom.

'I'll be through there, babe.' He nods to my Romeo, snatching his drink and turning on his heels to glide into the next room. I am cheered to see one of my friends drunkenly bump into him on her way to the toilet and splash her drink on his arm.

'That's my other half,' my new friend explains, almost dolefully.

It figures. Personality vacuums like that other guy always seem to be dating the hottest man for miles. There's no justice.

'What about you? Who are you here with? Boyfriend? Uh, girlfriend?'

I reply with a hollow laugh. 'Errr, no, I have no other half. I am, um, my whole.'

His eyes crinkle in confusion. 'You're a hole?' It really was a big gin.

'No, no, I'm two halves of the same whole. You see?' I'm floundering. 'Shit. No. I mean I'm single. There is no boyfriend. Not yet. No longer. Not now.'

He grins. I see him consider me differently. 'Ah, OK. Cool.'

That 'cool' is loaded with intent and we both know it, but I figure I should play dumb just long enough to come out of this with some dignity if I'm misreading the signals.

'Tell me about yourself,' I say. 'What brought you to this rotten old kitchen in south London?'

He laughs, stroking his chin in mock contemplation. Are these palpitations? Or is it just the gin relieving me of my marbles? He touches my arm. Nope, it really is getting hot in here.

We're finishing a fourth round of lethal gins when the boyfriend slithers back into view. I offer him a drink and his eyes narrow to slits as he accepts. My Romeo excuses himself to go to the loo. The boyf sips his gin suspiciously. It's too strong, but he's desperately trying not to show it.

He asks my name, even though I'm certain he already knows it. It's an old technique, pretending to forget someone's name, but I reckon his glories in life are few so I hand him this nano-victory and tell him.

He repeats it over and over, hissing in sibilant, Scouse monotone. On asking where *my* boyfriend is, and being told I don't have one, he fixes me with a chilly 'I see'.

'It must be so hard to meet someone these days,' he smiles, sourly. 'Everyone our age is paired up, I suppose. Well, I *say* our age – how old *are* you?'

I laugh out loud at this pathetic bargain-basement insult – the gin is well and truly kicking in – and tell him.

'Well,' he gushes in faux-sincerity, 'You don't look it at *all*. And I'm sure the right guy is out there for you somewhere.' But not here, his eyes say. Not *my* guy. Subtle.

Our young buck returns and his ball and chain gives me one last withering look and turns to his prize. 'Shall we go soon?'

My Romeo shrugs, disappointed. 'If you want.'

'I do.' The boyfriend shakes his shoulders like he is shaking cobwebs off them. 'One more quick boogie. Coming?'

'I'll get us a drink for the road.'

'Fine.' He waves at me dismissively as he walks away. 'Bye, then,' he says, giving my name one more swirl around his tongue like it's a particularly nasty-tasting mouthwash. And then he is gone.

My Romeo turns to me. 'Another?'

I nod, conscious our time is almost up. As he pours, he keeps glancing at me furtively. Like he wants to say something, but obviously doesn't feel he can. The sense of urgency is palpable, but I'm not quite drunk enough to drag it out of him, so I gaze back and smile like a simpleton.

'It's been great to talk to you,' he stutters. 'We should, uh, meet up or something.'

Interesting. And I am interested. My slight inebriation gifts me a brief frankness: 'Will you be bringing your boyfriend along?'

Our hero flushes red and breathes quickly. 'No, I definitely won't.'

My eyes flick over to the other room. I can see his boyfriend in the distance, his back to me, talking to a girl who's laughing uproariously at whatever he is saying. My drunken pal walks by and bumps into him yet again. What a woman. I come back to my Romeo, who has his phone in his hand, primed to take my digits. I look back again to his much worse half.

I should do this to you, I think. I should take his number, give him mine and meet him, just to spite you, you sour bastard. Teach you a lesson for looking down your nose at me for talking to your precious – and, yes, ridiculously handsome – boyfriend in the kitchen. I should meet him and meet him again and meet him yet again and finally take him from you, and prove it isn't really 'hard to find someone at my age' at all. Pairs can be halved. Before your very eyes. I should ruin you. I sigh. But I won't. I know I won't.

If my Romeo is to go a-wandering – and something tells me that eventuality isn't too far off – I don't want it to be with me. Plus, I don't want to be one day creeping through to the kitchen at parties to check my beautiful boyfriend isn't talking to another gin-pouring chancer with designs on my man.

I reel off my telephone number, switching out the

last 5 for a 6 so he won't get through to me should he try.

And as he walks away, I dismiss the creeping dread that I may well be chucking away my Last Romeo right here and now. He's perfect for me. I know it. And so does he.

He can't be the one, can he? That can't be the twist? Does the Last Romeo belong to someone else?

Well, I'll put this one down to experience. If we meet again, I'm taking him. Watch out. Shots fired.

post-date rating: 9 for effort; 1 for attainment.

7.

As Romeo's following grew, he soon became less a hobby and more a way of life – unfortunately, I didn't have enough life to go around. As a result, Roland hauled me into a meeting room to let rip with only the second bollocking of my career since I started at *Snap!* Last time, I'd been given the hairdryer treatment because a soap actress had called him to complain about me. I'd stood on her dress at a movie premiere, and she moaned I was a 'stupid poof'. Not recognising her, I retaliated with a very curt 'fuck off'. Dear Roly took my side but advised I try to spend a little more time reading the actual magazine – 'She's in it every fucking week' – and, you know, the actual news, so I'd know who people were. This time, however, the problem was all mine – my productivity was down and Hurley was outclassing me at every turn.

'Just because he's fast doesn't make him good,' I ventured, but promised to try harder, managing to persuade Roland it was all down to readjusting without Adam. The truth was, I was knackered because I was out almost every night. By the time I had got home from work, shovelled down a ready meal or a limp salad, thrown myself into the shower, picked out my clothes, and perfumed and potioned my poor excuse for a body, gone on a date, exhausted myself with small-talk, drunk too much, before either making my excuses or making my advances and getting home to bed – not always my own – there wasn't much time for regenerative sleep.

And in fact I was more productive than ever – just not for Roland. I'd been amazed when an email from the editor of the most popular magazine for gay men, *HIM*, landed in my inbox and – just like that – offered me a magazine column.

Toby was straight to the point:

> I'm sick of fabulous gays drinking expensive cocktails. I want a relatable person, like you. It doesn't always work out. Sometimes your dates don't like you. Maybe sometimes we won't like you. You're a bit older, you're not some gorgeous model.

> How do you know? I might be!

> Darling, nobody capable of stopping traffic with their devastatingly handsome looks ever hid behind a secret identity for long. You seem to have a story, something we can get behind. I like a man with a following – just as long as you don't expect me to open your fucking fanmail.

His final requests were pretty simple. If I got a boyfriend in the meantime, I was to tell him, and not lie, and the most important commandment:

> Never, ever, under any circumstances, refer to yourself as a male Carrie Bradshaw, because, honey, that's what they all say. And they're not even Charlotte's interior decorator. I think we should aspire to something a little more, something newer. I think that might be you.

I'd written for magazines before, occasionally, but this was actually *about* me. The day the first one came out, I raced to the newsagent and headed to the nearest coffee shop, installing myself in a quiet corner to read it. Holding it in my hands for the first time, I couldn't stop staring, and running my fingers over the type on the glossy paper. I flipped the pages back and forth, pretending I was just a regular reader. Would anyone stop at my page? Did I stand out enough? Would they read it? It may not have carried my name, or had a full picture, but *I* knew it was me, and that was all that mattered. An overnight success at last – only thirty-four years in the making, but all thanks to Romeo.

'Do you never think that the reason you're still sitting here is because my advice is so crap?' I asked Alicha as we sat, being very unproductive, poring over another of her job applications. Every few weeks or so I rewrote her CV, crafted a cover letter and came up with a few ideas she could send in. In return, she did the tea runs so I wouldn't be trapped in the kitchen with Hurley.

'Nah, it's the interview I always mess up. You're the only person I trust to help me.' She chewed the end of her pen distractedly. She was applying for jobs way beneath her ability, but she didn't care as long as she got away from *Snap!* So far, however, any prospective employers had seen through her ruse and knew she'd be bored and off applying for other jobs within six months – so they nicked her ideas and told her she was overqualified.

'I dunno, Alicha ... the fact *I'm* still stuck here too should give you a clue I'm not all that.'

Hurley looked over at us enviously from his desk, which he now called his 'news hub' since his promotion. Clearly bored, he wandered over. Hurley had the attention span of a toddler eating a bag of Revels at the best of times, often breaking off from what he was doing to lip-sync to a video off YouTube – not just music, sometimes entire scenes from *Neighbours* or old adverts that he'd memorised – or pretend he was modelling his outfit on a runway. Whatever he did, he was 'on' 24/7, often FaceTiming his entire day to any one of his equally distracted, entitled friends, who all had similar jobs with equivalent levels of responsibility and clueless bosses, but, in most cases I noticed, slightly nicer offices than ours. I would go over to Hurley's desk to query something and, on my way back to my own knackered chair, hear him say, 'Yeah, that's right, that's him'. He'd been broadcasting the whole time – filming me from below, the horror – and I was a recurring character in whichever dramas Hurley had dreamed up.

As he approached, Alicha and I moved away from each other and closed all the non-work-related windows on our screens.

'Jamie?' Ah, the sickly sweet voice. The 'Jamie' – my least favourite of all the derivatives for my name. When Hurley said it, it went right through me. I'd always try to combat it with as neutral a tone as possible. Like Gary Barlow reading out the football scores.

'Hurley.'

'How did it go with Roland? I hope you didn't get into trouble.'

Hurley placed his coffee cup down on my notepad. A ring appeared immediately. I watched the dark stain of wetness fan out across my scribbles.

'Mind you, he's always had a soft spot for you.'

I ignored the remark – a rumour I was secretly shagging Roland would be just the fuel Hurley needed for weeks and weeks of sly comments, fake concern and conspiratorial eyebrow-raising at the urinals.

'Did he mention me at all? I sent over some brilliant new feature ideas earlier. Was he telling you about them?'

'Feature ideas?' Alicha snorted. 'I thought you were all about the "breaking news" now, Hurls?'

I didn't look up from my screen. 'We didn't talk about you at all, Hurley.' Eyes up. 'We never do.'

Hurley flinched for a second but recovered, turning to Alicha. 'Guess who I saw last night? Only poor old Jamie, out on the tiles!'

Had he? I was nervous. Last night had been a late one. I could still smell booze every time I loosened my collar against the hangover heat. I thought of the guy. Cute, handsy after a few drinks. I never used to let anyone touch me in public, not even Adam. But Romeo did.

'He was in Bar To Be,' Hurley said brightly, innocently. 'You certainly looked like you were having a good time. We *all* thought so.'

Alicha momentarily forgot she was supposed to be my ally – it happened every now and again. 'Oooooh. Slutty Jim. Into it. Who were you with?'

Hurley barked out a laugh, precisely three seconds long. 'Well! He was out with an old friend of mine, actually. Well, I say *old*.'

Alicha and I exchanged a quick glance. She bit. 'What do you mean?'

'Billy, wasn't it?' Hurley roared. 'I remember him. *Everyone* does. From *school*. He was in Year Eleven when I was in sixth form, that's how I know.'

No way. He'd said he was *twenty-seven*; I hadn't asked to see ID. I assumed only older men lied about their age, and he wasn't trying to buy a bottle of vodka from me. Seeing my discomfort, Hurley ploughed on:

'I don't remember him being into antiques back in school but I guess we've all grown up since then.'

He sailed away from my desk like an ocean liner: graceful, triumphant, unsinkable.

I saw Alicha's gaze still firmly fixed upon me. I glared back. 'What?!'

She got up and walked over to me, clamping her hands on my shoulders like she was comforting a mourner at a funeral. 'You know what this means, James. You're a ... a *daddy*.'

Shit.

My obsession with my age was fairly recent. I knew I wasn't *old* old. Yes, the hair was greying and oh my goodness hello jowls, but I felt relatively youthful. It was everyone else who had an issue with it. Hurley, obviously, pensioning me off and asking me what it was like living through the war. The *Boer* War. But on dates, too. I was always honest about my age and kept my profile pics filter-free, but I still ran into problems. One night, I ended up with a miserable guy who, after an hour or so of the conversation not really soaring to the heights we'd hoped, accused me of lying about my age.

We were standing outside a pub in Covent Garden. He scrutinised me in the bright sunshine. 'You look younger in your photos.'

'I *am* younger in the photos. I'm older now than I was then. That's how ageing works.'

'Very good.' Sip. 'Yeah, but you look, like, waaaaay younger. How long ago were they taken?'

'The oldest one is about six months old.'

'Did you Photoshop them?'

Bloody hell. 'No. Obviously I've aged a decade between leaving my house and getting here.'

'I don't like it when guys lie about their age.'

'I didn't lie.'

Eventually he snarled at me and walked away without a word, leaving me standing there by myself.

Luca pinged me just minutes after it was published.

I felt really bad for you in that one. But you
really put him in his place. What a cock.

Oh, I made it sound much worse
than it was. Dramatic licence.

I was lying; I'd actually made it sound better. Tears had stung
my eyes as I slowly put down my drink and crept away before
anyone noticed I'd been jilted, and the blog's closing line – 'Oh,
by the way, you're at least three inches shorter than you said you
were' – was said only in my head. But it's what Romeo would've
said out loud.

Don't you ever wonder why you put yourself
through it? You seem to meet a lot of the
wrong guys.

It made for a good blog, though, didn't it?

And it had. Likes and shares were through the roof.

It did. It was brilliant. You do that really
well. Kind of sad but hopeful at the same
time. I wonder if it's good for you in the long
run, though.

Well, if you enjoyed it, that was the main
thing. Worth it in the end, right?

And at that moment, I truly believed it was. Better a night on
the town with an unsuitable Romeo than staring at the ceiling.
Living on my own meant meaningful interactions were few and
far between outside of work, and even then talking to Alicha was

the only normal conversation I could have all week. Everyone seemed to have their own lives. Sunday Club round at Nicole's was always an excellent release but it was once a month – the rest of their time was caught up in ferrying Sid and Haydn here, there and everywhere, and spending time as a family. Silvie offered to take me out any time I liked – 'I can do gay clubs but I promise not to treat you like a fag bangle', she promised – but something always stopped me. Whenever I was tempted to call someone, I wondered if I'd be intruding. Poor single, saddo James, I imagined them thinking – not him again.

But with *One More Romeo*, they all wanted to see me, didn't they? They had to turn up; they wouldn't think me intruding. And thanks to the column, I had a whole host of online buddies lining up to chat to me.

Bad Irish-themed pubs always have old proverbs scrawled on the wall – 'a stranger is a friend you haven't met yet' – and if the internet had been full of strangers before, we were certainly getting to know one another now. Their feedback made me feel good, every day. Too many dark hours spent browsing the comments section of *Snap!* had taught me the internet was full of chippy morons who got very angry about other people's grammar and the length of women's skirts. Being Romeo taught me … well, exactly the same, to be honest, but in among the manure there were true diamonds. The odd fly in the ointment, sure, like the guy who insisted on calling me 'Maeve Bitchy', but I decided to ignore it and take it as a very misguided compliment. A year spent working with Hurley had taught me garbage fires needed oxygen to survive; it was down to me to starve them entirely.

As long as I had Romeo, no matter how bad the dates got, I was never *totally* alone. I had all my friends with me. Didn't I?

The Prime Beef Romeo

pre-date rating: 7/10
age: 30
stats: 6'; black hair; grey eyes (I am gay for grey eyes in a big way – gey? gray?)
where: A bar-cum-restaurant-cum-cabaret in the most try-hard part of east London. Where else?

I have a rule: no food on a first date. It can only end in disaster, really. Sauces slop down your front a whole lot more eagerly if you're dining opposite somebody you're desperate to impress and vegetable-induced farts are all the more enthusiastic if they know you're sharing crudités with a stranger.

Unusual, then, that I'm meeting tonight's Romeo in a restaurant. He tells me he'll be waiting in the bar area and that he's just up for a few drinks – we don't have to eat if we don't want to.

And I really don't want to. Nobody ever got a hard-on watching someone work their way through your steak-frites after polishing off their own. Well, almost nobody.

Plus, my date tonight, Alex, is an actor – AN ACTOR! – so it's very likely his idea of pigging out differs from mine. If the opportunity arrives, perhaps I'll graze on some bar snacks, but that's as far as I'm going. Ten mouthfuls at most. No more.

I walk into the bar/restaurant/eatery/what-fucking-ever and there he is before me. Draped across the bar, angelically handsome and dressed in a denim shirt and chinos which I suppose would pass for edgy but are the vibrant colour of hangover piss.

His face is framed by black curls and should be hanging in the National Gallery. His eyes are a steely grey. A closer gander from top to toe reveals his head isn't the only part that got all the good stuff. But salt looks like sugar right up until it's on the end of your tongue, so I don't get ahead of myself just yet. The proof of the pudding is in the— oh, no, no, not back to eating again.

He's slugging JD and Cokes like they're going out of fashion and talking about himself a lot. It's like he's at therapy, or his entire childhood will be rendered void if he doesn't blurt it out to someone. But this isn't exactly unusual first-date behaviour – what else is he gonna talk about, tbh? – and he's quite funny and ever so pretty. It won't do me any harm to play the strong, silent type for one night only.

About three drinks in, he suddenly exclaims he's hungry. I'm not exactly surprised he needs to soak up the grog, but I don't want to break my no-grub rule. He insists, though, and did I mention he is very beautiful, so we make our way to a table. He slinks across the room like he owns it, the sexy bastard. Confidence pours from him, leaving stunned onlookers helpless and gasping for air in his vapour trail.

When he gets to the table he's a little unsteady. I

wonder how many JDs he's been throwing down that delicious throat before I got there. I'm not complaining too much. While he hasn't exactly been all over me, he seems friendly enough, my gaze unbroken for much of the date. Uncertainty hangs around us like a cheap pashmina – I really have no idea where this is going to end up. But back to more pressing matters: the food.

I cast my eye over the menu. What do you choose to eat in front of someone you've never met before? Noodles are out: I struggle with chopsticks and slurping soy sauce isn't sexy. Comfort food like pies and curries are verboten – they're full of onions and I want to make sure my breath is in tip-top condition for later. You never know.

After much deliberation, I go for a salad – what a copout, like I'm not boring enough – and my date plumps for a burger. With onions. I cringe a little. Our chat continues as before and just as I'm leaning forward appreciatively to hear him tell me I have nice eyes, a surly waiter gracelessly flings two plates in front of us and stalks off without so much as a 'bon appétit'.

I load up a forkful of salad, looking up just in time to see Alex take a huge bite of his burger, losing most of its contents on his previously exquisite and dimpled chin. He starts to tell me about a funny thing that happened to him during rehearsal, but I can't tear my eyes away from his open mouth and – horror – the burger within. He laughs. A speck of it flies out from his mouth and lands on my cheek. I close my eyes in silent mortification.

There follows twenty minutes of utter torture for me as I watch him swill and slurp and slobber. His beauty is now almost grotesque, ridiculous. It's like someone has drawn a great big cock on the Mona Lisa.

Once the bill comes, we go Dutch without a second thought – even though he had more drinks than me, I just pull my lips in tight and tell myself he's worth it. He suggests we leave in search of 'one for the road'. He's pretty much had enough for every road and motorway in Britain, and I'm still not sure what I'm going to do here. While his table manners were distinctly farmyard, he was certainly enthusiastic. I imagine him going in for a kiss and slurping his tongue all round my face, like an amorous cow. The thought is not unpleasant.

We find a cosy corner in a nearby bar, and he starts to look at me the same way he looked at that burger.

I pull him close to me and we kiss. It's passionate and satisfying. We go in again and again and again. After a couple of minutes, Alex gets up to go to the loo and I sit back in smug satisfaction and survey the rest of the bar. It's highly likely Alex is the hottest man to walk in here in the last ten years, and it was me who got to kiss him. Me 1, rest of the bar 0. I absentmindedly run my tongue over my teeth, in appreciation of the memory, and find something there. What is that? I manoeuvre it onto my tongue.

And then I taste it. Oh no. Noooo.

He appears to have gifted me one of his onions mid-snog. And, there, another. I wince and reach into my pocket to fish out a packet of chewing gum, popping a piece right into my mouth. Time for me to pass on a little something of my own.

post-date rating: 9. Mark knocked off for leaving an onion in my mouth. An. Onion.

8.

My nightly dates with strangers were like being back at university – well, I was spending most of the time drunk and learning a lot. For example, one man's 'dressed-up' was another man's slouchwear, and you should never arrange a hookup with a man who says he's 'looking for a room', because that means he'll be expecting you to pay for the pleasure – whether it was one or not. My biggest takeaway, though, was that you had to get the venue right. Where you took a guy, or let them take you, was your biggest tell, far more revealing than cologne, how you did your hair, the number of kisses on the end of your messages, or a fondness for textspeak. It revealed everything. You were naked, helpless.

But even getting it wrong could go in your favour. Bonding over bad lighting, a horrible crowd, or bar staff with the zesty charm of Victorian prison guards could be all you needed to bring you closer together. If a date dithered too long or suggested somewhere over an hour away from where I fancied waking up, I'd go for my default – an unassuming pub on Columbia Road, the scene of a bustling flower market on a Sunday but otherwise pretty quiet. It wasn't fancy and had zero wow factor, but it was warm, friendly, and perfect for setting nervous dates at ease. Plus, it gave away nothing about *me* whatsoever. It was the kind of place anyone could find themselves in: gay, straight, or anywhere in between.

'Are you still forcing them to meet you at that *bloody* pub?' howled Bella, her derision slicing through the thousands of miles and bad internet connection between us during one of our weekly marathon two-hour FaceTime sessions she'd taken to calling her 'homesickness booster shot'.

'I like it.'

'Yeah, and I know *why* you like it!' She paused to glug on her vodka. 'When that door swings open, everyone can see you. Like you're in the Wild West.'

'Errrr, and I can see *them* coming in, don't forget.'

Bella cackled. 'You never get the chance, Mr "I like to arrive three minutes late"! I do read the sodding blog, you know.'

I pulled my lips in tight in mock indignation but the signal was poor and the video call blurry so the subtlety was lost on her. 'Look, if the door is in the corner it doesn't have the same effect. I like them to see my entrance.'

Bella was almost hysterical now. 'Your *entrance*. Oh, they'll see your entrance all right.' She choked with laughter. 'Jim, if you want an audience, why don't you try panto. Break a leg, sweetie!'

But there was no chance of a big entrance tonight, in this dingy, unloved side street, blocks away from the sterile, reassuring gentrification of shiny hair salons, chain bars, and pop-up restaurants. My date's choice. I liked the idea of meeting somewhere unpretentious, but this was a *local*. It felt purposefully unlovely, like it wanted to keep you out rather than welcome you in. I gave the warped door a shove and stumbled into the narrow, U-shaped main bar – nobody turned to look. I snaked through the throngs to find a free table, quickly finding myself in another room, containing only a pool table, at which four men were having an argument – none of whom looked like the gay man called Tom I was supposed to be meeting, thank fuck – and two further smaller tables. Nobody was sitting at them. I went back out into the bar and looked around for . . . well, I had no idea.

Tom – or 'RegentsParkGuy' as he had been up until that morning – refused to give up a Saturday night for me, but said he'd do early evening drinks on a Sunday. This reeked of married man nipping out while the kids were getting their bath. I was lonely, but I wasn't that desperate. I asked him for another picture. He was cagey but I insisted.

It's me, I promise. It is genuine. I'm not phishing.

He meant 'catfish', I assumed. I thought correcting him might mark me out as a know-it-all so I ignored it.

The image came through. Grainy, again. This time he was standing in what looked like a leisure centre wearing a very unattractive tracksuit. He had what my grandmother would've called a 'nice face'. She would never call anyone handsome or good-looking unless he was her very own grandson (hey!) or a famous person on TV. Those were Gran's rules – the men in your family were the most gorgeous matinee idols in the world and all other males looked like a tomato turned inside out, whoever they were. 'Nice face', though, she could do. That was allowed.

I'm better in the flesh, just you wait. Sunday?

You'd better be.

This was me being cheeky. Assertive. It still felt like trying on a new coat, but it seemed to work.

I was worried about not recognising him thanks to those awful photos, but Bella's advice rang in my head. 'Look for a desperate bloke, all on his own. Just make sure you're not looking into a mirror.'

A woman was slapping the jukebox in frustration – not a Steps fan, I assumed – and as she gave it one final whack, I spotted a table in the corner with a man hunched over it, sipping a drink. He was wearing glasses, had his hair pushed to one side, and was shrouded in a grey hoodie that was far too large, but if I squinted and perhaps held a torch up to his face, and applied untold filters, I could make him out as my date. I could see he'd gone for a prize-winning lack of effort as his 'look', with product through his hair about the only concession to looking nice. I went over and stood right in front of him, casting a shadow. He did not look up. Wow. Really making me work for it.

'Tom.'

He didn't acknowledge me straight away, but he was clearly thinking about it, so I said his name again and this time he looked up, smiling nervously. 'James.' He half-stood and then quickly sat down again. This was going great.

'Seeing as I'm already up, I guess I'll get us some drinks, shall I?' I stood waving my hands in a 'drinky-drinky' motion. 'What is that? What are you having?'

He looked down at his glass. 'It's a lemonade, but I'll have a pint this time, thanks.'

He reeled off some lagers and possible alternatives should they not be available – I should've brought a notebook – and I made my way to the bar. I hated queueing at the best of times, but now I was gently stewing at my lukewarm reception. He hadn't even shaken my hand. Last-minute regret? Was I not looking at my best? I peered down at my stomach, only slightly distended. I really shouldn't have crammed in that last roast potato at Nicole's. Nor the thirteen before it.

When I returned, the hoodie was off and on the stool next to him. I took him in for a moment. Blue Oxford shirt. Sleeves rolled up. Comfortably, almost wilfully, dull. The shirt fitted him considerably better than the hoodie had and I could see, although I was trying not to peer too much, that there was what I'd call a 'body' underneath. He was sizing me up too, even more furtively, like he actively didn't want to look, glancing over at my torso at least fifteen times a minute. The specs, I could see, were just frames with clear lenses. How very 90s. The face behind them was fresh, but closed off – a few freckles dotted his nose, and his eyes were a muted blue. His reddish-brown hair looked like it had been cut very recently – certainly since he'd sent that blurry photo – as the sides were super-short. I could tell he usually swept his hair back, but removing the hoodie helped a thick mass of it make a break for it and flop onto his forehead. He timidly brushed it back to one side. His skin was very clear, in a way that came not just naturally, but with extra care and attention. Expensively. He had money, I could tell; supermarket-brand toiletries didn't make your skin zing that hard. I looked at his mouth last. Full lips, but pulled in tight. Shyness, awkwardness, anger; I couldn't tell which. He forced them into a smile for me. Despite itself, it was a nice smile.

'So.' I fiddled with my belt in the absence of anything else to do. 'Have you been waiting long? Am I late?'

'Not long, no.'

We both stared down into our pints for a second or two.

He spoke. 'Sorry for the cloak and dagger; you know what it's like. And the "Tom" thing – well, I can't be too careful, I mean, you know.'

I leaned forward and smiled. I couldn't work out why he'd been so keen to look as plain and ugly as possible – he was quite good-looking. *Very*, actually. A bit like a superhero. But I had no idea what he was talking about. The music *was* a bit loud. When in doubt, I always faked agreement and prayed it would work. I smiled wider. 'Of course.'

What had I missed? I wasn't the best at retaining information, and I'd only skim-read his messages – hey, I had a lot to get through – so there was a chance he'd told me something important and I'd forgotten, or hadn't paid attention. 'The Tom thing' – what could that mean? Maybe he preferred to be called Thomas and I'd ballsed up straight away. People could be funny about names. I certainly was, having so many derivatives of my own. James, Jamie, Jimmy, Jim, Jimbo, Jambo, Jam (which I insisted on at school, what a TWAT) and Jay had all been used to get my attention over the last thirty-four years.

I decided to press on. 'So, *Thomas*' – just to show I'd been listening – 'why did you choose, erm, *here*?'

He lifted his pint to his lips, his hand trembling slightly. 'I like to go where nobody bats an eyelid.' He laughed. 'Nobody ever recognises me here.'

Nope. No idea. Zero. I looked round to see if any eyelids *were* batting, as if it might give me a clue why they should be. A girl was being sick into a pint glass, but her eyelids remained fairly static. Closed, in fact. Rule two of not being a good listener: when in further doubt, just make a non-committal noise until somebody else starts speaking. 'Hmmmm.'

'And if someone did spot me, say,' he continued, his eyes darting everywhere, 'then we'd just be a couple of mates out for a drink, watching the game.' He nodded up at a TV on the wall. Some kind of sporting event was happening. It could've been football, shinty, hockey or the world crocheting championships – no glasses on, I couldn't see a thing.

'A couple of mates?'

'Yeah.' He brightened, smoothed back his hair again. 'Easier to explain than if someone saw us in a gay bar.'

Wait a minute.

'Tom . . . ' I began. I could tell he was concentrating very hard on listening. 'I want you to know, um, this is *fine*, but are you . . . not out?' He stared back. 'I mean . . . are you *in*? The closet, that is?' Stumbling over my words here. Big sausage tongue. 'Not out to . . . someone? Someone who might bump into us tonight? Your, uh, boss, maybe?' I was rambling, lost.

He looked back incredulously, shuffling on his seat. 'I'm not out to *anyone*. You know that.'

I knew? Had I already been on a date with Tom? Had I dated everyone and was now lapping myself? I had this recurring nightmare where I'd go on a date with a guy and not remember meeting him before. Was it coming true? I'd even started a spreadsheet compiling all my Romeos' stats and quirks, to make sure it didn't happen, but my updates had been sloppy. I gripped my knees hard in case he was about to tell me I knew him from a parallel universe or we were both avatars in a simulation or something. 'Not out to anyone?'

'Well, some friends. An old girlfriend. But, I mean . . . obviously I'm not.'

Obvious? OK, so he was pretty masculine and butch and restrained and all those other ideals all gay men are supposed to aspire to, or whatever, but I'd spotted that skincare regime straight away, and those specs, I could see, *were* Tom Ford, after all.

'Look, it's fine, I mean,' I searched for the right thing to say. I'd have made a terrible agony aunt. 'You know, it's something that takes time for all of us.'

I wondered briefly if I could date anyone so firmly in the closet. Not even the telling-the-parents bit over with yet. He was twenty-eight, for God's sake. I believed in doing what felt right for you, but coming out was a big deal and I wouldn't be the right person to support him through that; I was a wastrel who never paid bills and ate Bombay mix for dinner. This took responsibility, actual adults.

114

I remembered Adam hadn't told one of his grandmothers he was gay and it made family occasions laborious and, naturally, caused arguments between us. I'd come out at twenty-one – pretty late – but even I was still working my way through my own shit all these years later; taking on somebody else's wasn't part of my plan. I hadn't had those endless, execrable coming-out conversations with everyone I knew just so I could go scooting right back into the closet at the first sign of panic. One day maybe, I'd even be able to stop repressing myself and enjoy a brightly coloured cocktail without being embarrassed it made me look camp; so long as my baby steps were going in the right direction – forward – I could live with myself.

But I was bounding way ahead of nature as usual. I hadn't even finished my first drink.

'I don't know if I'll ever be able to come out,' he said, sadly.

'Aw, mate.' My hand slid across the table but he sprang back so hard he elbowed the guy behind him. After muttering apologies in a ridiculously gruff voice, he turned back to me, his eyes narrowed.

'What is it you do again?'

He'd obviously forgotten. I didn't feel so bad about skim-reading his messages now.

'I'm a writer. On a magazine. Well, a website. Long story.'

'Oh.' His voice was small, his face pinched. 'Which one?'

I steeled myself. '*Snap!* You know, the sidebar of sadness, that one.'

He recoiled. 'You're fucking kidding me.' His eyes searched the bar. 'Is this a wind-up?'

His face drained of colour. I was used to people wrinkling their noses in disapproval, but this was anaphylactic horror.

'Tom, look . . . it's just a job. I don't rake through anybody's bins or anything. I write about famous people.' I lifted my head a little higher, to show defiance and also make sure he could see I was flaring my nostrils. 'What do *you* do, anyway, Tom?'

He seemed to be trying his best not to panic. 'Are you taking the piss? Why do you keep calling me Tom? Actually ... I've got to go.'

Without saying another word, he calmly stood up, picked up his hoodie and walked out of the bar. I sat in shock for a few seconds. The fruit machine's shrill beeps and bells blared out to indifference. My first walkout. I looked around the bar. If anyone had noticed I'd been jilted, they were unfazed. I gathered myself, pushed back the stool, and left. I was surprised to find Tom outside, putting his hoodie back on. He regarded me with haunted eyes.

'You work for *Snap!*? You're a tabloid journalist?'

I sighed heavily and began my often-rehearsed speech. 'I don't camp out on doorsteps or hack phones or chase princesses' cars on a moped. I sit at a computer writing *captions*. I never get any free champagne and I don't care *who* does cocaine.'

To my surprise, he smiled. A thaw. Wow, he really was handsome. Those blue eyes weren't dull at all – they'd come alive.

'Are you good at your job?'

What a question. 'Ask my boss.'

'You don't know, do you? I mean, if you *do*, you're a fucking amazing actor.'

'Know what?'

His eyes bored into me, searching for a lie.

'Tom?'

He laughed again, mimicking my voice. 'Tom, Tom, Tom. You really don't know. Fucking hell, this is brilliant.' He bent in two, in hysterics. 'I don't believe it. Amazing. You don't know who I am!' He came close to me until our noses almost touched. This was unprecedented. His hands on my shoulders.

'I'm Nathaniel Harris. Nate.'

Nathaniel Harris. Wow. Nathaniel Harris. Of course. Nate. I

took a moment to let this sink in. Mind-blowing. In the flesh. Just as I'd imagined. Erm. And then, I had to be honest: 'Who the fuck is Nathaniel Harris?'

He laughed so hard he started coughing, doubled up again. Shaking with laughter. There were tears in his eyes. Someone in the house opposite looked out of their window. When he composed himself, he breathed out deeply and stuck out his hand for me to shake.

'Can we start again?'

I wasn't sure I wanted to. 'This is very weird.'

'I know. I'm sorry. It's just ... it's fine. *Please*.'

I shook his hand.

He cleared his throat, pushed his shoulders back like a soldier and mimicked a TV voiceover.

He was Nate Harris. He had won his first Olympic gold in the triathlon when he was twenty and had another five to his name. 'You may recognise me from ... or perhaps you don't.' I guffawed. Awkward. He was the face of a range of bikes, a brand of trainers he had to wear at all times. I glanced down at his feet. 'But not tonight,' he laughed. 'I'm also the *face* of Amber Oak' – a fragrance collection that I'd never so much as sniffed – 'and I'm in talks to design a range of pants. Like, boxers. Oh, and a smoothie maker. Well, a juicer, really. Basically a big blender. I always forget that one. Ring any bells?'

I squinted at his face. 'I ...' Nada. Where was Alicha when I needed her?

He reached into his pocket for his phone. Tap tap tap. Wikipedia. There he was.

And then ... 'Oh, I think I remember you from the Amber Oak advert. In the shower? And, like, some random branches wrap around you or something?'

'Yes, that's the one. Are you sure you're a journalist? I've been in your magazine!'

'Um, I don't *do* sports, I'm afraid. And ... well, do you often fall over drunk in Soho? Are you going out with a reality star or a model?'

He grinned. 'Well, no. Tonight I am out with *you*.'

Seriously, how could I not know who this person was? 'All Olympic medallists look the same to me. I only really know—'

He interrupted. 'Let me guess, I bet you only watch the diving?'

Bang to rights. In my experience, famous people didn't like it when you didn't know who they were, but this guy seemed positively overjoyed.

He laughed and looked up to the sky. 'Sorry? Don't be. You're my fucking *dream* come true.' He jerked his head toward the pub. 'Go back in or ditch this dump for a cab and a good time?'

I pretended to mull it over. And then: 'Taxi!'

9.

Before we got into the cab, Tom – sorry, *Nate* – asked that we didn't speak during the journey. Like, not a word. He wasn't joking. He said we should sit looking at our phones to put the driver off talking to us. I sat so stiffly in the back of the cab, I could feel every bump in the road. Nate scrolled on his phone, but looking right through it.

'I used to love talking to cabbies,' he told me later, wistfully, 'but they always ask if I'm shagging any of the female athletes. I get asked who I'm dating a lot. Not speaking in the first place is the best thing I can think of without lying.'

'So you just look like another rude celebrity who's totally wrapped up in themselves?'

He chuckled, but it felt empty. 'Yep, exactly that. But I suppose I'd rather they thought I was up my own arse than ...'

'Than finding out you were up somebody else's?'

We both laughed out loud, like old friends, and clinked glasses for what would be the first of about a hundred times.

Most famous people I'd met over the years – and I'm not talking A-listers, by the way; my access to Hollywood was restricted to Netflix and the local Odeon like everyone else – were pretty nice, so it wasn't entirely a surprise to find Nate was friendly, witty and sharp as a pin. The shirtiest celebs were usually the ones on their way up and unsure of their place in the hierarchy – those lower rungs of the ladder were pretty wobbly – or those so famous they'd become used to sycophants, devotees and spin doctors who convinced them of their own hype.

But when you're that famous, everyone wants a piece of you; it's only right you should keep some for yourself, and if that manifested itself as diva-esque or eccentric behaviour then so be it. And luckily, there was everyone else somewhere in the middle: a little spooked by their fame, but grateful for it, and anxious to remember who they were and where they'd come from. And so far, with two of the best martinis I'd ever tasted inside me, and propped up on one of the comfiest sofas in London, I'd decided Nate was definitely in that happy middle zone. But not so happy for him.

We were in a private members' club in Soho that I'd been to only once before; I wasn't very well connected. Last time I was here, an American woman had mistaken me for a coke dealer and followed me round all evening. 'Sweetie, just connect me to the ching, would ya? Honey?' The place was just the right side of tacky and opulent. Not quite Russian oligarch level – I was sure Bella was sitting in some much finer establishments on her travels with her zillionaire employers – but there were over-stuffed sofas, stripped back wood and bookshelves crammed with leather-bound tomes that would never be read, flashes of gold in the upholstery, and many an ostentatious candelabra.

'Nobody bothers me here,' Nate had said as we'd been waved on in, 'because when I wear these glasses I look like that guy off the decorating makeover show.'

'Alasdair Jones! Oh, so you do! Yes, I can't imagine anyone would want to talk to that miserable pie.'

He shot me a withering look. 'Oh, so you recognise Alasdair sodding Jones. But not me. Great.' Fucking celebrities, honestly.

Fame came unexpectedly for Nate – triathletes weren't the usual pinup material, after all. And looking at Nate in this light, with reassuringly expensive booze slicking my throat, I could see that was definitely an oversight. Nate's notoriety began when he started unzipping his top to the waist or, later, whipping it off altogether, after winning a race. 'I was hot!' he protested. Boy, was he. I watched his wiry, toned body twitch beneath his shirt like a cat eyeing up some pigeons. Anyway, he won a lot, so off came the top, again and again. At first he liked the attention; it led to a couple of parody sketches and adverts, which turned into more serious ones and then the inevitable sponsorships and endorsements. He was a star of sorts. 'Now if I don't take my top off when I win, they boo,' he sighed, 'so I do.'

One of the few perks of his form of celebrity sprang from this, however: with a shirt on, or out of Lycra, he went pretty much unnoticed. 'But I'm still cautious. Like before.'

He didn't like being recognised. Even the smallest of things, like going to the loo in a pub, turned into a nightmare.

'I have to wait for a cubicle in case anyone takes a picture of my dick,' he explained, half-laughing. 'And even then I can't get any privacy – I have to sit down on the toilet to make sure they haven't popped a camera over the top of the partition.' He saw my shocked face. 'It happens! You of all people should know that!'

Keeping his penis off the internet sounded like a full-time job.

'How have you got to twenty-eight, and this level of fame, without someone outing you? It happens all the time.'

'Yeah,' he murmured. 'Sometimes in *your* magazine.' I was cowed momentarily. 'And as for level of fame ... well. *You* had no idea who I was.'

I bristled. I wasn't proud of being out of the loop. 'We need to move on from this.'

He giggled mischievously. 'We do. We have. Anyway. Um. Why have I never been outed?' He glanced around the room to make sure nobody had heard. 'Well, it's not in the public interest, is it? I'm sure there are rumours, if you know where to look. But, y'know, I've never pretended I was in a relationship with a woman or paraded myself on the cover of magazines.'

I sipped my drink carefully. 'No, of course. But, and this is just me playing devil's advocate' – God I hated that expression – 'but you do flog fragrance and . . . whatnot, based on your image. I mean, men must want to be like you. Like, straight men. And women, I guess, want to sleep with you.'

Nate sat back and looked at me icily. 'I don't "flog" *anything*, let alone "whatnot",' he snapped, making air quotes with his fingers. Oh dear. 'And I'm selling products, not *myself*.' He shook his head.

I turned away from him in embarrassment. A guy I vaguely recognised walked past me to the bar and dipped his head to me by way of a hello. I shrank into my seat a little.

'I'm sorry. But it's what some people would say.' Oh God, I'd upset him. Suddenly everything was on fire and I was made of wood. '*I* don't think that, though.'

'Don't you? Then what do you think?'

My glass was empty. Another? Or should I just put my other foot in my mouth and have done with it? 'I think it's your personality and your achievements that people are buying into. If people fancy you, that's a bonus. And, you know . . . ' Come on, I could do this. Come on. 'I think there's something a bit dumb about only fancying celebrities if you think you've got a chance with them. I mean, you're no less available to them sexually if you're gay than you would be straight. It's never gonna happen, is it?'

Nate raised his eyebrow mischievously. 'Isn't it?'

I laughed. 'You know what I mean. Straight or gay, they can still appreciate your body, and everything else that makes people fancy you. It's just aesthetics. When you come out, you don't turn into this kind of … Quasimodo that only straight people can see. You're still you.'

He smiled. 'Thank you. That's what I think, too. My agent is harder to convince. If people only like me because they think they might get to fuck me one day then I'm screwed anyway. I won't look like this for ever. And if it puts men off from buying my trainers, then … ' He shrugged. 'It says more about them than it does me.'

'Then what's stopping you?'

He swallowed. 'I'm not ready. I don't think I ever will be. It's still something I'm working out. And my mum and dad … they're religious, quite traditional.'

'How religious? Church every Sunday? Or just a midnight mass at Christmas?'

'Sometimes twice on a Sunday. It's my mum's main way of socialising. Like, everything is centred on it.'

'That doesn't mean she'd be against you being gay, though, does it?' Nate flinched and I lowered my voice. 'You tend to find that when things happen a little closer to home, family trumps God.'

Nate eyed me over the rim of his glass. I felt a chill. 'You *tend* to find? Do you? Anyway, there are precedents. I'm not sure it's a chance I want to take.'

'Precedents?'

'Things they say when a gay bloke's on telly. What they've warned me against. I have a cousin, he was gay, it … '

'Was it awkward? What happened to him?'

He looked off into the distance. 'I've seen what happens when someone famous comes out. I've watched it play out on

123

Twitter. Five minutes of "well done you" and the slating begins. "Why didn't he come out sooner? Why was he hiding? How could he lie all those years?" All the judging. Even by gay men.' He looked straight at me. '*Especially*, in fact. They'd think I was sneaky, deceitful or selfish. I know. I've done it. So have you. I don't think I could cope.'

Nate noticed my glass was empty. 'Another drink? Let's talk about something else before this becomes an interview instead of a date.'

'Sure.'

'You won't put any of this in the magazine, will you?'

Now that was a promise I could keep. 'This is not going in the magazine.'

'I don't trust a lot of people. I ... I'm just not ready. I don't want to be a role model, not like this. Not yet. Do you understand?'

He ran his hand across his chest. I watched.

'How about kiss-and-tells, though?'

He laughed. 'I don't kiss.' He waggled his eyebrows. 'Well, I do, but I don't let them see *everything*.'

I reddened. 'Oh, why?'

He signalled for the waiter, who appeared like lightning. Alasdair Jones, my arse – nobody would move that fast for his torn, Z-list face. They knew exactly who Nate was, the lying toad. 'Well, Jimmy,' he slurred my name out lazily like Marilyn Monroe in slow-motion. 'Maybe you *will* see, later. Two more martinis!'

The next few hours were punctuated by two more silent phone-staring taxi journeys to different, even safer spaces. A seasoned player, Nate didn't break character at all. When he sensed I was on the brink of getting the giggles, he caught my eye and gave me a look. It wasn't a threatening look, not a warning, nor pleading, but it was serious. 'Don't,' it seemed to say. 'It's not worth it. Don't.' And I didn't.

It was kind of exhilarating, like a game. How would I know if I'd won? And what was my prize?

It was getting late. At the last bar, the waiter yawned theatrically as he placed two vodka and tonics down in front of us. The heavy clang of the sturdy tumblers on the glass-topped table jolted us slightly, like we'd each forgotten we were there. Our eyes met conspiratorially.

I leaned on my hand and it slipped gracelessly off the arm of the sofa. It was way past my bedtime. 'Isn't it hard not to be yourself?'

Nate stared into his drink. 'Nobody's ever themselves all the time. What about you? Are you like this all the time? Are you like this at work?'

I was certainly never this drunk at my desk, but I knew how it felt to be someone else. I'd always thought I knew where James ended and Romeo began, but tonight I wasn't so sure. I was so drunk I may well have adopted a third persona and not realised. I pawed my drink lethargically.

He breathed deeply. 'It's time to go.'

'I've had a really nice time,' I said, truthfully, as I tried to focus on my watch. It was quarter past whenever. No idea.

He leaned over and took my hand. I glanced down at it. 'You're nice. This is nice.' He lowered his voice. 'It can still be nice.'

'But you said it was time to go.'

'It is.'

Holborn, the City, Wapping. It all rushed by as we sat once more in silence and as far away from each other in the back of the cab as we could manage without actually hanging out of the doors. How did we cope with stultifying silences before phones? I absentmindedly checked some messages. One from Luca, a few hours ago, asking why I hadn't tweeted since I'd arrived at the date. Was I OK? What was going on? I fired off a breezy non-committal reply – he'd be offline now anyway. One of my detractors was on duty, too: *I see Barbara Fartland is at it again.* Working on a Sunday. Such commitment! Oh fuck 'em. I was on my way back to Nate Harris's house, with enough sexual tension fizzing between us to light the Eiffel Tower all the way to the top. Nobody else in the world, I imagined, was having this much fun, and on the brink of even more.

I coughed to get Nate's attention. He looked up from his phone. That look again. And then he spoke. 'Just here on the left.' The cab swung into an underground car park of a huge modern tower block, and after he handed over the money and we got out, he nodded for me to wait. We watched the taxi leave. 'It's this way,' he said, leading me back out of the car park and across a small, immaculately tended green to an identical tower directly opposite.

'You get cabbies to drop you off at a different house when you bring a bit of stuff home?' I laughed.

He turned to me, suddenly appearing deadly serious and sober, despite his drunkenness. 'I know you think this is *stupid*. Believe me, so do I. But this is how much my life means to me.' He put his hood up. 'And don't ever call yourself a bit of *stuff*, James. You're much more than that.' He raised his hand as if to touch my face, but a dog barked, so he withdrew it quickly. 'Come on.' He sprinted off, and I followed. I'm more than that, I thought. He thinks I'm more than that.

The next morning I felt way *less* than that. A million minus zeros. My hangover was so powerful I could see through time, and my body felt like I'd woken up midway through abdominal surgery. Nate's bedroom, I noticed through the gloom, was impeccably decorated yet utterly without personality. There were no flourishes or embellishments. It was safe, functional, sexless, like waking up inside a furniture shop.

Nate was lying under me, awake, his hands behind his head. I gently pulled my face away from his chest and prayed there'd been no drool joining us together. I quickly cast my eyes over his body, one last longing look at the work of art that had been all mine for the shortest and the longest of nights ever.

'Have you ever been anything other than ridiculously fit?'

He smiled at the sound of my voice and ruffled my hair, looking down at his chest. 'No.'

'Amazing.'

He narrowed his eyes good-naturedly. 'I live in the gym and only let myself get wasted once a month. It's no life.'

'Only once a month? Was *I* your once a month? I feel honoured.'

He laughed. 'You should.'

'Do I have to sneak out?'

He touched my face. I couldn't read the look on his. 'Not quite. I'll call you a cab and it will pick you up next door, like last night. I can pay for it.'

What I really wanted to say was did he think we would see each other again, but I stayed practical. 'Nate. I can't have you handing me money after a one-night stand. That *would* get in the papers.'

If he was going to say anything about 'one-night stand' or 'the papers', he thought better of it, and simply nodded, swinging himself out of bed. One more sneaky look from me. Wow. He reached for a robe and left the room. I heard a kettle click on and the cheerful chime of a teaspoon in a cup.

'Peppermint.' He handed me a mug as I staggered through to the lounge. 'Good for your stomach.' Clearly I had been farting in my sleep. He was opening post that looked like it had been stacked up for days. His old school was naming a new sports pavilion in his honour. 'Insane. I got an athletic scholarship; they wouldn't have had someone like me anywhere near otherwise.'

I stood shivering with hangover and awkwardness. He noticed I was barefoot.

'Your socks are in the kitchen.' What had I been doing in the kitchen? Nate grinned. I felt a flutter in my tummy at the memory.

I wanted to ask him what he'd do if he ever met someone – *the* someone – but I didn't want him to think I was angling to *be* that someone. I couldn't be that someone, could I? Could I? I mean, he had a really nice toaster and I could tell he had his own cleaner because the products on his bathroom shelf were gleaming and dust-free. But what about everything else? Sneaking around, silent in taxis, fake addresses and lowering my voice, pretending my 'friend' was Alasdair Jones? I had butterflies at the thought – bad ones and good ones. And the body, what about the bloody body? Could I let him see mine sober? Would I not die with nerves every time we had to 'do it'? Because, you know, I'd probably want to do it a lot.

As I was leaving, he stood behind the door so he couldn't be seen from the hallway – I tried my best not to make a face at the ridiculousness of this – and kissed me lightly on the forehead. 'You're a good guy. And thank you.'

There was so much I wanted to say. Now did not seem the time. 'Goodbye, *Tom*.'

As the car took me back to Camberwell I thought of Nate's plea that our date wouldn't go in the magazine. I'd resolved never to break two things: hearts and promises. Adam would be a witness for the prosecution for the first, but I could keep my word on the second. But there was that *feeling*. A good story was a good story. And if I changed a few details about the night – just enough to keep it the right side of credible, like his name, where we went, his sport – then surely it wouldn't hurt to . . . ? No, I shouldn't. I couldn't let Romeo have this one. It was special, meant something.

There was hope. Then I remembered the crosswinds lashing at me as I trudged back over to the car park to be picked up incognito by the taxi. That empty feeling. 'One night.' He hadn't protested, or said he wanted to see me again, he'd just called me a good guy and given me a brotherly peck on the noggin. Not even a vague 'see you around' – just 'thank you'. The blog was about *my* life, after all, and this was something that happened to me. That was the bonus about being anonymous: it protected us both. What harm would a little preparation do, in case he never called?

I sat back in the cab and began to type on my phone. I got in the car as James, but I'd be getting out as Romeo. Thanks to rush-hour traffic, the cabbie going the wrong way and roadworks at Elephant & Castle – plus my nimble, excited fingers and the wide-eyed hysteria of a hangover – by the time I got back to my teeny tiny flat with the cobwebs and the stray noodles of Bombay mix on the floor, it was done. My night with the celebrity. A little something for my loyal few. It was going to be fine.

Definitely.

10.

How long should you wait before someone you describe as a 'one night' calls you? Seven hours? Seven days? A lifetime? To stop myself thinking about Nate, and dreaming about his body and his smile and the smell of Amber Oak from his skin – yep, he really wore it – I distracted myself by filling the miserable tundra that was my diary with social engagements. It was a struggle.

Day one, I went to dinner with Seonaid and Carrie and despite being massively preoccupied, I managed to greedily chomp my way through a delicious vegan version of beef wellington while everyone pointedly avoided mentioning Adam's name. On day three, I met Curtis for drinks where he told me how lucky I was to be single. Perhaps he was hinting all was not well with Parker, but if he'd wanted me to know, he'd have told me, and he seemed more concerned with work issues.

'The young writers we've got now, they just don't care,' he sighed. 'They didn't grow up with decent magazines. They don't know how to interview; they just read off a set of questions. When they come back to the office brandishing their Dictaphone like it's a gold bar, the interview sounds like it's been done by a Dalek. I can't cope.'

'I'm sure they're not that bad. You could teach them.'

Curtis whooped in horror. 'They're my rivals! That would be like giving a pyromaniac a set of matches and your home address.'

Day four, I ran and I ran and I ran until my knees gave way and I couldn't think about anything. Day five I helped Silvie paint her kitchen, and would not be persuaded to go shirtless under my overalls. 'I could take some pictures of you, post them to your dating profile,' she said. 'Manual labour – I thought that was a turn on?'

Day seven, I played dutiful godfather and took Sid and Haydn swimming and then to the cinema, sitting through 150 minutes of a Hollywood adaptation of a comic book I'd never heard of, and blew a day's pay on popcorn, drinks, an affiliated toy and a pizza afterwards, which included a bottle of prosecco just for me. 'Is someone else joining you?' smiled the waiter as she hovered with the bottle and two glasses. Sid and Haydn looked up at me. The Earth fell briefly silent. 'No,' I said, finally. 'But leave the second glass in case I break the first one.'

Did I really think there was a future if Nate called, or did I just fancy the idea of going out with an Olympian? I could've called him, of course; there was nothing stopping me. Except my pride. And the worry he'd act like a stranger. When the phone didn't ring, I felt that pang of loss from no longer being in the spotlight that kills all fading stars eventually. So on day fourteen, after a weekend spent completely alone in anticipation, I fired up Seizer and arranged a date with someone else for midweek.

'I can't tonight,' he explained. 'I only drink coconut water on a Sunday. I can't have anything else in my mouth.'

The next day, on the way to work, I looked over the draft of the blogpost. I hesitated. I agonised. I read it over and over, as if staring at the words and correcting the zillions of typos might will Nate to call me. He did not. I made some small changes, tapping at the screen hard in frustration, and, as my tube train pulled into the station, I posted it.

'Publish and be damned,' I said, accidentally out loud. The man waiting to get off beside me moved away ever so slightly and held his copy of *Metro* closer to his chest.

When I got back from lunch, Alicha prodded me and pointed at my phone, which I'd left on my desk. 'Your phone has been freaking out, Jim. It sounds like someone's got a vibrator on the go.'

As we watched, it jerked into life, buzzing at what seemed to be a flurry of notifications.

'You gone viral, babe?'

'Huh?'

Alicha pointed at the phone. 'You must be getting a lot of retweets. I didn't realise you were a Twitter celebrity. You post a picture of a dog or something?'

I had a bad feeling about this. Did she know? I tried to read her expression, but she had chicken katsu round her mouth and it was very distracting. 'I think it must be broken.' I grabbed it and ran to the loo to turn my notifications off and see what the hell was happening. Comments, tweets, emails – there was some serious postbag going on and I needed to see. Another hit on my hands, perhaps.

The only available cubicle smelled like a wild animal had gasped its last in there so I grabbed the rusting can of air freshener beside the loo, made the sign of the cross with its spray and barricaded myself inside to get up to speed. I smiled as I flicked over the fans' feedback, heart-eyes emojis and plaudits. Messages from Luca, and other online pals, calling me an inspiration, saying it was a thrilling read. All five-star reviews, gushing with praise. Everybody needs a fan, don't they?

> I read it on the loo, walking to the shops and even tried
> to take my iPad into the bath with me. I was gripped.
> Please. Never. Stop.

I chuckled. And then I noticed another message from Luca.
The wind changed.

> Look, don't worry about what they're saying. Don't
> listen to them. You've every right to tell your story. I'm
> here if you need me.

I scrolled on to see some more recent messages.

> @OneMoreRomeo i hope yr face is a lot less nasty than
> yr blog
> Here she is, Scarlett O'Horror!

> @OneMoreRomeo This is a disgrace.
> Who cares about some random queer's love life?
> Those lips of yours look chapped in that close-up btw:
> must be all that POISON.

> Just another Carrie Bradshaw wannabe looking for
> fame. GARY BRADSHAW lol you sad fuck.

And on and on and on. My post about Nate had finally broken
me out of my loyal circle, but landed me in hostile territory. It
was like driving down a road and suddenly noticing all the cars
were coming in the opposite direction. Had I got this wrong?
Was I going down a one-way street? Would I only know for sure
once I crashed?

They ... hated it. And me. It wasn't until a small fly buzzed
around it that I realised my mouth was gaping open in shock.

I read back over the comments, the accusations and jibes. People were really pissed off. I'd factored in that people would wonder who Nate was, which was why I'd changed a few details, but I'd naively missed the fact they would actively guess – out loud, in public, fake-outing just about any sportsman in the country. As I slumped against the cubicle door, reality hit me – how could I not have seen this coming?

To spare his blushes, I'd reimagined Nate as a successful swimmer called Tom – a quick look at the British Olympics website told me there weren't any of those in real life. While some people took notice of my disclaimer – 'I have changed some of the guy's details, in particular those that could easily identify him' – some obviously assumed I *wanted* him to be discovered, and that I hadn't hidden him in deep enough cover.

> please please please tell me who the famous swimmer is. i've been through all the olympic medallist swimmers of the last 20 years and can narrow it down to 4 people. if i send the initial can you just confirm that one of them is right? i promise promise promise not to tell anyone!!!! pls say it's TP and not MC!!!

Sadly, I had no idea who either of these people were and this was no time for me to try to decipher the code. What had I done? And how did I make it stop? But that was the thing: toothpaste doesn't go back in the tube easily. My special, sexy evening with Nate now felt cheap and salacious – the tabloid fodder he'd feared so much. And I was the sleazebag making it happen. This was out there. This was a *thing*. Everywhere. Everyone was talking about it. Journalists, celebrities, long-time readers, haters, someone I recognised as working at the big Topshop at Oxford Circus. A great big oil spill, and I was sliding all over the place.

It wasn't even that good a post; I'd rushed it, anxious not to forget any of the details before the tidal wave of post-martinis hangover took away my brain cells for ever. I kept reading, hoping to find some love amid the derision but it was sparse. The same kind of comments kept coming up over and over:

> Who IS this guy anyway? Are you a famous person too? You should reveal yourself!

> You do realise that outing in this way puts your date at considerable RISK?! Why not show your stupid face so we can JUDGE YOU ourselves?!

> We DEMAND to know who you are!
> Wherefore art thou Romeo? Show yr self!

When you know the punchline, jokes aren't as funny. I knew who Romeo really was, that I was about as exciting as stale toast jammed between the wall and the bin. I never imagined anyone would care, but they didn't just want to know who my 'mysterious swimmer' was – they wanted to unmask Romeo too.

I had a pain in my chest. I sat shaking on the loo (trousers pulled up, OK, I wasn't a savage). I looked at my watch. I'd been gone fifteen minutes. Just a quarter of an hour and it felt like the floor had been falling away from underneath me since the dawn of time.

I staggered back out to the newsroom. Hurley and Alicha regarded me with bemusement.

'What did you have for *lunch*? You've been gone ages. You got IBS or something?'

Hurley turned back to his screen. 'Digestive system packs up once you hit middle age. I expect the same will happen to my dad when he's as old as James.'

Only one thing to do in this kind of situation: drink tea. Alicha watched my hands shaking as I poured the water into the cups.

'You gonna tell me what this is about? Have you killed someone? Do you need help burying a body?'

I shook my head. 'Nothing, right, but *hypothetically*, how would you deal with a big social media shitstorm?'

Alicha looked puzzled. 'We haven't done anything like that today. It's been dead. Literally nobody has so much as shown their knickers. What's up?'

I explained it was something I'd written for another client that had blown up, that I'd done it on work time and could get into trouble. I felt bad lying to Alicha, but it was actually pretty close to the truth. She looked hurt when I refused to give her any more details.

'Can't you just give me your Twitter handle? I won't tweet anything stupid at you.'

'But how would you deal with it?'

Alicha stirred her tea. 'Is it racist, Jim? Have you had a big white-supremacist meltdown? 'Cos I can't be helping you with stuff like that, y'know.'

Once I'd assured her there was no racism, misogyny or making light of her gluten intolerance, she shared her wisdom. 'This will sound like really shit advice, but just ignore it. Let it play out. If you know what they're saying isn't true, trying to clarify will only make it worse. It'll prolong it. Just ride it out.'

Could that possibly work? Just do nothing? 'Of course,' Alicha smiled as she waved the biscuit tin under my nose, 'if you told me your Twitter account I could just steam in there and handle this for you . . . ' She laughed. 'Nah, look. Nobody can stay mad at more than, like, three things at a time these days. It'll be someone else's turn tomorrow.'

*

136

It was tricky trying to explain to my friends about how big this was – only Nicole, Richie, Silvie and Bella knew about *One More Romeo*. Bella was only on Instagram to follow the latest trends in almond milk, Nicole thought Twitter was really boring and full of journalists 'who could do with a job that involved them actually getting dressed' and Richie's online life was restricted to viral videos and following American reality TV stars and footballers on Snapchat. They all thought my newfound infamy was hilarious and exciting. And in a way it was. People were reading me, sharing me and my follower count had ballooned. I even made it into the 'Everybody's talking about' section in one of *Snap!*'s rivals, and at Sunday Club Richie howled as he held *Style* magazine aloft and read out the 'going up' column of their barometer: 'It says here that Romeo is "the secret sassy, clued-up GBF with dating advice no woman should be without". I mean fucking hell, that's YOU.'

Even Sid was impressed. 'You are basically Spider-Man, uncle J. But gay.'

'It's weird,' I said as Sid was ushered out of the room. 'Look at this message I got the other day from some guy who reads the blog.'

> I would LOVE for you to take me out on a date and write about me! I'm sure I could give you plenty of material.

'And another one.'

> The way you write makes me think you would be pretty good in bed. Promise not to tell anyone who you are if you let me find out for myself.

Richie grabbed the phone from me. 'Men are actually offering you sex. This is the *dream*, isn't it?'

Silvie flicked ash in her wine glass. 'They're offering it to Romeo, hun, not Jim.'

From a safe distance of thousands of miles, in a country with an alphabet that reads like it was created during a messy divorce, Bella couldn't believe I wasn't enjoying this more.

'It's actually been quite hard having to wade through all the messages the last couple of days,' I complained.

Bella screeched. 'Oh my heart bleeds! So much *fan mail*. You could always shut down your social media, stop doing the blog. You know, if it's bothering you so much.'

She and I both knew I was way too thirsty to do that. I immediately switched tack.

'When are you coming home for a holiday? It's been ages.'

Bella's filthy-rich bosses were building a house in Miami and the poor thing was going to have to go over with them and watch the baby while they picked out gold-plated toilet-roll holders, but she assured me it was far from a vacation.

'After the first few times, turning left on a plane lost its appeal.'

I fluttered my eyelashes. 'Ooh, so *desensitised* to first-class travel already. So *accustomed*!'

'Shut up. So has your favourite Olympian got in touch?'

He hadn't, and I guess I was relieved – I was starting to think he'd make a better anecdote than a boyfriend.

'Are you worried someone's going to work out the blog is about him? Has anyone guessed him yet?'

My stomach churned. 'I haven't seen anything. What do you think will happen if they do?'

Bella shrugged. 'Between you and Nate? Absolutely nothing. There's no going back from that, is there?'

I was about to agree when my phone started ringing. No way.

'Bella, I've gotta go.'

Bella put her hand to her head in mock distress. 'Fine! Leave me here by *myself* in Moscow while you answer your stupid phone. Who the hell calls people directly anyway?'

I looked from my phone back up to the laptop and glared right into the camera. Bella instinctively knew there was something wrong.

'Nate Harris does, that's who. It's ... Nate.'

Bella's mouth went canyon-sized. 'Oh. My. *Fucking*. God. Answer it immediately.'

'I can't. What have I done?!' I flapped for so long the call went to voicemail.

Bella put her hands over her face. 'You fucking idiot. Nobody ever leaves voicemails.'

Ping! 'Again, Nate Harris does.'

I played it on loudspeaker. Bella peered right into the camera on her laptop so all I could see was her eye. The message began with a deep sigh. This had been a call he didn't want to make. I steeled myself for a nuclear rage. 'James. I ... it's me. I ... ' A long pause. 'I'd love it if you would call me back. You see ... ' I sensed he had broken his 'I only get drunk once a month' rule. 'You see I ... I can't stop thinking about you. Please call me.'

Bella looked into the camera, her eyes like dinner plates. I gawped back. 'What do I do?'

'This is Hollywood romcom big. Call him. Now.'

I felt a rush of panic. 'I *can't*! But what about the blogpost? What if he finds out? You were just saying ... '

Bella shook her head. 'Forget about it. I talk shit. He never needs to know. End this call with me immediately,' she said. 'And go make that fucking adorable boy's day.'

11.

Nate gave a little whinny of excitement as he heaved the distinctive eau-de-nil carrier bags onto the worktop and began to peek inside at the treats within. He took them out one by one, presenting them to me for my approval.

'OK, so I know you said you were giving up sugar or whatever, but I remembered you telling me about the jam your gran used to make, so I thought this tayberry one from Fortnum's would be perfect. A little bit different.'

I took the jar from him. 'Nathaniel, this stuff is about eight quid a jar.'

'And then I thought for the morning we *could* maybe go out and get fresh croissants but then I remembered these' – he showed me a tinfoil tray of small white blobs in packaging written in French – 'they're so cool. You basically shove them in the oven and they turn into croissants. That way we can, uh, stay in our pyjamas.'

'Are you allowed croissants?'

Nate looked at me with serious eyes. 'Are you going to expose me on *Snap!* for eating bread?!'

Weekends with Nate, when he was in London and not away

either competing or training or being an ambassador for shower gel, followed a pattern. On whichever day constituted the beginning of his 'weekend', sometimes Fridays, maybe a Tuesday, while I was at work, he'd head into town and do a huge shop, buying all manner of things we never found time to eat. His diet was crazy and more strategic than fun, but he always popped a small bag of Bombay mix in for me because 'I know it's your favourite – I saw crumbs of it all over your flat'. I would bowl over there, swerving any post-work drinks, and it would all be waiting, lighting perfectly dimmed, music playing at just the right volume, the curtains closed and the smell of something wonderful coming from the kitchen. The rest of the world was a million miles away.

It had got to this point fairly quickly; Nate didn't mess around. For our second date – was it a date? Does it count if you don't go out? – he cooked for me at his place and I didn't leave for two days. I insisted our next date be at my flat, so that I could return the favour, and while I could see it made him slightly uneasy to be somewhere unfamiliar, I appreciated he'd made the effort. It was funny to see him in Camberwell, torn from the faceless, high gloss of his purpose-built block and the functional gentrification of its neighbourhood, but as we sipped coffee in the local deli and hummed and hawed over menus the next morning, I saw him begin to unwind.

'Nobody's looking,' I said, to calm him a bit more. 'And even if they were, we could be cousins, brothers . . . '

'We don't look anything alike!'

I laughed. 'OK, brothers from another mother, maybe. Anyway, it's fine. I'm glad you came.'

Nate smiled over his cup and took a drink. Cappuccino froth on the end of his nose. I remembered Bella saying to me that this was 'romcom big'. It felt that way.

'I certainly don't feel for my brothers like I do about you.' He raised his eyebrows suggestively. He hadn't mentioned brothers plural before, but I was already learning not to ask too many questions, plus I didn't really want to get into a conversation about the incestuousness of our relationship this early in the day, so I let it go. 'Thanks for going to so much trouble last night,' he said. 'I know I'm not easy to cook for.'

I beamed. 'Oh, it was fine.' It was not fine. I'd taken the day off work – unpaid! – and spent it sweating, knackered, trawling round Borough Market. I'd had to drink three Coke Zeros just to summon up the energy to cook.

As I'd cleared the plates that night, he'd asked about Adam, and even though I didn't want to kill the mood, I told him. I felt lighter almost immediately. He absentmindedly tapped his fingers on the back of my hand.

'Is it wrong that I'm jealous? That I wish I'd met you before he did?'

I moved my hand to his leg. He carried on tap-tap-tapping. 'Anyone who says they don't get jealous is a liar, and *usually* the most jealous person alive. I'm glad you were honest. But . . . well. Meeting Adam when I did made me who I am. I think I'm in a better place now.'

Nate looked around my small, squalid kitchen-lounge. I could tell he was about to say something. My cleaning had been rudimentary – I figured it was more important to hide all the dirty laundry and make the surfaces as clear as possible. Now I looked at it again, through a stranger's eyes, and a very handsome one at that, I saw it for the dive it was. I blinked in silent horror as I noticed my fish slice had fallen down the side of the fridge; I hadn't used it for at least three weeks. Nate turned away from it, and back to me.

'I know my life is a bit unconventional,' he said, softly. 'But I'll never treat you like Adam did.'

I swallowed uncomfortably. 'Forget Adam.'

Nate shook his head. 'I don't want to. I can't be, um, everything you might want me to be but I want you to know I'll be as much as I can.'

'That's quite poetic. I'm impressed.'

Nate ignored my patronising compliment. 'Y'know, let me look after you a bit. You do so much, I've seen it. The way you talk about your mates, and your godsons and . . . ' he took a deep breath which I already knew well enough would be because he was about to talk about my job, 'uh, the *office*. I think it's time somebody was nice to you.'

'*Everybody* is nice to me.' I thought for a second about my internet critics.

Nate drew me nearer to him. My sofa creaked in appreciation. I didn't dare open my mouth, in case rainbows, streamers and love hearts flew out. 'Fine,' he whispered. 'Let me be *nicer*.'

And he was. When he was away, his texts were sparse and at first I assumed he didn't trust me to go into details, but it turned out he was one of those weird aliens we hear so much about who doesn't have their phone clamped to their side. He wasn't on any social media and avoided the internet like the plague. 'My involvement ends with approving adverts with my face on. I never see them. I haven't got time to go online.' He was too busy training instead and, I admit, a part of me was relieved I seemed to be getting away with it. I'd wondered whether to take down the post about our night together but it was so popular and people seemed to have come round to loving it again. One day, if there ever was a day when he came out, I could show it to him and we'd laugh, maybe. Maybe.

Romeo's followers soon noticed I'd gone a little quieter. I dispelled any rumours that I'd met #LastRomeo by posting a couple of blogs I'd had in reserve, and kept my tweeting fairly neutral. It didn't help that I wasn't really sure what was going on between Nate and me. It was beautiful and it was fun but were we going out? Whatever it was, I cancelled all my other dates and didn't log on to Soulseekers, even if a message was waiting. I owed Nate my exclusivity, if nothing else.

Luca got in touch, worried.

> You haven't jacked it in, have you? After the
> swimmer blog? I think people have calmed
> down a bit now.

He'd noticed the blogs I'd posted were older; he remembered the tweets. This was something I hadn't really counted on: people actually recalling what I'd said and done. I reassured him I was just busy with work.

> The weird thing is that even though we all
> want you to find the last Romeo, we kind of
> don't as well!

Why?

> Because then it'll be all over won't it? We
> won't get to hear about what you're up to
> anymore. We don't want it to end.

At first, Bella was beside herself with excitement. 'I can't believe you're dating someone off the telly.'

'Erm, he's an Olympic sportsman.'

Bella tutted. 'Yeah, but he's basically the Amber Oak guy. Amazing!'

'It's so sweet, y'know. As soon as I walk through the door on a night, he's got the whole evening planned.'

'As it should be.'

'Yeah, yeah, but even better. Like, it's miraculous how right he gets it. I always felt Adam was dragging me to stuff I didn't want to go to, but Nate actually listens to me. Things I don't remember I've said. Some off-the-cuff remark about liking jam? There it is. Maybe mentioning that great steak tartare me and you had that time—'

'Ooh now that *was* good.' Bella rubbed her tummy. 'I am fucking sick of the food here.'

'Well, yeah, that. He had the restaurant bring some over.' I waited for Bella to be impressed. 'They. Don't. Deliver. He just called them, and they brought it.'

'Wow.'

'I know. Nobody has ever done this for me before. Made me feel this way. I didn't know it was possible.'

Bella looked straight into the camera, and said again: 'Wow.'

Every time Nate and I met, it was a wow moment. His thoughtfulness, his knack for romance, his sense of humour – he amazed me every time. And yet there was something in the back of my mind that made me think it was such a waste. Wasted on me, wasted on him. He would be the perfect boyfriend for someone – if only he'd allow himself to be one. Because it was only when we were alone. The silent taxis continued, the respectable distance when we went for drinks at his club. We never went to any of what he called my 'gay places', and the visit to my flat was a one-off. 'It's just easier here,' he would say. 'And I thought it would be nice for you to get away.' He was too perfect for me in a way, but I went with it because he made me feel I deserved it.

I didn't want to pry too much into Nate's past because I could see it pained him to talk about his family, or previous experiences, but I got a sense he hadn't had this level of intimacy before – everything we did was straight out of a storybook, like he was eager to try out as many romantic clichés as possible.

'What about Paris, for the weekend? Or maybe Venice.'

'Well, that would be lovely, but I'm a bit strapped for cash at the moment.' Plus we'd only just started going out, or whatever this was. Wasn't it a bit too early for the big romantic gestures before we'd done all the normal stuff, like kissed in a nightclub or had an argument in a kebab shop?

'Don't worry about it. Shall we go for a picnic this afternoon?'

'Picnics are quite … public.' His brow would furrow at this reminder that we were not like other couples.

'A day trip, then! I wanna find a lake, and a boat, and sit in it. With you.'

So he did. And we did. We sat at opposite ends of the boat, shoes off, a bag of lager between us, as it was the most laddish thing we could think of to drink. Any onlookers would, by our reasoning, just think we were two normal blokes knocking back cans. On a boat. In the middle of a beautiful, romantic lake. As the very last heat of the summer burned off to make way for autumn.

I tried to bring things back down to earth as only I could. 'That water is filthy.'

Nate peered over the edge. 'I have to swim in worse, sometimes.'

'I like my swimming water chlorine-bright and free of beasties.'

'Oh yeah, you take your godson, don't you? Is he any good?'

I chuckled. 'I don't think he's going to be much competition for you for a while yet.'

I stretched out and lifted the hem of his T-shirt with my toe and peeked at his pale tummy, which I was cheered to see rolled very slightly over the top of his trousers. Mine rolled a lot more, of course. Not that I felt remotely self-conscious anymore. Any worries I had that Nate would judge me for my lack of six-pack were quickly dispelled. 'I like your body,' he said one night, as he watched me trying to hide under the duvet under his bright bedroom light. 'It's ... unexpected. Sexy.'

I spluttered in disbelief. 'But you're so buff!'

He gently peeled back the covers. 'And you're so *you*. My body helps me win. It's a machine. But I don't want to date myself.'

I dipped my hand in the water and smiled at the memory. Nate had a thought. He was the king of not saying what he was about to say. 'Let's row ashore, I ... uh ... I don't want to sit this far away from you anymore,' he said, his voice rich with intent.

A week later I was trying to persuade Haydn dive-bombing off the top board was just not OK for someone his age, and asking could he maybe set his sights a little lower and let me teach him the butterfly or something, when I heard a cough behind me. I quickly turned round – no mean feat in water, in too-tight trunks, with a hangover, and a nine-year-old boy hanging off your arm – to see Nate, resplendent in navy-blue swimming shorts and a matching swimming cap. Round his neck, his tiny St Christopher gleamed.

'Um. Surprise.'

I wasn't sure how to greet him so I good-naturedly rubbed his arm. His eyes tracked down slightly to my hand. I was so pleased to see him, but frightened I would ruin everything by being too gay around him. I tried to keep my voice as low as possible. 'Nate! How did you know I was here? I thought you were away.'

'Process of elimination. And you're a creature of habit, Mr Brodie.' He grinned at Haydn, who suddenly decided he was shy and hid behind my back. 'Anyway, I wanted to check out your technique, see if you're as good in the water as you are on the, um, field.'

I introduced him to my charge and soon the two were firm

friends, as Nate taught Haydn all kinds of complicated and dangerous moves that he made look effortless. I was happy to play gooseberry, and watched them like a proud dad from across the pool, until there was a piercing scream and I heard someone shout Nate's name. A teenager in a Team GB swimming cap was racing toward the edge of the pool as Nate and Haydn took a breather on the side. The guy's mum and sister padded behind him – obviously not regulars to the pool, as their mistrust for the supposedly non-slip tiles was palpable.

I couldn't hear what they were saying, and I thought it best not to swim over, but it looked like they were fans, and wanted to know who Haydn was. Nate ruffled Haydn's hair and pointed over at me, and I heard loud and clear. 'He's my cousin's godson. I haven't seen him in a while so we're catching up.'

The fans lamented they had no phone with them for a selfie, and that they had to dash, as the youngster was in a tournament in the junior pool. I saw Nate pretend to sympathise, although I could tell he was overcome with relief. And then they were gone.

We walked to the changing room in silence. Until: 'Cousin?'

Nate looked around the pool, then at me, and winked. 'Very *close* cousins. It's better than brothers.'

In the cafeteria Nate and Haydn stood at the counter drooling over the junk food while I grabbed a seat. Just as the server plonked a huge hot dog the size of HMS Belfast on Haydn's plate, my phone buzzed.

> James, hi, it's Finn from the party a while
> back. A month? Two? Kitchen gin and
> tonics? I said I had a work opportunity
> for you so Seonaid gave me your number
> because for ~some~ reason I had the wrong

> one for you. I was wondering if you still
> fancied meeting up? Grab a drink. Etc etc. x

Well well. I looked up at Nate, who was holding up two cartons of juice for my approval. I mouthed 'orange' at him and typed.

> Hey Finn! How lovely to hear from you. Work
> opportunity sounds exciting. What is it?

I dallied over whether to add a kiss. He'd put one. I didn't.

> Aaaaaahhhhh well that may have been a ruse
> tbh. Would you still be interested in catching
> up anyway?? x

It would've been easy to say yes, but why complicate my life even further by going for drinks with a guy who had a boyfriend, behind the back of a guy who might possibly be *my* boyfriend? I had no idea. Either way, I'd be swapping one secret for another and, in a twist of morality that surprised me, betraying the sweetest man I'd ever met. I thought of Finn's crumpled half-smile and his relaxed laugh as he poured the gin, his other hand in his pocket, his whole being oozing with confidence. Beautiful, beautiful Finn. Then I watched Nate athletically glide toward me, despite his steady hand the tray wobbling with all manner of junk he'd bought for Haydn, a huge smile on his face. My stomach went tight.

A ruse, indeed.

> I'm pretty tied up at the moment
> with work and other stuff – can I
> let you know when I'm free?

I thought for a moment. Deleted. Sighed. Typed the exact same again. Added a kiss.

Understood.

I read it just as Nate took his seat. He unloaded the goodies, caught my eye and smiled. 'Happy?'

I smiled back and turned my phone face down with a satisfied sigh. 'Yes.'

12.

Which club are you going to?

Sweetie. Do you know it?

I've never been. We don't go out much.

Wrangling with my shirt over my head, I tried to use voice recognition to dictate a reply to Luca. The result was:

How come you don't go out much then
stop me as much about Amber?

Eh?

Great. I tried again, with actual fingers.

I meant to say, why don't you go out
much, are you a bit of a homebird?
Prefer to stay in like a cosy couple?

There was a long pause. I spritzed on my Tom Ford, worried about my hair for a few seconds.

> I'm not a homebird by choice. Let's just say
> my boyfriend goes out a lot.

It seemed there was something he was trying to tell me, and I started to type a reply but I had the feeling this would be an all-nighter and I was running late.

> Well, you should definitely get
> yourself out for a boogie! Or so
> my friends tell me! Night! x

At Sunday Club the week before, Silvie shoved a cup of tea in front of me. 'Look, I don't mean to get all "u ok hun", Jim, but it's time we had that night out. You need a night off from going on dates; it's time to join the real world and socialise with other humans.'

I hadn't told anyone other than Bella that I was seeing Nate. I wasn't lying, as such, I was just, erm, not saying anything about it. I trusted my friends, but Silvie had become uncomfortably matey with Curtis since Seonaid's party – his Instagram was full of pictures of the two of them pouting with pornstar martinis in Soho – and while she'd assured me she hadn't revealed I was Romeo, and I believed her, Curtis had a nose for scandal and a mouth eager to spread it. Nicole and Richie too lived for celebrity gossip and as I was usually so useless at providing them with it, they wouldn't be able to help themselves, I knew. So to avoid giving the game away, I agreed.

Nicole and Richie said they'd come too. 'You'd better watch out, princess,' said Richie as we planned our evening. 'I might get turned by a gorgeous gay bloke.'

Nicole rolled her eyes. 'Rich, I will literally pay them to take you away from me.'

Nate sounded disappointed when I told him my plans. He was away, and his voice was tinny and businesslike over the phone.

'It's just that I'm back on Saturday.'

'I know, I'm sorry. But my friends are trying to do something nice for me.'

'By taking you to a *gay* club?'

I chewed my nails. 'You could always . . .' Could I really suggest this? I decided to go for it. 'I mean, you could come. Wear your glasses. Do your hair different.' I realised it was a stupid idea as soon as I said it. Curtis, for one, would be all over him.

Nate's voice sounded strained and dry. 'It's just not something I'm gonna be able to do, James. You know that. It's not the kind of thing I *want* to do. I didn't think *you* did, either. Do you even *go* to gay clubs?'

I didn't want to get into this now. Or at all, really. 'Every now and again. It's a laugh. The music is good. I don't do drugs or anything.' It was like coming out all over again, reassuring elderly relatives I wasn't like the gay men they read about in the paper. It felt stupid and dishonest. What *was* wrong with going to a gay club? 'I can cancel. Do it another time.'

'No,' he answered, sharply. 'You go.' We chatted a while longer but his tone was clipped. When we wrapped up the call I noticed he didn't end with 'Night, handsome' like he usually did.

I noticed Bella's tune was starting to change on our catch-up call.

'I think I'm in the doghouse for the first time,' I moaned as I scoured ASOS for new outfits that could be delivered within twenty-four hours. It had been a while since I'd been in a club full of gay men and I wanted to look as sharp as possible without looking like a tumble dryer had exploded in a glitter factory.

'Look, I know he is really gorgeous and this is exciting and he treats you like you're a king but ...'

'How can there possibly be a "but" in that sentence?!'

Bella cringed in anticipation of the truth bomb she was about to detonate. She couldn't even look into the camera. 'The last thing you need is someone forcing you back into the closet. It took you so long to come out and feel comfortable with yourself ...'

'Who says I feel comfortable with myself?' I laughed. 'I'm still a burning mass of contradictions and insecurities.'

'Yeah. You hide them really well,' deadpanned Bella. 'But you know what I mean. Every day I see a new you, a confident you. A million miles away from who you were with Adam. Don't let anyone ruin that for you, even if he does seem like a dream come true.'

Nate would come round, I knew it.

Sweetie was one of those clubs that had been in the same venue for years and saw no reason to move, even though it was one of the most popular LGBT nights in London. Basically, it was packed every week. I hadn't been for a while but it felt like home. Held in a ramshackle old pub in Vauxhall, it was hectic, loud, full of characters and, if Richie's face was anything to go by, thrilling. 'It's absolutely fucking full of men,' he gasped. 'I can't see a single woman.'

Silvie nudged him in the ribs and pointed to herself and his wife. 'What about us, you arsehole?'

Richie looked her up and down. 'I've been looking at you so long you're just part of the furniture, to be honest, Silv. You're like a wardrobe to me, basically.' Richie downed his drink, raced off to the dance floor and started pogoing to the music. Nicole rolled her eyes. 'I'd better go after him and make sure he doesn't say anything inappropriate.'

We knocked back a few shots and danced a while, before a drunk Curtis bounced over to us. 'Hi, you miserable bitch,' he trilled, kissing me on both cheeks. 'You're out having fun, so tell your fucking face.' He nodded down at the lurid yellow cocktail in his hand. 'It's called a Golden Shower. Want one?'

I was about to answer when he grabbed a bearded guy who was passing by, and started to dance with him.

The results were not stellar. If the other guy had been slightly more out of time or awkward, it might have been funny, but this was just painful. He was leaden and mortified, his sole concession to acknowledging the rhythm of the song was a self-conscious hand wave that looked like he was trying to shake a wasp out of his bedsheets. Curtis was never going to feature in a chorus line but his hips knew their way around a tune, and he stared back in horror. In what I assumed was an effort to contain the damage, Curtis pulled him closer and they started gyrating closely and snogging really aggressively, like they were tearing each other's jaws off. Silvie nudged me. 'What about his husband? Parker, isn't it?'

They looked like two watermelons smashing into one another. 'Parker isn't here, though, is he?'

As Silvie and I danced, I thought I saw some familiar faces. You know that thing when you see someone on the train and are unsure whether you actually know them in real life or they've just been on TV or something? My recall of celebrities was pretty amnesiac, but I didn't feel I'd met these people in person. They all looked slightly off. And then I got it. More of them. Most of them. I looked at them all again and they appeared to me as little avatars, or profile pics. Usernames and Twitter handles flooded my head. They were followers. They read me. I laughed at the outrageousness of it, at being able to shimmy alongside the entire comments section of my blog while they stayed oblivious. I felt almost regal. Maybe this was my kink, to be in a room filled with strangers who knew everything about me but didn't even know I was there. It was so weird. Too weird. As Sid had said, it was like being a gay Spider-Man.

One very familiar guy banged into me and did a double-take. Did he know me too? Where from? We hadn't dated. But he'd really *looked* at me, like a painting in the National Gallery. I instinctively, ridiculously, covered my mouth. Had he recognised it from my photo? Surely not. My tummy somersaulted and I hurried off the dance floor for a breather.

The place was busy, and the fight for space at the bar involved a lot of elbowing. One guy barged in and rolled his eyes, before shooting me a quick smile and an apology. It took me a second, but I realised he was one of the guys who'd been slagging off Romeo on Twitter. Compliments and plaudits I could never recall, but I remembered this man tweeting Romeo. Tweeting me.

> @OneMoreRomeo ur just another basic bitch slutting his way through soho. Gurrrrrl nobody gives a shit

And after my blog about the swimmer.

> @OneMoreRomeo bitch I hope ur better at suckin dick than u r at keeping secrets and WRITING

And there he was, large as life, ordering a rum and Diet Coke and a vodka tonic. He even said 'Sorry babes' to me as he nudged past, leaving me shell-shocked. I looked round the room again, and saw more men I remembered leaving bitchy comments.

I recognised some of them, but what about the anonymous commenters, the pseudonyms, the guys who used a close-up of their eye or a cartoon character? Any one of them could be here right now, watching me. The room spun, the air felt threatening, my jaw clenched. I had to go. I pushed back to the dance floor where Nicole, Silvie and Richie were losing their minds to 'Gimme More'.

'Guys, I have to go.'

Richie snorted. 'What? It's a sodding sausage fest in here, are you mad? I wanna take them all home *for* you.'

Nicole pushed him aside. 'Are you all right? What is it?'

I was confused. Drunk. 'I think I saw someone who follows me.'

Curtis tore himself away from his bearded limpet. 'Someone's *following* you?! Where? You haven't been anywhere but here!'

Thankfully he was so drunk he wouldn't remember any of this in the morning. I just wanted Nate. I wanted to say sorry, tell him he'd been right, and forget about Romeo. Everyone tried to persuade me to stay, but quickly gave up. There's nothing worse than someone telling you they want to leave when you're having a good time; sometimes you have to let them go. They relented, Silvie shooting me her best puppy-dog eyes in a last-ditch attempt to get me to stay. I queued at the cloakroom, desperate to chew my fingernails but unwilling to look too anxious, trying not to catch anyone's eye. My phone buzzed. A notification, but from my work email. Whatever. It could wait until Monday. But then I saw the subject line: *Hello Romeo*.

I quickly opened it to find nothing but a screenshot of my Twitter account. But sent to my work email. Weird. Why? There were no words, but the message was clear: *I know who you really are*. I only noticed there were tears in my eyes when the cloakroom attendant asked me if I was OK.

As I headed for the exit and struggled with my coat, a hand came out of nowhere and grabbed my wrist. I didn't dare look up.

'Hello handsome,' I heard him say. For a second I thought it might be Nate, but when I looked up his face was the wrong kind of familiar and I couldn't focus. I wrenched myself away and made for the door again. He called out. 'Hey! Jim!' I pushed on, almost sprinting to the taxi rank.

I rode home in the cab with my head between my knees. 'It's a hundred pounds straight away if you puke, mate,' warned the driver as he took a sharp turn at Oval.

The guy had known my name. How the hell had he known my name?

I looked at my wrist. He had left a mark. I called Nate but he didn't pick up. He'd told me never to leave a voicemail in case his agent heard it. I'd already upset him enough, so I didn't break the rule.

I texted a couple of times but no reply. I looked at the email again, zoomed in on the screenshot in case there was some weird hidden message or something. Was it the same guy who'd grabbed my arm? I felt a rush of panic. If someone knew who I was, what if they knew about me and Nate? It wouldn't be long until they worked out who the blog was about, if they didn't know already.

I listlessly pushed open my front door and, too wired to go to bed, poured myself a very large vodka and stared at my screen, willing Nate to wake up and message me.

I saw Luca was online.

> What was the music like at Sweetie? Last
> time I went out the top tune was a wax
> cylinder of Charlie Chaplin coughing into
> a microphone.

The floodgates opened. I told him about coming face to face with my trolls and the weird email. Why would anyone care who I was? I was nobody. Luca seemed to understand.

> I can't speak for the creep who sent you
> the email, but I think it's the curiosity of it.
> You're anonymous, it creates a mystery.
> Everybody wants to be ahead with the
> gossip. Knowing who you are . . . it's a
> status thing.

The email had seemed pretty calculating to me. It wasn't sent by someone wanting to be friends.

> This guy is probably trying to show you
> how clever he is. They want you to see that
> they're interested.

But how would anyone work it out? I thought I'd been careful. But then I really thought about it. Anyone could look at my tweets and find out where I was. My last tweet had said 'going clubbing in Vauxhall – what are the chances?' Hardly under-cover. And while I'd never shown anyone my face, I'd described myself in great detail on my blog. My appearance, my age, what I did for a job. Assuming I wasn't lying – which I now started to wish I had done – anyone could play detective and unmask me. Being anonymous wasn't the same as hiding. I was out there in plain sight. Suddenly I felt sick.

> I've been an idiot. Look, Luca, level with
> me: did you already work out who I was?

There was a long pause. I got up to get a glass of water and instinctively closed the blinds and double-checked the door was locked. When I got back, Luca's reply was blinking for my attention.

> I was wondering if you'd ask. I couldn't
> decide if I should tell you. I had a feeling it
> would upset you.

Fuck. I felt a jolt through me, like when you trip up and get that jolt of adrenaline that stops you falling over.

> I didn't do much digging. I didn't need to. I
> was worried you might be someone I knew in
> real life and didn't like, for example. It turns
> out we used to chat years ago on an old
> messageboard. Remember LowPop?

Fuck. Yes, I did.

> The weird thing was I never even bothered
> poking into it. You gave it away yourself. I'm
> a big reader of *Snap!* you see – pls don't
> judge – and I read something that really
> jumped out at me.

I dreaded to ask.

> Go on, put me out of my misery.

> How many writers do you reckon use
> the phrase 'he had all the foresight of a
> comatose lizard'? Clue: two. Romeo, and
> James Brodie.

I sat back and breathed deeply. The guy who'd called out to me at Sweetie – he'd called me Jim, so he knew me. And he looked nothing like Luca, as far as I knew from his avatar. I squinted at it again. If indeed that was his real picture. And as for the email? I had to ask.

> Given you seem to know a lot about
> this, I just want to check: you didn't
> send me that email as a joke, did you?
> I promise not to be pissed off.

No, mate, honestly. I wouldn't do that. I'm on
your side. Last thing I'd wanna do is freak
you out.

I believed him, but still I felt exposed, unsafe. I needed to be with Nate. More than anything. But my secret was unravelling – what if his was next?

13.

'OK, so I need every picture we've got of Tim Prentice with another man – no women anywhere in shot. It doesn't matter who they are, how old they are or whatever. Just Tim and a bloke. The more furtive the better.' Roland was on a roll. Only a bit of insider information could get him this excited.

'Get them in a gallery, with some cheeky captions – not too dirty – and then whack it over to me, like, yesterday.'

I shot Alicha a look. Who the hell was Tim Prentice? I scanned the highlights she sent me.

> Olympic swimmer. 20. Abs to die for. Likes tight trunks.
> We never put him in the mag because he never does
> anything or ANYONE. Literally no girlfriends ever except
> rumours he was shagging Victoria Cordon (also swimmer).
> Two things to check out: Wikipedia (FFS you are useless)
> and Hurley's desk calendar. He is a total fanboy.

It was probably the reason Nate and I had managed to stay dating so long – celeb magazines just weren't that interested. Olympians didn't get drunk in public or dress up and make idiots of themselves; they just went to training and posed with javelins or medals. Not thrilling. I glanced over at Hurley's desk and saw Tim's beaming face under a shock of bright blond hair and not much else. His only concession to October was a strategically placed pumpkin. I swear it was the first time I'd ever laid eyes on him.

'He's about to come out. He's filmed a confessional or something and is putting it online.' Roland scrolled furiously on his phone. 'There's a press conference after but they won't say where until he's done. All they've said is he's broadcasting a video message for the fans at . . . ' he checked his watch. 'Oh, like now. So hurry up.'

'How do you know he's coming out?'

'He's been to tell the family already.' Roland looked slightly downcast. 'Let's just say those Prentice cousins couldn't hold a fart, let alone a secret, Jim. And they like money. And we *have* money. I needed that photo-story ten minutes ago.'

I looked at Roland. 'Don't you sometimes think we shouldn't do stuff like this?' He stared back blankly. 'You know,' I continued, losing my faith a little, 'as *gay men*?'

Roland gave a hollow laugh. 'We're not "gay men" today, we're at work. We're just *men*. And if we don't cover it, someone else will.' He tapped on my desk. 'They probably already are. Don't forget gay men are readers, too. It's what they want, even if they never admit it in public.'

I was just finishing off the story when Hurley screamed: 'It's live! He's doing it!' He yanked his headphones out of the computer and hit play, frantically live-blogging along as the crackly audio piped out of the speakers. Hurley whacked up the volume and Tim's voice reverberated around the office. People nearby wandered over to watch what was happening on Hurley's screen. 'Fucking slaaaaay them, Tim,' he yelled.

I watched as Tim, sitting in an immaculate, tastefully decorated hotel room, sighed and stared into the camera. It was a far cry from my own coming-out to my mother – done at Christmas because me me me – when I'd brightly reassured her that no, I didn't do drugs and, no, it wasn't a phase, while she calmly boiled eggs for my breakfast.

The vastness of the hotel room made Tim look tiny, and I noticed he glanced off-camera every now and again, either at cue cards or whichever PR person had the dubious honour of coaching him for the event. Tim talked about 'endless speculation' and how things had 'come to a head recently' – I was about to make a joke about oral sex but looked up and read the room; some people had tears in their eyes, and I thought better of it – and how he'd felt under increased pressure to 'reveal the truth before somebody else did'.

He assured his fans he'd never wanted to live a lie, but that he hadn't been ready, and he knew they'd understand. He looked once again off-camera – I could almost see his eyes scan the script being held up for him – and closed with an impassioned speech, perfectly rehearsed. 'Nasty people who out others or break confidences for their own entertainment, or for gossip, or for attention, are the lowest of the low.'

When it was over, I could hear ripples of applause from some of the teams on our floor, while the rest bowed their heads at that final burn. Almost everyone in that room, in all four corners, had played their part in a story like this at one time or another. I thought of Nate. Should I text him? Would he know about this?

The screen went to black and Hurley stood on his chair and whooped, 'Drag those bitches, honey!' He turned to me and Alicha excitedly. 'I knew it! This is it! My chances of being Mr Hurley Prentice-Fox just went up by a million.' For the first time, I was almost happy for him.

Roland strode over to me, emotionless. 'Right, cab it over to the press conference now. Soho Hotel. Alicha, take the camera and see if we can get reactions from fans – they'll have arranged for a rentamob to be down there waving teddy bears and fucking balloons. Let's do caring and sharing and wait for the backlash online. Be good experience for you.'

Hurley leapt up, dramatically. 'What? What about me? I know more about Tim Prentice than anyone in this room.'

Alicha heaved the camera bag onto her back. 'You're breaking news, remember, hun? Well, it's broken, so leave this to the professionals. I'll email you the footage and you can get to work. Excuse me.' She winked at me jauntily and sauntered out to the lifts.

Hurley looked at me with utter contempt. 'Why does *he* have to go? He's not even staff!' But Roland was already back at his desk. I shrugged and walked away from him without saying a word.

In the cab, I tried to swot up on Tim Prentice as much as possible. Alicha, as ever, was better than Google.

'In his video there, the announcement. What did he mean "speculation" about his sexuality? I didn't see anything. I've never even heard of him.'

Alicha tutted and popped some chewing gum before offering me the packet. 'Trust me babes, you need this. Your latte addiction is out of control.'

'Alicha! What did he mean?!'

She leaned back in the seat and let the bag containing zillions of pounds-worth of camera topple over. 'How can you not know about the Tim Prentice stuff? The blog?!'

My tummy did a bunny-hop. 'What blog?' I knew my voice was shaking. Surely she wasn't going to say it.

'The Romeo guy,' said Alicha, looking down at her phone

and thus missing my panicked expression. 'The blogger guy. Anonymous. He wrote about going on a date with some weird and uptight swimmer who was in the closet and it was *blatantly* Tim Prentice all along.'

My throat went pinhole-tight. How could this be happening? I hadn't even really heard of Tim Prentice two hours ago and now *this*? Yes, I'd *said* Nate was a swimmer because we'd joked about only knowing the divers – how hollow and long ago that laugh felt now – and I had called him Tom, not Tim. Who had said it was about him? Why had nobody asked me outright? I'd been ignoring a lot of emails and messages recently – there'd been too many to get through.

As she carried on filling me in, I started to cough so hard that as I reached into my bag for a tissue to cover my mouth with, I retched and had a very slight vomit kind of situation. Alicha peered at me in horror.

'Are you hungover? It's a bit shitty though, isn't it?' she said.

'What?'

'Well, to out someone. It's dark. You can't go around doing that.'

'But if he changed the details . . . how do you know it's Tim?!'

Alicha put her phone away. 'He didn't change them *enough*. Tim/Tom. He wanted everyone to know. Don't you think?'

I retched again. Alicha handed me a bottle of water and I drank. 'Keep it.'

'Thanks.'

We sat in traffic for a minute or two. Alicha didn't take her eyes off me. 'OK, don't get offended, yeah?' I stared back blankly. 'I've been wanting to ask you this before but I thought it might be, like, stupid but, well, y'know, you have *literally* just been sick into your bag in front of me so I feel I can say anything now.' I knew what was coming. I considered springing out of the cab but we began to move. 'You're Romeo, right?'

Now was not the time to lie. Somehow, I couldn't wait to tell the truth.

'Yes. I'm so sorry.' I breathed out for what felt like the first and longest time ever.

Alicha leaned back and whispered a wow. 'OK ... putting aside the fact you never told me this, what on earth were you doing shagging some lame-ass *baby* like Tim Prentice?'

'I ... how did you know it was me?'

'I got a bit suss that day you were giving me all the "hypo-theticals" about Twitter shitstorms, remember? And you were so weird about giving me your Twitter handle. Like, unless you were calling me an ugly bitch or something, why would I care?' She was talking at a million miles an hour – her investigations had been thorough and she had receipts to spare. 'Anyway, the only thing happening that day that wasn't politics and Kim K's no-make-up selfie was the Romeo thing. And I know you *still* couldn't pick Kim K out of a line-up so ... And I read it, him. You. And it's ... pretty much you. It's brilliant, by the way. You're a legend.'

I somehow managed to mutter my thanks. 'I promise you, it isn't about Tim Prentice. I've honestly never heard of him. I wouldn't have left so many details the same.'

'Then who is it about?'

'I, um, I can't tell you.' Alicha frowned. 'Seriously.' As I gar-bled my explanations, I sounded more and more of an idiot, more thirsty for likes than thoughtful of feelings. I checked my phone in case Nate had heard but he was either oblivious or planning my murder. How could I have been so stupid? However, Alicha, surprisingly, got it.

'Look, Jim, it was a good story. Sexy. You shagged an athlete. My Instagram stories would've been fucking flames for days, mate. And, yeah, it was irresponsible.' She shrugged. 'But it's what we do, isn't it? Problematic for a click or two. And now you're seeing this guy?'

'This is the thing.' I noticed the cab was swinging round the corner to the hotel. 'If this gets out, if I'm connected to this in any way and he notices it, then … I'm done for.'

Alicha gathered up the camera bag while I paid the driver. 'Jim, babe, it sounds like you are already. Come on.'

We shlepped down thickly carpeted stairs to the hotel's basement and were herded into a small auditorium – more accustomed to private screenings of movies nobody wanted to see than events like this. Alicha and I took a couple of pics of the staging area and rushed to the back as everyone filtered in. Soon the room was thundering with the sound of exaggerated whispers and everyone pretending to be very serious.

I flipped open my iPad and prepared to type as Tim Prentice was ushered into the room by a group of flunkies. His face wasn't the bright, hopeful one I'd seen in all his photos, or even the brooding one on Hurley's calendar. He looked startled, haunted. I felt a rush of regret. Had I really done this? Did they really think this timid little sparrow was the same guy from my blog? His parents followed and each took a seat either side of him, while a terrifying woman with a side-ponytail stood behind, scanning the crowd for questions.

I nudged Alicha to ask a question, but she shook her head and drew her finger across her throat. I knew Roland would be mad if one of us didn't, so I raised my hand and caught the side-ponytail's eye. She sprang to my side with a microphone. I tried to control my voice. 'Uh, James Brodie, from, um, *Snap!*' I murmured, my mouth too close to the mic.

Tim leaned forward into his own microphone. 'Sorry, can you stand up? I can't see you.'

Shit. I shakily rose to my feet. Our eyes locked. 'Er, yeah, hi, so, um, Tom – Tim! – was it your decision to come out? Why now?'

Tim looked back at me defiantly. 'I wanted the story to come from me, not anywhere or *anyone* else.'

The mic was snatched from my hand and I heard a familiar voice ring out. Curtis, trying to contain himself so hard he was squeaking like a rocking chair. 'So Tim, hello dear, Curtis Jacobs, from *Oh My Goss*.' He'd changed jobs again, then. 'Was your big decision ∴ oh and well done on that by the way, I know how hard that can be . . . but, was it anything to do with a certain anonymous blogger?'

Alicha and I slowly turned to look at one another. The audience started to get a little rowdier – clearly half of them had no idea what Curtis was talking about. But we did. I saw Alicha typing on her phone furiously. Buzz!

> Oh my fucking God. James. We have to get
> out of here.

I turned and grimaced at her.

> I feel like I'm gonna shit myself inside out.
> I'm having 20 panic attacks and wanna
> dieeeeee. Can I be ARRESTED for this?!?!?

> I'm scared we're going to give it away. I
> daren't speak in case I start screaming
> ROMEO ROMEO ROMEO and pointing at
> you! How the FUCK can this be happening?
> TO YOU?!?!?!?11!1??

> I missed what he said?! How did he answer?

> He said 'no comment'.

BASTARD!!! He knows the blog isn't
about him! Why would he do this?

I dunno. OMG look at the screen.

Projected behind Tim and his parents were screenshots of
One More Romeo. I saw my words – and my mouth – jumbo jet-
sized, while Tim gurned like Prince Charles, as if recalling the
memory of something that, we should remember, never actually
sodding happened.

OKAAAAAAAY so I am now
in an anxiety dream.

!!!!!!!

It's like I can see danger coming
and wanna scream but no sound
comes out. And everything
is inexplicably on fire.

This is wild. You are the worst kind of
famous. Like a serial killer. One thing and I
promise I will back you 100%: Are you telling
me the truth? This is NOT about Tim? Defo?

I realised if I couldn't convince Alicha, there was no way anyone
else would believe me. Although one other man would certainly
be able to vouch for me. The one man I didn't want to find out. I
tried to type my response but my fingers were numb, I couldn't
breathe and tears were doing their best to escape from my eyes.
Nate Nate Nate Nate.

> I am, I swear. Please. BTW I really am
> going to vomit and shit myself at the
> same time if we don't leave now.

As we milled around in the lobby, Curtis sashayed over. 'What are you two whispering about?'

Alicha nodded at him curtly. 'We were just saying how scuffed your trainers are.' I knew there was no love lost there. Curtis had patronised her and tried to touch her hair once at a premiere and Alicha didn't have time for him.

Curtis took the barb and gave me the once-over. 'You look awful. Come for a quick coffee!'

He found a cosy corner of the hotel bar and clicked his fingers for a waiter. Alicha gave him a death-stare.

'I can't believe you do that,' I stage-whispered as I finished typing up the story and hit 'send'. 'You'll get us chucked out.'

Curtis sat back in his seat like a monarch. 'So what did you think about all that drama, then? It seemed very *staged*, didn't it?'

I didn't want to think about it at all. Coming face to face with Tim made what I'd done to Nate more real. 'He'll have been briefed beforehand.' I tried my best to look nonchalant as Curtis's eyes searched me for a reaction. 'Nothing unusual about that.'

'No, I suppose.' Curtis beamed widely as three huge cups of coffee were placed in front of us by a very handsome waiter. 'And this whole business with the blogger is very ... *disconcerting*. There's always a reason people come out, isn't there?'

We all knew how it worked. Many gay stars didn't choose to come out – it was forced upon them by a journalist with information, an indiscreet or spurned former lover.

I could see Alicha's mind working overtime. 'What about this blogger, eh?' She kept her voice steady, uninterested but she was obviously trying to find out how much Curtis really knew.

Curtis clapped his hands in glee. 'Everyone loves a mystery, Alicha, darling, especially me. And if Tim can spin it that he was *forced* out it makes his adoring public more sympathetic.'

I sighed, forgetting myself. 'Not to the blogger.'

Curtis eyed me uncertainly. 'Yeeeees, well if he blames the blogger he can still stay onside with all the journalists. Nobody likes a blogger, darling; they're destroying the industry.'

I toyed with the sugar cubes on the table. Alicha sprang back into action. 'Yeah, but is it definitely him? Why wouldn't he just confirm it?'

Curtis pursed his lips. 'Hmmm, yeah, that's the one thing I'm not sure about. The guy in the blog sounded mature, like a sad soul who'd been battling with his sexuality for years, living in secret.'

I cringed at how accurate a picture of Nate my words must've drawn. Curtis carried on: 'Prentice, though, has the depth and charm of a packet of crisps, and he's been fiddling with his what-sit on those *apps* since he got his GCSE results.'

Alicha tutted. 'His *whatsit*?! What's that got to do with anything?'

I butted in before it got nasty. 'You should know better than to start slut-shaming, Curtis. None of us is whiter than white.' I thought of Romeo's dating spreadsheet and the triple aster-isks that meant he'd – well, *I'd* – seen rather more of my date than anticipated.

'I'm not slut-shaming him, you fucking dolts. I'm saying he's never hidden in the shadows – he's just chosen not to say until now.'

'Until now,' repeated Alicha. 'Until he was outed.'

'Yes.' Curtis exasperatedly plonked his coffee cup back in its saucer and the noise rang out across the room. 'This is why this *idiot* blogger is perfect.' I winced. Curtis was in full flow. 'Playing the victim like this . . . it gets people backing him. I'm sure his straight fans might have a bit more trouble processing what he really gets up to.'

'What *we* really get up to.'

'Mind you . . . ' Curtis looked away from me and bit his lip. 'Being outed is horrible. It happened to me. It ruined my life.'

Alicha giggled, assuming he was being dramatic for effect. 'But, Curtis, were you ever in?'

I sat back as Curtis recounted the story I'd heard many times before – his idealistic, disastrous crush on the school football captain that had been revealed to everyone when a young, drunk Curtis confided in the wrong person.

His eyes were moist. 'That was just it, you see. Everybody else had an opinion on my sexuality but me. I didn't even know I was gay.'

Alicha leaned over and rubbed Curtis's arm. I saw the beginnings of a detente. The last thing I needed was those two becoming best friends. 'But what if Tim isn't the guy in the blog? Like you say, it sounds like someone else entirely.'

Curtis drained his cup. 'It doesn't matter now. That Romeo twat has planted the seed, made people question it. The damage is done.'

I suddenly felt the urge to hide my hands in my lap; it was like they had blood on them.

We rode back to the office in silence, until Alicha looked up from checking the footage on the camera and prodded me across the cab with her shoe. I felt sick, and not just because I was facing backwards.

'Jim. What are you gonna do? I mean, your secret is safe with me so don't worry about that.' How many times was I going to hear that? I reached for my phone and pulled up the three-word email I'd received to my work address. Screenshots of tweets. *Tut tut, Romeo.*

173

'It's not just your secret to keep.'

Alicha handed me back the phone. 'Shit, that's fucked up. But, this guy ... Do you, like, love him?'

I looked at my screen. 'I think I've ballsed it up. If he finds out ... he's super touchy about it. I ... his mum and dad don't know, and ... his career. It's ... I don't care about me anymore but I *cannot* be identified. It would be a disaster for him.'

I realised I couldn't even deny the blogpost was about Tim. As painful as it was, and as bad as it made Romeo look – especially with Tim's puppy-dog eyes staring out from the front pages of all the tabloids, as they definitely would be the next morning – if everyone thought it was about Tim, Nate would stay protected. For now.

Alicha huffed dramatically. 'Unless you've been meeting in a nuclear bunker, somebody will have seen you together. If someone already knows, it will come out eventually. Pardon the pun.'

'So what would you do?' I knew the answer. It didn't matter what Alicha said. But she blew a huge bubble with her gum and told me anyway.

'You gotta let him go, Jim.'

Right on cue, my phone buzzed. Now was my chance.

We went to one of the quiet bars by the river out near Nate's flat, the first time we had gone anywhere local. It was one of those places that looks like the set of a TV show – it felt temporary, and unwelcoming. The furniture looked like it had been rescued from a flooded leisure centre and the lighting was airport levels of oppressive. Laminate from floor to ceiling and practically empty save for the bored bar staff and the local drunk who was clearly resisting the gentrification of the neighbourhood. We drank our pints quickly – I knew this was not Nate's night of the month to drink, but didn't comment – and waited for conversation to come. Small-talk dribbled from us until we gave up and left, bracing ourselves against the first very cold night of the autumn. Unexpected, short gusts hit us from all angles.

Finally he came to it: 'My agent phoned. Did you hear about Tim Prentice?'

I nodded but Nate wasn't looking at me, so I caught his eye and said yes.

'Are you going to write about it?'

I wanted to scream in fright but I kept it together and sneaked a look at him. I knew his face enough that it told me he didn't know about Romeo. My mind wandered and I imagined telling him, and him throwing me into the murky Thames beside us.

'Uh, yeah we covered it.'

'Were you nice?'

I thought of the spiteful gallery of every man Tim had ever been seen in public with, and my salacious captions that managed to stay just the right side of tasteful but were certainly open to interpretation.

I swerved the question. 'How do you feel about it? Does it make you feel any closer to . . . you know?'

'What?'

'Well, coming out.' I coughed nervously. 'I mean, if Tim Prentice can come out, then maybe it would be easy for you. I mean . . . ' I was rambling. 'Well, he's got loads of sponsors and stuff and they seem to be OK with it.'

Nate's face was stone. He narrowed his eyes as a blast of wind hit him hard. 'This again.'

'Nate, don't say "this again" like I'm whinging at you for not emptying the bin. And it's not as if I bring it up all the time. I don't. I daren't. But if Tim Prentice can come out, then why can't you?' I stopped and Nate paused beside me.

He turned to face me. 'I don't give a fuck about Tim Prentice. And this is not about my sponsors and *stuff*. I have enough *money*.' He was so angry I had to move back from him. 'I ... I thought we understood each other.'

I leaned against the railings. 'Then what is it? I *don't* understand.'

'No, and I can't tell you how ... devastated that makes me.' He grabbed his head with both hands, before looking about him to see if anyone was around. 'I'm not ready. I said. Remember? Nothing has changed. This ... only makes me feel *less* ready. I just don't want to do it.'

I turned from him, looked out at the river and tried to be soothed by its stillness. I could only see its filth. I needed to be calm.

'*Some* things have changed.' I felt my throat turn to stone. 'You have me now.'

Nate cried out. 'Fuck! Fuck, James! I knew this was too good to be true.'

I knew what I had to do, to protect us both. I turned back to him.

Nate coughed. 'James, I don't think we should do this now.'

'No,' I said. 'Let's go home.' Better to tell him there than out here. It was freezing anyway; my teeth were chattering so hard I didn't trust myself to get the words out properly.

Nate shook his head and stepped toward me. 'No, I mean, do *this*. Us. Any of it. Not now.'

'Do you mean ... ?'

'I'm going to go home. By myself. I think you should, too.' He reached out and touched my face. Further along the riverbank, a dog barked – just like that first night – and he drew back, quickly. 'It was so much fun, and I ... care about you. But it can't go on. I've too much to lose.'

I felt myself do a huge about-turn. No, not like this. Not by the river in this characterless part of town. I wanted to ask him: wasn't I a lot to lose? To tell him I could help him through this, that we could stay secret a while longer if he wanted. But I knew that wasn't true. Sooner or later it would come out. The earlier we walked away, the better chance we had of keeping a lid on it.

'I don't want you to call,' he said softly. 'I won't change my mind. Night, handsome.' He didn't touch me again, just walked away. The wind whipped up as his footsteps faded. I looked up at the streetlight to see the first spittles of rain in the orange glow. My umbrella was in Nate's flat. The wind howled and screeched, and nipped at my face as I opened my mouth to scream the three words I'd never managed to say to his face. He would never hear them; the wind took them away.

14.

What was it about getting in the shower and having a revelation? First, Adam, interrupting my singing and convincing me to pull the plug on him, and now, trying to wash away the vestigial night terrors after a sleepless seven hours pining for Nate I realised I had to snap out of it, and fast. Everything had to change. I was thirty-five in a matter of weeks. Christmas was coming up. What magazines liked to call cuffing season was zooming into view, and I was alone. It was difficult to admit you were lonely, especially if you lived in a big city, surrounded by people, going to sleep inches from your neighbour's hacking cough, through a cheaply built wall. They say in New York you're never more than a foot away from a rat, but it seemed in London I was always only ever a few inches away from someone else having the time of their lives. But I was that peculiar, tiny corner of the beach that the sea never reached – just day after day of dry sand.

I'd been isolating myself since Nate and I finished. It didn't help that Tim Prentice had been everywhere, his bush-baby eyes blinking out from every daytime TV show, telling his story. After yet another night on my own in the pub feeling sorry for myself, I turned to Luca for some clarity. Now he knew who I really was, there was a new honesty between us that felt a comfort after all that time pretending to be someone else.

What's Romeo's next move?

I could deny the blog was about
Tim Prentice, maybe?

Mind you, calling Tim a liar didn't feel like it would help my case; he was basically untouchable now.

Once you take Tim out of the equation,
people will only start poking around again.
'No comment' seemed to work pretty well for
Tim. Maybe it will work for Romeo too?

On a scale of 1 to 10, how much do
people hate Romeo right now?

About a 7. It'll blow over. You've always
said you would never reveal your Romeos'
identities. Stick to it. Show integrity. If you
don't give your critics any meat, they can't
tear it from your bones.

I hoped he was right.

And as for Nate, well. You know that thing where you come across a word for the first time, or it's explained to you what it means, and suddenly you hear and see that word everywhere you go? The Baader-Meinhof phenomenon? Nate was that. Everywhere I looked: hoardings, magazines, on TV talking about a charity he was involved with – it must've been an old recording, as I didn't recognise the haircut. But Nate Harris was pretty much everywhere except in my inbox and my bed and I was determined to wallow.

I was so miserable, it was embarrassing. I was cancelling plans. Ignoring calls. Stacking up pizza boxes beside the dustbin, just as I had after Adam – it was a comfort to play to type, and I was determined to play the tragic hero. I sat swiping this way and that on Seizer until my knuckles locked, lost in a sea of clumsy openers from men who I decided, depending on what mood I was in, were worth ten of Nate Stupid Fucking Harris or, more usually, especially after chucking the 'six cans for a fiver' deal down my neck, couldn't hold a candle to him. Nate stayed true to his word and didn't contact me, and while I would get my phone out and stare at his name every now and again, I stayed away – although if the police were tracking Google searches about him then I would have some explaining to do. I had an inkling I might need to stage some kind of intervention with myself when Alicha dropped a hint that perhaps I wasn't quite with it. Well, I say hint, she screamed across the office, 'Jamie, your hair looks like a squirrel slept in it – when was the last time you ran some product through it?' and I saw Hurley sit back with smug satisfaction.

And then there was that day in the shower. I was soaping myself, doing the usual holy cross of the male toilette – face, neck, underarms, along the arms, torso, the main event and up and round to the aftershow – when I realised if I slipped now and put my back out, or broke my neck, nobody would find me. Everyone who cared about me was far away or too busy to notice. I quickly – but not too quickly in case I did actually slip – jumped out of the shower and sat on the sofa, shivering in the dark, while outside it sounded like the rest of the world was falling in love and having the most fun it was possible to have on a major bus route through Camberwell.

Where had they gone, all my old friends? All my gay friends? The guys I danced with in my twenties, shared secrets, traumas and bumps of something speedy in the last cubicle on the left? Hadn't I had my own squad once upon a time? Had I driven them away? Bobby and Will swanned off to Australia and never came back. Bruce and Innes headed back to Scotland to start a family. Some of the boys were gone for ever: beautiful, funny Mitch had ascended to a better place after a long, slow climb that was painful for us all to watch. A hit-and-run claimed acerbic, clever Gareth. Curtis was still here, of course, and despite his outrageousness, he was thoughtful, kind and hilarious, but he came and went like the seasons – hibernating with his handsome husband for months on end – and was hard to talk to on a deeper level. My straight friends were always surprised I had no cabal of gay pals to hang around with, assuming we were a hive mind who bonded over sassy gifs, Beyoncé's back catalogue and mutual love of vests that showed your nipples. But I couldn't remember the last time I'd opened my heart to another gay man – Adam had taught me they were careless with them.

It occurred to me as I trembled on the sofa in just a towel, feeling my hair frizz up as it dried naturally, that I had access to a mine of gay men with friendship potential. Not every date had ended badly. Not all the 'thanks but no thanks' men had been toxic. My contacts groaned with the weight of all these guys who'd been great but just not 'the one'. I was a nice guy, right? I could be pretty funny. I was reliable. I knew *great* places to grab lunch. It should be possible for a man to be friends and not fall madly in love with me, surely – plenty had resisted me so far. I quickly dressed, ran that all-important wax through my hair, curled up on the sofa and got scrolling through my phone contacts.

*

Niall. Niall. Who was Niall? From Cork, shining green eyes and hair the colour of dishwater and a winning smile. My memory jump-started. He'd punched me good-naturedly on the arm on arrival – nervous, maybe? Whatever it was, it activated a shooting pain down my arm so I'd spent the rest of the date convinced I was seconds away from a fatal heart attack and struggled to concentrate. We'd texted vague plans to meet again sometime, but hadn't.

> Hey Niall. How are you? Wondered
> if you fancied meeting for a
> drink next week, maybe?

Was it clear this would be a matey drink and not a precursor to sex? I hadn't put a kiss on the end, after all. Within thirty seconds, I had my answer: a picture of an erect penis (model's own, I assumed).

> How about dinner instead?

Very forward. I'd never taken a picture of my pecker – I mean, I called my dick a pecker, I was practically a born-again virgin – and I wasn't about to start now, but for some guys it was no big deal, no worse than firing off a selfie. I mean, it was just a penis. Maybe he sent it by mistake.

> Did you mean to send me that picture?

> Wait, who is this?

What? Great. So not only had he erased my number from his phone, he was also sending out pictures of his knob to whoever landed in his inbox. Suddenly I felt very unspecial. I stared back at my phone before getting busy with my fingers.

It's Father Mulcahy from chapel.
Wondering if you'd like to join our
scriptures study group. I'm guessing
not. Peace be with you, son.

Next. Sheridan. Handsome, with a slight underbite and eyes
that had never witnessed the inside of a Burger King. If Sheridan
were a stick of rock and you cut him in half, he'd have 'privilege'
written all the way through. Not that he knew it, or cared – but
that was usually how it worked

'I've toiled so hard all my life.' He was thirty-one and as far
as I knew had no discernible job. 'I've earned the right to pull
back a bit, enjoy my success. Especially now I've managed to
buy my own place.'

Now, in London, this *was* an achievement, especially where
Sheridan lived, in Notting Hill, on one of those streets where all
the houses are painted different colours, like really swish Lego.
And he had a car. He was entitled, seemed to be substituting
access to a good barber for a personality and was gloriously
tactless, but he had a dry laugh and wasn't afraid to get the
drinks in.

'Oh, wow, well done,' I had gushed. 'You must've saved
like mad.'

Sheridan looked skyward as if totting up all the sacrifices he
had made to get his foot on the property ladder. 'Yeah. I mean,
it took me ages to convince Dad to lend me the money.'

'When do you start paying it back?'

I was speaking a foreign language as far as Shezza was concerned. '*Back?* I ... it's going through my dad's business. It's
an investment.'

'It's just when you said you worked ... oh never mind.'

No, Sheridan may have had wheels and a bank balance, and
I had gone home with him that night to check out the electric

doors on his wardrobe for myself, but my class envy would poison any joy I derived from being his friend.

Connor, then? We'd spent a sedate three hours in a spa together and managed to keep our hands to ourselves. If we could stay platonic after being half-naked, slathered in mud and pummelled to within an inch of our lives by two sadistic masseurs, surely we could be pals. He'd cast his eyes over my body about as lustfully as you'd look at a traffic cone and seemed more engrossed in the guy working on reception than me. Connor's weapons-grade indifference might make me feel even more worthless but at least I could trust him not to throw himself at me during a Netflix binge. A reply came back quickly. Promising!

> Jim! A drink next week? Yes, of course. But I have a question. May I ask it?

> That would be amazing. And, yes, ask away!

> What took you so long to get back in touch? I assumed you weren't interested, tbh. Did you meet someone else? If so, fine. I was puzzled is all.

Someone else. Even the sight of those two words together brought a lump to my throat as I remembered the someone. Someone. But I swallowed it hard and took a beat to compose myself before getting back on the horse.

> No, not really. Nothing serious. I was getting back in touch because I enjoyed the date and I thought it would be great to meet again.

A lightning-fast reply.

> Forgive me, Jim ... but this all sounds very
> fraternal. Are we meeting because you want
> to be bros/homies/gal pals? Or do you want
> to see what's under my towel this time?

Hahaha. Shit.

> Keep the towel on. I thought
> we'd try being friends. :)

The unthinkable. Like a smiley could save me now. Did anyone even send those anymore?

I saw he was typing his reply. And typing. And typing. I went off to make another cup of tea. Typing. Finally:

> I didn't join a dating site to make friends,
> James, and I don't think you did either.

I imagined how many times he must've typed and deleted various scathing retorts. I could practically smell the vinegar through my phone screen.

> I just thought it might be nice
> to see each other again.

This time, he went with his first draft. It was there, sizzling on my screen within a minute.

> You're a timewaster, James. Do me a favour.
> Save us the trouble and update your profile
> to LOOKING FOR FRIENDS ONLY. I'm sure

> you'll be inundated with replies from men
> who'd much rather just THINK about fucking
> you than actually DO it.

Once my palpitations subsided, I thought it best to leave it there.

Hang. On. What about Finn? Poor beautiful Finn. I undid two buttons on my shirt at the thought of him. But when I remembered Finn, I remembered Nate walking toward me as Haydn tottered alongside him. I remembered the pair of them building skyscrapers out of French fries. I remembered feeling like a heel for being curious. And I remembered that gelatinous toad of a boyfriend of his – Antony. I couldn't fuck my own pain away. Breaking up a relationship wouldn't glue my heart back together and the last thing I wanted to be with Finn was friends.

I threw my phone aside, reaching to my left for a long-ago-opened bag of Bombay mix and tipping half of it right down my throat.

Maybe I needed another week or so on my own and I could try putting myself out there again? I was just getting used to the idea of another few days shovelling all manner of self-pitying unhealthy snacks down my throat when Toby sent one of his infamously direct emails.

> Hey Romeo
>
> So I'm assuming your relative radio silence has been because you're licking your wounds after the Tim Prentice thing. All very dull, but I wouldn't worry. He can't be that mad at you . . . he's agreed to be on the cover next month so either he doesn't read *HIM* at all and doesn't know you're a columnist or he doesn't care so long as he gets to parade about in his speedos. ANYWAY literally tens of people are dying to know who the fuck Romeo is. I have replied to so many messages about you I'm considering

186

invoicing you for my next manicure. SO what I am saying here is more please. Thank you. Obviously I can't bring out any more issues of the mag a month so I am also putting you online, WEEKLY. Three dates a month and one week you can talk about an issue important to you – the Suez crisis, carrier bags, dealing with halitosis, I don't care. Just get DATING immediately and get writing even sooner. First one goes up on Monday. Thanking you. x

Wow. That was settled, then, my public needed me. Suddenly I felt like I had a *purpose*. Romeo didn't have to be about love, did it? I could just *say* I was looking for the one. A weekly column? One a month about anything I wanted? I could live with that.

I thought about FaceTiming Bella or messaging Nicole to tell them the good news. Alicha would be thrilled, surely, but it was Saturday; they'd be busy. Party for one, then. I trudged over to the fridge, hauled out a bottle of champagne I'd been saving for a special occasion and cracked it open. Well done me. Back to the sofa, phone out, I opened up Seizer. There was no time to lose – winter was coming and I did so hate to be cold. I arranged to meet someone in a just about bearable bar within the hour.

Romeo would be reborn.

The Filthy Romeo

pre-date rating: Errrr, look, we just met, but I'm not a slut or anything. We had a connection

stats: I don't have a tape measure but he is tall and has two eyes and some hair. It's dark

where: The bar. The taxi. His place. Don't get judgey

I'm in a taxi, speeding away from logic, reason, and safety, with someone I met two hours ago. Harry, apparently. Who cares? Anyway. Hello Harry.

It shouldn't have been you, Harry. But the gods brought us together. When I arrive at the bar, I'm looking for somebody else. I peer into each of the bar's dark corners but find only the wrong faces. Despite arranging to meet only an hour ago, my supposed Romeo has got cold feet. I go to scroll back through our messages, to see if we'd had an error in communication, but his profile is gone. Ghosted before we even meet; that must be a new world record. No matter – I'm this close to the sea, I may as well go for a paddle. See if I can come out with any fish. And then Harry's eye meets mine and vodka does its best to make the whole thing history.

I don't know how long we've been in the car or where

we're going. I don't recognise these streets. Suddenly, he bids the taxi stop, and we get out on a fairly run-down high street. 'I just need to get something,' he mumbles and slopes off ahead of me.

I can't think what he's after. Drugs? Suddenly I imagine myself on a missing-person poster – am I about to be doped up and killed? He suddenly stops – I hold my breath – before striding right into a chip shop. Oh. Chips, really?!

My stomach heaves; I wait outside. Nobody ever broke off from kissing me to get *food* before.

Finally he comes out, armed with a huge portion of fish and chips and a battered sausage. I'm amazed.

'Are you going to eat all that?' I gasp.

He looks down at what is essentially a meal for six. 'Well, yeah. I'm a growing boy.'

We walk down the street. It's our first time under a bright light together, so I gaze at him anew.

'How much growing have you got to do?'

'I'm twenty-six,' he shrugs. 'You?'

Quick as a flash, my first lie of the evening: 'Thirty.'

I wait for him to start laughing, but he doesn't. I exhale. Thank you, vodka and darkness.

'Older man, eh? Like it.'

Silence from the peanut gallery, thank you.

We arrive at a ramshackle block of flats. A jangle of keys. And in. A hallway that smells kind of mildewy. And dark. Very dark. Like midnight one billion leagues under the sea.

'There's no light,' he whispers. 'Just go straight ahead.'

I stumble in a brave attempt at a straight line and

find a door-handle. I am in a candlelit room. I feel like I'm in a 'choose your own adventure' book – and sure enough, there is a sentry waiting to tell me my quest. Well, not quite. A girl is sleeping under a huge quilted jacket on the only piece of furniture in the room – a battered cream leather sofa. She is surrounded by cigarette packets and mugs. It is apocalyptic.

'Erm, Harry?' I call out, his name feeling weird and formal as it leaves my mouth.

He appears behind me. 'I thought she'd be in bed. My room, then.'

'Wouldn't that be, uh, better anyway?' I ask, reaching behind me to place a hand on his thigh.

He scratches his chin and grinds into me for a millisecond. Hello. 'Um, yeah. It would. You wait there.'

He closes the door to my sleeping angel and darts off, leaving me in the dark. I'm starting to sober up now – all my realities are coming back to me at once. I am in a stranger's flat, God knows how far away from home. I feel the stupidest I have felt in ... oh, I don't know. Since I last did this.

Another door creaks open like Dracula's coffin and I can see Harry's silhouette in front of a dull, sickly light. I move toward him with all the enthusiasm of an aristocrat walking into a plague pit.

Once I'm in, it's pretty hard to tell where I am. It's a bedroom, I imagine. I can feel stuff all around me. It's oppressive. I've no idea what any of it is, though, as Harry's room is lit by two tealights, ten miles up, atop a huge stack of what I think are books.

'Harry, why is it so dark?'

'Um, ambience?'

He lights another candle. The room may as well be illuminated by a cigarette dangling from the ceiling.

'Fucking hell,' I exclaim, frustrated. 'Where is the light switch?' I trip over something – something that moves, reacts – and hear a seriously fretful miaow out of the darkness.

'Is a *cat* in here?'

Harry scratches himself. 'Possibly. Look, don't turn the light on.'

But he is too late. I shriek in surprise and horror as the light switch fizzes to my touch like a firework. I leap away from it.

'I did say,' he sighs. 'Look, I'll put a lamp on.' A furry tail brushes against my leg.

Suddenly, the room is 'bathed' in slightly brighter, but still hazy and ailing, light. I very quickly see why Harry was eager to keep me in the dark. He is super untidy, like, stratospherically. This isn't just the odd coffee cup and a few magazines flung about – this is the kind of messiness that could lead to an outbreak of a Victorian disease. There are pizza boxes piled everywhere, and plates with the remnants of some very sloppy meals dried on like ancient magma. Overflowing ashtrays adorned with, I can now see, balls of old chewing gum stuck to their sides. A laundry basket that long ago gave up any hope of containing Harry's smalls and T-shirts and instead spews them violently out all over his floor.

Not only that but the whole place looks fit to be condemned. One of the windows is broken. The wallpaper is trying to escape from the crumbling plaster beneath, and the ceiling sags like a scrotum.

There is a TV, screen thick with enough dust to make

a cardigan and, on top of it, tail swishing menacingly, the mangiest cat I have ever seen in my life, brimming with ill-concealed loathing.

The one tidy part is the bed, which has been made and looks clean. I flop down onto it in disbelief. 'I assume it's your cleaner's year off.'

Harry shrugs – 'It's a flat, not a show home' – and noisily finishes off the last of his chips. He scrunches up the papers – I wince as he chucks it over his shoulder and I hear it plop somewhere on the floor unseen – and gets on the bed with me. He touches my face tenderly and for a second we are lost in each other. I pretend it is fine that his tongue is vinegary and that I can feel the salt from his lips as he kisses my chest. He breaks away from me as his stomach grumbles, and he lets out a belch inches from my face. I look over his bare shoulder to see the cat still staring, looking ready to pounce.

It is just the wakeup call I need. 'I need to use the bathroom.'

'Straight across the hall,' he smiles, then pulls me toward him for a final kiss.

I shlep to the bathroom, my hangover starting to kick in. I find the light cord and pull, expecting instant electrocution. Instead a dim bulb sputters into life and I quickly realise I'm standing in hell.

The walls are covered in black mould and the room reeks of it. The bathtub is brown and has almost certainly been the scene of a dismemberment. The wretched shower curtain looks like the Turin shroud. There is toothpaste all over the sink and the pedestal mat around it carries the hair of a thousand coconuts.

I know what it is like to have no money, and my

own attitude to domesticity is 'leave it two weeks until either it cleans itself or I can no longer stand it', but this is wilful neglect. Harry's ick threshold is a concern to me. I am about to take off his trousers and investigate him closely – if this is Harry's idea of house-proud, what personal grooming terrors await me once I unzip his fly?

I squint at the filthy loo, desperate to pee. My desolation is vast. Suddenly, a bang at the door. A voice. 'Harry!' it cries. I am guessing the girl in the lounge has arisen at last. 'Will you hurry up? I need a shit.'

I blanch like I've just found a bluebottle in my wedding cake and open the door to push past her, propelling myself forward and landing next to what I hope is the exit. I spin round again to see Harry standing there. His shirt is back on.

'You all right?'

'I've ... I've got to go, Harry,' I gasp. I think he's disappointed; it's too dark to tell.

'Why?'

'Because, well ...' I groan. 'I'm just too sober.'

I feel for the latch and pull open the door. I rush down the stairwell, ignoring Harry's pained calls, and bound outside to see a bus that goes right past my house pulling up to a stop.

I clamber on it, elated, and realise I must've been really, really drunk in that taxi.

I live four streets away.

post-date rating: 4.5. Cleanliness is next to sex-godliness, Harry, even if you are the hottest hot mess I've ever met.

15.

If my job taught me anything, it was that a publicity machine needed feeding, and Romeo's belly was certainly getting fuller. I had to change my whole outlook to dating – this wasn't just about finding 'the one' anymore, I had pages to fill and glory to collect. I pushed myself, said yes when I would ordinarily say no. Sometimes it was unpleasant – an uncomfortable two hours with Peregrine the racist; a mixology class; a running date with a very sweaty Jasper who I suspect shat himself during the last kilometre – but I powered through.

The trouble with being out of your comfort zone is the discomfort isn't necessarily just your own. I was doing pretty well at keeping Romeo out of my day-to-day life, but as my – sorry, *his* – popularity grew, I saw more and more opportunities for him. It bled into my real life, too. I'd never been one for openly flirting – not without a vodka-infused confidence boost anyway – but soon I found myself batting my eyes at guys in the gym and laughing so loud at the new intern's bad jokes that Alicha heard it over Little Mix blasting through her headphones.

*

At her Christmas party, Seonaid handed me a drink and told me I seemed like a new man. Adam, thankfully, was away for the festive season so there would be no repeat of our last meeting.

I played dumb. 'Do I? Good.' I exaggeratedly craned my neck to eyeball the rest of the room before swinging back to her and fixing her a mischievous grin. 'Finn not coming?'

I saw the glimmer of realisation in her eye. 'I'm afraid *not*. We don't see much of him these days. Not since he and Antony broke up.'

A beaming smile took over my face before I could stop it. Seonaid pursed her lips. 'That's not how you're supposed to react to bad news.'

'Bad news for whom?'

My renewed vigour had me saying things I wouldn't say and doing things I'd never do – but it was about to get me into trouble.

It was my first swim of the year with Haydn, and after days of Christmassy cabin fever, Sid wanted to come along too, because he was 'bored'. Like that was a new development; my godsons were always bored. Switch on a movie, first five seconds you'd hear a chorus of 'bored'. Any new toy would fall from grace from 'best thing ever' to 'really really boring' within an hour or two. I was a sucker for a bored child, though, having been one myself, so I let him join us. The trouble was that with Sid there to entertain, race, instruct, and, to be honest, torture him, Haydn didn't need much from me, so soon *I* was the one who was bored. I was paddling about at a safe distance from my two charges, when I saw him. The man.

He was sitting on the edge, leaning back on his hands, calves in the water, moving them slightly so I could see his thigh muscles bubble up and retreat with every stroke. Of course he could've been dad to any one of the boisterous brats squealing in delight in the water, but if he was, he wasn't a very good one, as he wasn't paying any of them the slightest bit of attention. Instead, it was all on me. I faked fascination in whatever Haydn and Sid were doing, occasionally calling out to them, pretending to chastise them for crimes they weren't committing, just to show I was actually with them and not a paedophile chancing his arm. Every time I stole a glance, and saw his unbroken stare, my heartbeat groaned a little, like a cog in a grandfather clock making that last bit of effort to get to the hour. After five minutes, I saw my spectator smirk slightly, slide gently into the water and begin to swim over.

I looked down at my body. How were we doing these days? Was I still carrying any weight from Christmas? Could you tell I hadn't been to the gym in ten days? I told myself I was waiting for all the New Year resolution signups to get bored of the gym and return to their sofas, boxsets and calzones, but in reality I didn't have time – I was out on dates whenever my diary would allow. In fact, I had a window that very evening – was it about to be glazed? I looked fine, but I sucked my stomach in anyway, to show willing.

Soon, he was by my side, and speaking. American. His name was Chase. I did what any other gay British man would do when confronted by an American in green speedos – I went full Downton Abbey.

'Chase? A noun *and* a verb, yes, but not a name, surely?'

He was here visiting his sister and, being a keen swimmer – I quickly banished all thoughts of Nate and Tim Prentice – hopped down to the nearest pool to check it out.

'You haven't done much swimming.'

'Ah. I was looking at the hotties.'

I stifled a flinch at the surfer-bro patter. 'Find any?' He had the good grace to pretend to be shy, looking down into the water while he drawled, 'Sure did.'

It felt like I was somebody else. I'd never have talked to a stranger anywhere before, let alone flirted in a swimming pool. I spent most of my twenties running in the opposite direction from men trying to get my number. This shyness had kept my bedpost relatively light on notches before I met Adam, something I'd been making up for ever since.

As we talked, he moved closer and closer, but I wriggled away. I had no idea what was normal in this Californian's local lido, but we were in a leisure centre, not a Castro bacchanal during Pride Week. I had class – not to mention my two godsons in earshot.

'I'm gonna want your number.'

I couldn't quite believe it. This would happen to Romeo, yes, but not me. I wasn't anything special. I was wearing a swimming cap and shorts faded from the sun of two summers ago, my last holiday with Adam. Four days in Morocco in early June: when he booked it, he hadn't realised it would be so hot, so we argued the entire time about who should've realised sooner. I prayed he'd get dysentery from having ice cubes in his Diet Cokes, just to give him something else to think about than gaslighting me into admitting it was all my fault.

Chase invited me to the changing room so he could retrieve his phone and take my 'digits'. Again with the fromage-esque lingo. I glanced over at Sid and Haydn. They were giving synchronised swimming a go, and getting on more famously than ever. A miracle. Romeo would've gone, wouldn't he? 'OK, let's go.'

I shouted to the boys I wouldn't be a minute, and eased myself out of the pool, while Chase's gaze tracked my knackered old body from neck to ankle.

Water dribbled down my thighs unsexily as I shuffled toward the locker room. He strode ahead, confidently; I trudged behind. Nervous, excited, stupid. A stray child ran out of the changing room screaming, leaving it deserted.

197

He opened his locker, towelled his hands dry and grabbed his phone, before motioning me to follow. He slipped off into the shower area out of sight. I poked my head round the corner and he sprang at me, somehow manoeuvring me against the wall. The tiles felt abrasive against my still-wet back.

I looked again to Romeo for inspiration. What would he do? Lean in to kiss him, maybe? Hoping the sheer force of his hand against Chase's arm would hide his trembling, before turning his head away and instead pulling Chase's swimming trunks away from his belly and looking down into them? Chase would gasp. So would Romeo, then he'd say something clichéd, like: 'Well, I'll definitely be giving you my number now.' These things wrote themselves.

In real life, however, I falteringly read out my number – too nervous to think of a fake – as I watched his chest heave in time with his breathing, way calmer than my own. I moved my hand toward him. Then I noticed the screams. They quickly got louder.

I heard the locker-room door swing wide open, hitting the wall with a thump. I inexplicably twanged the waistband of Chase's trunks. The surprise and sting of it pinging back against him hard made him spring away from me, so things looked almost innocent by the time the lifeguard scrambled in with Sid, whose face was snow-white and screwed up in fear.

'Uncle Jim! Come quick! Haydn's hurt himself!' And then he looked from me to Chase and back to me again, and he knew.

Silvie drove us back from A&E while Haydn told his mum how he'd tried to jump into the deeper pool but lost his nerve seconds after his toes left the poolside, so he turned back, smacking his chin off the tiles and plunging into the water anyway. He was very lucky it hadn't been his head – but not as lucky as I was – and he'd remained conscious throughout. He'd cut his chin and had been fished out of the pool very quickly by a lifeguard. According to the handsome nurse – Romeo was always on duty – it looked much worse than it was, and was unlikely to scar.

I'd never seen Nicole look so panicked as when she burst into the cubicle where Haydn's chin was being mopped up. She was generally pretty easy-going and unfazed by most disasters. One night at university when I'd borrowed her bike, drunk, and managed to get clipped by a car on my way home, writing it off completely, she hadn't batted an eyelid. 'Sure I never rode it anyway and I guess you won't be doing *that* again.' But this was wild-eyed concern, and I could tell she needed someone to blame, even if it turned out to be herself.

'God, Jim, you must've been freaking out when you saw all the blood.' Nicole knew how squeamish I was. Even a hangnail had me reaching for the co-codamol. I eyeballed Sid in the rear-view mirror. He looked right through me. 'Mmmmm.'

'I mean, you must have been shitting yourself – you're a worse mother hen than me.' Despite Nicole's protests that she wasn't like the other mums, when it came down to it, she was just as protective. She wanted all the gory details, to torture herself even more. 'What was going through your mind when you saw Haydn hit the side? Were you hysterical?'

I think I could've just about explained the thing with Chase away if Haydn hadn't also mentioned 'Uncle Jim's other friend' he'd met at the swimming baths, the one who'd shown him how to do tumble turns and bought him a giant hot dog afterward. To hear Haydn describe Nate so innocently, brimming with hero-worship, made my chest feel a little tight but I had no time to wallow in sentiment.

We arrived back at Nicole's and the children were dispatched upstairs. Silvie grimaced at me in sympathy as Nicole stomped ahead into the kitchen, slinging her bag onto the breakfast bar where Richie was sitting reading a paper, knocking over his cup of coffee.

'Aw, I just made that!' He attempted to salvage the soggy pages before giving up and chucking it all to one side. 'What the fuck is going on?'

Nicole filled him in, while she stared out of the window into the back garden, her shoulders surging and collapsing fast with every angry breath. She made it sound filthy and depraved, like I'd gone there specifically to cruise – not the gentle flirting or mild fantasy sequence I still had in my head.

Richie had always struck me as a teddy bear, but he *was* straight – I mean, would he, under the right circumstances, tear my head off? He looked at me. 'Was you *wanking*?'

'No! We were just talking. He was some random guy, visiting. I'm allowed to talk to men!'

Nicole angrily dropped tea bags into mugs. 'No, Jim, you're not. Not when you're looking after my son, not when you're being Uncle James. These are my fucking *babies*.'

It seemed my dating scrapes, which usually had them rapt around the dinner table, lost their lustre when they involved the children's safety. Chase, with his funny name, and tight speedos, and cheesy chat-up lines – we'd have laughed about this weeks ago. Wouldn't we? And Haydn was fine, just a bit spooked.

Nicole's eyes blazed. 'I mean, what the *fuck*? It isn't even something you'd do. It's so tacky. Picking someone up in a pool!'

She glared at me as I pulled up a seat, so I backed away. Seating privileges were clearly denied until I had taken my bollocking.

'You know what?' Nicole stirred the tea. 'This is a Romeo thing, isn't it? Huh? This weird shit you're doing. Having a bath with a *stranger*, dating supposedly famous *swimmers*, chatting up guys in the *locker room*. Something to write about in one of your columns. All good material. A little bit of filth for your readers.'

That final 'filth' felt like it would leave a scar.

'What about Haydn's cracked skull? Will that make the cut or are you keeping that clean, too? Nah, I forgot, you edit out all the bits that make you look bad, don't you?'

I didn't have anything to say. Nicole and I had never argued in all the years we'd known each other. Richie laid his hand on her shoulder. 'Come on, Nic. Let's not get personal.'

Nicole shook him off. 'It isn't just one guy. He's done it loads. Introduces them to Haydn. They go off and buy chips.'

I wanted to explain quickly it was just *one* other guy, and that it wasn't seedy, that we'd dated – but it was detail nobody cared about and it got lost in my throat. 'I made a mistake ... but ... I was flattered. I never get chatted up.'

Nicole drank from her mug slowly. 'Yeah, well, you need to do *that* on your own time, OK?'

I felt the sting. My own time? And when would that be? Had I not been a good godfather the other 4,379 days before this one? Always dropping everything at a moment's notice, giving up my Saturdays, always being there whenever they needed me? I felt heat rising.

'When have I ever had something for myself like this? That's been all mine? And made me feel good? Never! There isn't anything I wouldn't do – *haven't* done – for you.'

Richie looked from Nicole and back to me. 'Are you saying this is our fault?'

'All these *secrets*,' cried Nicole. 'For fuck's sake, Jim. We've known you nearly half our lives but I barely recognise you these days.'

'Yeah,' Silvie chimed in. 'You're always staring down at your bloody phone when you're here.'

'That's on the rare occasions we *do* see you,' moaned Richie.

'I mean,' sighed Nicole. 'Yes, you got the *HIM* column and that is *incredible*, and we're all really proud of you, and excited. And sometimes I'm, like, oh dear, Jim is famous ...'

Richie coughed. 'Only Twitter-famous.'

Nicole shot him the kind of look that's legally allowed only if you own a marriage certificate. 'Twitter-famous. But is this really who you want to be?'

Where the hell had this come from? This was no thunderbolt – clearly they'd been discussing this in my absence. I finally pulled up a stool and sat down. I told them about the negative comments, and the creepy emails someone had been sending me. Understandably, sympathy was thin on the ground.

Silvie ripped a nicotine patch off her arm and lit a cigarette. 'Just stop being such a fucking baby. Who gives a shit about a troll?'

Richie nodded. 'You're crap at being famous. You should be up to your neck in groupies and coked out of your dome 24/7, not crying in my kitchen because of some internet wankers. Boo fucking hoo.'

Nicole breathed out. 'It's just a blog. It doesn't seem to be making you very happy, Jim. And you're not yourself.'

'Maybe that's the whole fucking point, Nic.'

She scowled. The north face of the Eiger would have looked more forgiving.

I felt anger start to swell, so switched to contrition. 'I'm sorry. I don't want you to think I'm irresponsible.'

Nicole tutted and gave me a light hug. 'That's the thing. I know you're not. This is why I'm so mad.'

Later, Nicole and Richie saw me to the door. Sid poked his head through the banister to say goodbye, but our usual fist-bump was missing.

'I just want you to know,' said Richie as he handed me my scarf, 'I'm not your weird internet stalker. If I was, I'd have gone really extreme. Dick pics. Photos of you with your eyes scratched out. I'd be sending you dead animals and spooky tapes of kids screaming in terror.'

'Well,' said Nicole. 'He knows what that sounds like for real now.' Her face was unreadable in the glow of the streetlight. I stepped out into the cold.

'Are we good?'

She nodded.

'I'm guessing you won't be letting me take Haydn out again?'

Nicole sighed heavily. 'I'm not saying no, but maybe you should go away and be Romeo for a bit, eh? When you're ready to act like Uncle Jim again, we'll be here waiting.'

I conceded defeat, went to button up my coat and started to walk away. Then, I turned. 'You might be waiting a while.'

I was halfway up the street when I heard her finally close the door.

I sat on the bus and thought of the empty flat waiting for me. I was just wondering whether I could interest UNESCO in proclaiming my pile of dirty dishes a World Heritage Site when a drunk couple clambered up the stairs and sat two seats away from me. She was eating a pasty and he was chowing down on a burger. Nobody sober ever ate on a bus, and I began to tune out their drunken chatter until I very clearly heard them say 'Romeo'. We all have an inbuilt reaction to hearing our own name, don't we? I sometimes wonder how people placed in witness protection cope. Imagine it: they're doctors from Manchester called John or Julie for forty years and then BOOM, they're Nigel or Belinda and living in Sidcup pretending to work the tills at Asda or whatever. Do their ears still prick up when someone calls to them using their new name? Maybe they do, because mine did, on hearing that 'Romeo'. I waited for the inevitable qualifying Juliet, or Shakespeare, but instead heard 'dating' and 'blog'. Readers. *My* readers. I sat very still in case any sudden movements disturbed them. It was my very own wildlife documentary. So that's what my readers looked like, but were they friends or foes? OK, well, they were reading out my tweets. Tweets I'd sent the night before, during my date with a guy I'd called Esteban. Something about the way he fiddled with his collar made me wonder whether he was fantasising about strangling me. Then they were reading out an old blog from the early days, where I'd answered the phone while in the toilet, peed all down my leg and had to leave my date sitting there. They were laughing. Fans. *Friends*. I felt brand new.

And then the guy said, 'I bet he's ugly, though.'

The girl laughed so hard I thought her throat was going to make a break for it. 'Yeah! And he probably makes them all up.'

I shrank back into my seat.

'Still . . . he's good.'

I smiled so wide the rest of the way home that everybody was too scared to sit next to me – even when the bus was full.

But I had to stay focused. One night after work, with no date lined up, I stayed late to catch up on my Romeo correspondence – I'd only get distracted at home and there was a lot of venom to wade through. People said weird stuff online – as brave as people were at the other end of a fibre optic cable, I knew that in reality they'd be meek and reverent, maybe even complimentary. I bet they'd shake my hand, their face would show the trickle of a weak smile, and they'd say, 'Nice to meet you.' It'd be the same with the ones giving me a dodgy compliment or the guys who'd say they wanted to have sex with Romeo. The guy who messaged me regularly to say, 'I wanked over a picture of your mouth last night' would not, I imagined, say this to my mouth in person.

I was sighing in front of my screen at yet another email from my 'weirdo stalker', as Alicha called them, when she appeared at my elbow.

'Why don't you write a diddums? Make some money out of it?'

A 'diddums' was what we jokingly called those popular pieces where famous journalists or other celebrities would bang out a quick thousand words on what it was like to have the internet turn against you. They'd speak of trolls, basically people who didn't agree with them, quoting their bile in the hope – or so they said – that it would make people who were nasty on the internet realise the effect of what they did and think again. And if any sympathy should come their way while they did it, well, they would gladly take that too. They knew what they were doing. Write a provocative think-piece, wring out a further three or four marvelling in mock-horror that people might actually take it as it was intended. And get paid. Aw, diddums. Of course, now the shoe was firmly on the other foot, I could see why they might want to vent. And could I honestly say I'd never sent a mean tweet or slagged somebody off? My glasshouse was down to its last shard.

'First of all, I don't think I'm famous enough to write a diddums, Alicha. Plus, it would, uh, compromise my artistic integrity – and they're really boring to read.'

Alicha spritzed herself in perfume. 'Oh, but you *are* famous enough. Anyone who gets as much hate as you do is automatically famous.' I winced. 'You've seen *The Real Romeo*, right?'

Indeed I had. *The Real Romeo*, which, despite its shameless rip-off of my name and concept, was very careful not to mention me directly, carried the tag line 'I'm a real guy and don't hide behind a secret identity'. Ouch. Instead of my close-up of my kisser, he used a picture of his full, actual face – I probably would've reconsidered this had I been him; I could imagine horses rearing up as he passed them – and *invited* guys to go on dates with him. He had a contact form! He'd then waste a thousand words – and everybody's time – giving these thirsty Kirstys a glowing review, with selfies of the pair of them holding matching flat whites or enthusing over eggs benedict, usually somewhere in Clapham. Not only that, the places he ate were bunging him free food and drinks while he did his strangely sexless wooing, in return for the advertising. He was actually making money from offering himself as an alternative to me. 'The nice way to be a dating blogger,' he liked to say.

Well, you know what they say about 'nice'; it says nothing at all. The guys who dated him loved it because it fed their ego, and my haters were lapping it up. Was this really how my big downfall was going to come? From two Instagram-ready boys pouting for the camera over zero-calorie noodles? Real? REAL?! I had eyes. I could see those filters. Skin simply didn't come in that colour, unless you ate nothing but carrots for a year – all his pics had at least two runs through the Nashville filter.

'I don't care about him,' I lied. 'He's an arsehole and anyone who accuses someone else of being an attention-seeker is usually only jealous they're not getting any themselves.'

Alicha whooped. 'Ooh, you're *my* real Romeo anyway, you sassy bitch.' I could feel she had news to break. And then it came. 'The real sign you've made it is a parody anyway, isn't it? Don't you think?'

I groaned and held my hands up to my throat like a feeble heiress in an Agatha Christie. 'What are you on about? I'm tired. Shouldn't you be going home? Leave me to my *public*.' I pointed at the umpteen unread messages on my screen.

'Haven't you seen it?! You must've!' She knew I hadn't. She pulled up a chair, gently nudging me out of the way of my keyboard, and began to type. 'It's a parody of *you*. Of *One More Romeo*.'

My mouth went dry, my tonsils turned to raisins. I tried to speak. It came out as a shriek. 'Me?!'

'Yep, you. Here it is. *One More Homeo*. Genius, really.'

Fucking hell. There it was. A close-up of a really chapped mouth, resplendent in cold sores; blog posts with sarcastic titles.

It looked almost exactly like my own blog. I got pins and needles everywhere. My fingers, my eyes, my balls. 'I don't think I want to read this right now.'

Alicha hooted with laughter. 'Obviously you fucking do! And you *should*. Know your enemy.'

I stared into the screen. Alicha logged me off. 'Not here though. Come on, you look like you need a drink.'

'I need two.'

'Let's go to the pub and I'll hold your hand while you read it. You should be flattered, really.'

For the first time, I understood what fame really meant. It wasn't a pill you could just stop taking any time you liked. You didn't control the dose; they did. And it was time for my medication.

ONE MORE HOMEO: THE GUY WHO MADE ME FEEL EMOTIONZZZZZZZZ

I feel conflicted. Like maybe I'm kinda sad but a bit happy as well. I am nervous but dead confident and I am exuding an air of what you might call 'don't give a fuck' as I saunter gingerly into the bar where I am meeting tonight's contestant. The lucky fellow's profile pics didn't exactly light an inferno in my pants – tasteful denim, and other adjectives – but I was feeling quite jaded but also excited and so I decided to grant him the once in a lifetime opportunity of an audience with my very brilliant gay self.

Did I mention how nervous I am? I don't mean to be self-deprecating or anything but wow it's like I don't really know how beautiful I am. Anyway, just imagine about 500 words of the journey to the bar here where I describe in great detail the bus, the passengers on the bus and even the sound the bus makes as it vibrates so the seat causes my (toned) buttocks to jump on and off of it. I wonder if they'll be bouncing off something else tonight but obviously no I don't because I never talk about sex because that is dirty and RUDE and I am just an innocent guy going on dates and sex makes me blush. I'm so embarrassed about what I call 'doing it' that I have left my penis at home. It's on a shelf next to all my EXPENSIVE colognes that I wear to make men fall in love with me and guess what? It works EVERY TIME.

So here I am, finding myself in the bar talking to Benito, 32, who does something very MEDIA for a living, which immediately puts me at ease because I too work in the media. Did I mention it? I do. Don't ask me what I do though because I prefer you to just imagine it. Because you do think of me, don't you? Thought so.

Benito is very MASCULINE and I feel a bit self-conscious because even though I too am masculine I think I might be a bit too girlie and that is not what men really want, and I will PRETEND that I'd date any guy but really I do want to go out with someone who's never even heard a Kylie record. Benito is drinking a pint and I order a G&T. I like to do that because in a little while, when I am trying to say how awkward things have become – maybe he will, like, not ask me a question for a whole 30 seconds or have really bad taste in books (I am an intellectual who has read *Wuthering Heights* 18 times) or perhaps I will decide I fancy him – I will stir my G&T and it will be SYMBOLIC.

Food? Are you MAD we can't eat food; I only eat one salad a week.

He is flirting with me, I can tell. He looks at me a lot. And coughs. And takes sips of his drink. And goes to the bar, and then to the toilet. He looks at his phone once and I bet he is texting all his friends saying wow this guy is hot and Facebooking it and tweeting it. I would say my privacy was being invaded and that I don't like being objectified but I don't want to be a hypocrite. Even though I am one. Actually, no I'm not because what I do is different because I am anonymous and also I have a lot of emotions. Loads. I'm quite a complicated person. I can't believe anyone would want to date me. Did I mention I wasn't that attractive? I sniff my wrist and get a waft of Tom Ford's Domtoppio for a bit of Dutch courage. That's better.

We talk about how I go running and drink stuff with kale in because I am a HEALTH PERSON. Then we have two drinks and then three drinks and soon the conversation turns *interesting*. You can tell because of all the *italics*. I won't quote directly because I got so drunk I can't remember and really only my thoughts are important tbh but let's just say he is being very flirtatious with his talk of 'having to be up early in the morning' and 'not wanting to miss the last Tube home'. I know a come-on when I see one so I lean forward – sucking my big fat stomach in, of course, because as regular readers will know I am now over NINE stone and just a middle-aged whale with a great career please like me – and suggest we move to another bar. He looks at his watch to make sure we have enough time together and shakes his head – in amazement at how confident and bright I am, I guess. Then he says something like how amazing I am or how unusual – I can't remember which – and I give a wry smile and STIR MY G&T.

We walk to the next bar – a gay bar so I can let this guy pounce on me – and I lean against him sexily. I do a lot of leaning. Forward, against, over. It means I am INTIMATE. He is so caring, worrying I'll fall over and saying I should stand up straight and walk by myself. Then he starts yawning so I know that means he wants to cut to the chase and go home right now, so I hail a taxi.

This is the part where we kiss but I'm too PURE to actually say those words out loud so let's just say our faces *meld together* as one and in the taxi they stay melded or moulded or welded – whichever you prefer, they're all nice words, don't you love my writing?!? – right up until we tip out of the cab and rock up at my hovel bachelor pad, which is such a dump even though I can somehow afford to live alone – ALL ALONE – in central London.

'I can't believe I'm here,' he says, in a mock-disappointed tone to hide his delight. I drag him in by the tie I have just decided he is wearing and he flops onto my sofa, which is red. If this sofa could talk it would probably get its own blog. Suddenly I get a feeling of emotions. I stare at the kitchen sink – full of mugs because I'm a creative and don't wash up – or the fridge or some other household object to convey bathos and ask myself if I really want this? What am I doing here? And other doubts and conflicts that come with being an imperfect angel just tryna make his way.

And then I go through with it anyway because it's been a whole forty-eight hours since a stranger saw my pecker – I call it a pecker because I am QUAINT – but I'm sorry you don't get to read about it going in and out.

Here's a last line that makes me look intelligent and tortured and sad and beautiful. Sigh.

16.

As much as I was grateful to Romeo's fans, I'd learned not to trust the approval of strangers. It could be won and lost on the strength of one tweet. It was flimsy, fickle; gratifying but ultimately unimportant. I'd ridden out storms and surfed the crest of a wave, but when I lost the approval of people I cared about, whose faces I could see – or at least imagine – it dulled my sheen slightly. I saw things for what they were. Hollow.

Silvie reassured me over text that I probably wouldn't be in the doghouse with Nicole and Richie for long, but I was too embarrassed to see them. I imagined them staring at every beep of my phone and I knew what they'd be thinking as I waved them goodbye after Sunday Club – 'he's probably going off to another hookup'. While I was polite by text, and would send Sid and Haydn my love, I thought it best to take Nicole's advice.

So I still kept going on the dates. Night after night of Mr Wrong. My dates' hopeful smiles had started to make me heave and their outstretched hands on meeting made me feel weary and isolated. I spent my evenings staring into space trying not to catch their eye in case I gave them the wrong idea. One night, I was on a date with a very sweet guy who had trouble keeping a conversation going. In the end, he quietly put down his glass and prodded me out of my daydream.

'I don't go on dates very often,' he said, so gently I had to lean in, half-smiling. 'And I was really looking forward to meeting you.' Then he looked around him and dropped his voice slightly. 'But I have to say you are the biggest cunt I've ever met. I hope not all men out there are like you.'

I raised my glass to his departing back to toast his honesty – and the fact he'd given me something to write about.

My excuses for rejecting men were getting ridiculous. Sometimes they'd look so puzzled as we said our goodbyes at the end of the evening – like they'd blacked out and done something horrendous that they couldn't remember. But in reality all they'd actually done was not be who I pretended I was searching for. One guy looked like he would be nasty in an argument, another said he didn't have a favourite kind of pie. One man was practically perfect until I heard the way he pronounced 'luxurious'. Of course, the real reason nobody was making the grade was much simpler than any annoying habit or quirk I'd made up – I had a magazine column to fill and, despite the backlash, plenty of people reading my blog and a promise to myself never to fake it. I was playing Romeo to create my own content. A soap opera with a cast of one.

Curtis was usually so wrapped up in himself the world could be on fire and he'd ask you to turn the central heating up, but even he started to pull at my threads as we jostled for space at the worst gay bar in Soho, ordering two-for-one Brambles in plastic glasses.

'What's going on, Jamie? So sullen. Bitchy. Not quite yourself.'

I slurped my drink. 'I am only ever myself.' What a lie. 'Maybe you're the one who's changing.'

Curtis adjusted his specs. 'I've seen you out with different men.

Never the same one twice. And I know you've spotted me across the bar. I see you huddle in, pretending you haven't seen me.'

This was true. I was an expert when it came to middle-distance staring. The last thing I needed was Curtis taking over a date with his uncontrollable recitals, spilling my secrets – the equivalent of your parents tagging you in loads of 'naked in the garden' baby photos on Facebook.

'I see you and I wonder if you're too good to talk to your old friend Curtis now? Hmmm.' He looked over my shoulder as if waiting for someone to walk in.

'I'm talking to you now, more's the pity.'

He ignored the slight. 'I've seen it all before, y'know. You're like one of those boys who moves down from Yorkshire or Lancashire or Cumbria or somewhere equally squalid. They come to the bars, skinny and eager and smothered in guyliner and cheap anti-perspirant, they tell you they're lonely, they let you buy them drinks, and tell you all their problems but never listen to yours. They say they don't know *what* they'd do without you. And then,' Curtis slammed his drink down on the bar, but the dramatic effect was lost as the plastic glass landed with a light thud and half his drink escaped over the rim. 'And then they have a little haircut, start drinking Tanqueray and getting noticed by everyone else. They find someone more fun, closer to their own age, or sexier. Join a gym, get a *body*. They become identikit versions of each other and then they start to see you as you saw yourself all along – a big, gay joke. And suddenly you don't exist.'

I finished my drink. 'You're describing yourself though, aren't you, Curtis? Didn't you do exactly that? Except a hundred years ago? Looks like your boomerang finally came back.'

I was alone in a taxi, on my way home and scrolling through Seizer, within twenty minutes.

*

My malaise was seeping into my work. Whenever someone tells you not to 'take something the wrong way', it's a bad sign. Same with 'to tell you the truth' (a lie is coming), 'I'm not being funny but ...' (you can bet your arse this won't be funny, but it will be offensive) and 'I'm not one to gossip but ...' – all of them qualifiers or disclaimers meant to assuage the guilt of whoever is about to speak and deny you either the right to reply or complain. Luca had noticed a shift in tone, and it was clear he considered it a downgrade.

> It's just you seem a bit more blunt recently.
> I don't want to say bitter but you know what
> I mean.

> You just *did* say bitter ...

> Haha OK but I mean, you never seem to like
> the dates anymore. You never used to be so
> harsh. You're a bit meaner. A *lot* meaner!

My blogs sounded *bitter*? No, not at all. That didn't sound like me. I was going for debonair, man about town, light disdain – a kind of aloof sexiness, the knowledge I was way too smooth for these wannabe lotharios. Your hero on the frontline. I mean, the last guy called me the c-word; I was the victim here, surely?

> There's a fine line between cockiness and
> arrogance you know.

Just as it had on Nicole's freezing cold doorstep, I felt the red mist descend upon me once again.

Don't I fucking know it. I dance across
it daily, and so fucking what? I didn't
sit at home for six years waiting for
a bad mood in chinos to get home
just so I could lie down and die when
some goon in a button-down shirt
deigns to tell me he likes my smile.
It's a jungle out there, you know, and
I'm not the only one out for a kill.

Right ... well ... your readers don't know
about the six-year thing because you've
never really opened up about yourself.

A pause. Neither of us willing to blink, albeit digitally and fig-
uratively. Then: the knockout blows started.

You're just starting to come across as a
bit of a ... twat. And I know that's not who
you are. It's getting pretty one-dimensional,
you know?

Look, you might know my real name,
but you don't know what I've been
through. Remember the weirdo sending
screen caps of things I've done – to my
work email? Still doing it. I've got trolls
slagging me off. Christ. I've even given
up GOOD men, all because I'm Romeo.

We never asked you to give anything up! Talk
about ego!

I clattered on my keyboard so hard that Alicha looked up from her screen. I refused to catch her eye. I should've. A friendly face might have saved me from the giant fire I was about to start.

> Oh FFS Luca, what are you following me
> for anyway, then? What do you *want*
> from me? My ego isn't so big that I
> need YOU or anyone else. Who are you
> anyway? Just another fan trying to fuck
> me, perchance? Well you can forget it. In
> fact, you said it wasn't YOU sending me
> the emails, but how do I know for sure?

I should've stopped. Why couldn't I stop?

> For all I know you could be typing
> these not *that* witty messages with
> one hand, and wanking with the other.
> What would your BOYFRIEND say?

The cursor blinked. It was coming.

> My boyfriend probably wouldn't give a fuck,
> James. I don't have one. Not anymore.
> Things have been going badly for a while.
> Which is why I've liked your blog and our
> chats. A bit of escapism from the shitshow. I
> thought you might notice. But you didn't.

My head met my hands.

> OK, I'm sorry.

I can't believe you would accuse me of
doing something so disgusting. I thought we
were friends.

I wasn't sure how to answer. I'd grown up with the internet, and
become buddies with countless avatars over the years, but were
they actually friends? If anything happened to them, would I
mourn? Would I have a right to? Did I owe them the same duty
of care as I did with my 'IRL' friends? The ones who'd got drunk
with me, grown with me, sobbed with me, fast-forwarded the
boring bits of films with me? If I did, I'd failed Luca. Big time.

We've been together five years, but it means
nothing to him. It's been over for ages I
suppose but I was too scared to admit it. It
was like a game of chicken, seeing who'd go
first. And now he has and I feel like shit.

I'm sorry.

Yeah. You said. All these months I thought
we were talking, you and me. But it wasn't
a conversation. You were just broadcasting.
I'm not your friend. I'm your *audience*.

I tried to pull it back.

We ARE friends, honestly.
You've been such a help.

Yeah and your writing helped me. But I think
that's as far as this is going to go. I need to
look after myself and find someone with time

to listen. You ask me why I bother following
you? You gave me a bit of hope. But now I'm
not so sure. Night, Romeo.

                    Hey, don't go! Look, let's break the
                  fourth wall. Actually speak! FaceTime?
                    Meet up, maybe?! I don't just do
                       that for *anyone*, you know!

Nothing.

I shouted his name out loud, like it would make a difference.

Alicha listened to my woes as she buttered a scone. Once finished, she licked the knife and chucked it in the sink. We flopped
down on some beanbags in one corner of the breakout area.

'OK, here's what I think. Romeo is like your comfort food,
isn't it, your security blanket? Things get a little shit and you
can go out and be Romeo again, turn the charm on, be someone
else.' She paused for a reaction. I stared blankly back at her. She
bit into her scone and carried on: 'You think going out on dates,
and getting off with blokes and being confident or *whatever* is
something you'd never do on your own. So you act like you're
doing it for the blog. Am I right? It's about having a power you
don't have anywhere else.'

How was it possible to both love and hate being psychoana-
lysed, at the same time? It was, like, the ultimate attention grab,
yet I felt like more of a waste of space with every word. 'I don't
think so. I don't know. You make me sound awful.'

'Well you don't have much power *here*' – she gestured over
in the vague direction of the rest of the office, crumbs from her
scone flying everywhere – 'and it obviously upsets you.'

'Am I power-hungry? Am I not nice to *you*?' I was devastated
at the idea Alicha didn't like me anymore either.

'Nah of course you are, you're a gent, my problematic but lovable dating queen. But there's the sense ... I dunno, it's obvious you ain't happy here and I think you keep on doing Romeo because you hope he can take you out of it.'

'Take me where? I don't want to be famous.'

'Nobody does. Nobody sane, anyway. But you *are* famous. Kinda. Isn't it frustrating not being able to tell anyone who you are, to take the glory, like that time you were on the bus? Sitting right there with the fans?'

'I guess.'

'You're carrying on being Romeo because you want to be discovered. Own it.'

'It's because I'm lonely.'

Alicha's face twisted as she attempted to excavate scone from between her teeth. 'How can you be *lonely*? You're out with a different guy every single night. You walk in most mornings smelling of sex.'

I shrugged. 'It's not always good sex.'

Alicha laughed. 'Cry me a fucking river, Jim. Bad sex is better than no sex some nights.'

I couldn't raise a smile. 'Maybe. But even when we're talking, or drinking, or laughing, or even fucking, all I can think of is how temporary it is. And that I'm going to be lonely again the second it's over. And I immediately *feel* that loneliness. Like when people who have their leg cut off still feel it, but in reverse. I miss it before its gone.'

Alicha whistled through her teeth. 'Sheesh. Fucking hell, that is deep. And I probably wouldn't use that analogy in the blog, hun. It's shonky as.'

I pressed on. 'But you know, don't tell me I can't be lonely because I'm never in. You have no idea. I'm at my loneliest when I'm having the time of my life.'

Alicha looked thoughtful. 'OK. Well, it seems to me to be

making you lonelier. Just an observation. It's getting in the *way*. Isn't there some way you can make Romeo who you are all the time, rather than be a secret? Break away from it?'

But what if it all came out about Nate? I'd come too far now. 'I'm sticking to my mission. It has to mean something. Last Romeo or no Romeo.' I owed everyone a fairytale ending.

'Well I reckon you owe yourself a little bit more than that, but OK.'

I was too embarrassed to say why I was doing it; perhaps I didn't really know. Maybe I did want to be famous, after all? I imagined it: limos, furs, fucking A-listers. Gold-plated everything. Why not? But wasn't there something sad about someone my age vying for attention, especially among all the younger, hotter, more talented pretenders out there trying a lot less hard than I was? Alicha seemed to read my mind.

'You don't have to pretend you're doing it for some *lofty* reason, you know, just as long as you know why you're doing it. *Everyone* out there logging on and calling you an attention-seeker is full of shit – every single person who tweets, or your gran posting on Facebook, or boring basics on Insta, is doing it so someone will notice them. Otherwise they'd get a fucking diary. I suppose you need to make sure you're getting noticed for the right reasons. If it can take you away from here, I'm all for it. Just make sure it does.'

I leaned back too far on the beanbag and spilled my tea.

'I think I've lost sight of what it was supposed to be about. I'm afraid to meet someone. Romeo isn't going to save my life – he's going to ruin it. I'll lose the column. I'll lose … myself.'

'Yeah, well maybe it's time you got back on track, then. At least act like you're trying to look for the last Romeo bloke. No more make-dos. That'll get you the real content, baby, and that'll get you out of here.'

'Isn't it usually my job to give *you* career advice?'

'Yeah, well let me give something back to my favourite daddy.'

'Uuuuuuuuuuurrrrrrrrrrrrrrrgggggggggggh.' Bella's guttural screams bounced off my kitchen walls, drowning out the traffic outside and making my pile of laundry tremble.

'Sorry if I'm boring you.'

I heard the splash of vodka in a glass. A big measure. 'Fucking hell, Jim, how are *you* not bored of this? Why haven't you called that Finn guy yet?'

Bella was obsessed with Finn being the one who got away.

'Because I have a second date with Oliver tonight.'

Oliver was my first attempt to take Alicha's advice, look beyond content and settle on a Romeo. Yes, he was slightly cold and a bit of a know-it-all, but he was free on a weeknight. On our first date he told me great bars to go to in my hometown, which beer I should try instead of the one I'd chosen, and, when I inevitably told him I was a runner, had loads of pointers and recommendations for energy drinks. He was like a smartphone, and only slightly sexier, with nice eyes and a kind of lopsided smile. I hoped he had a considerably better battery life.

Bella pulled a vinegary face. 'Fuck Oliver, he sounds dull as shit. Finn sounds fucking amazing and you've regretted not taking that further for *months*. Ever since . . . you know.'

'Well, it's not all about Nate, or Finn, you know. I've got quite a lot to deal with at the moment – not that *you'd* know.'

Bella visibly deflated as I recounted what had happened with Nicole, Luca, and my personal emailing troll. 'Why didn't you tell me? I thought we told each other everything.'

'I'm telling you *now*. And you haven't been returning my messages,' I replied, sharply. 'We hardly talk. Have you been avoiding me? You don't read the blogs anymore. Are you just not interested?'

222

She started to cry. Fuck.

'Oh, please don't cry. I'm sorry, I ... I don't care if you don't read the blogs.' (I did.)

'It's not that, Jim. Christ. I'm tired, I'm homesick. And ... and ...' She stopped to compose herself, trying with all her might not to cry again. 'According to Facebook, Drew is getting *married*. Before me! To someone uglier!'

The job was hard, she never had any time off, and couldn't make any plans because she was on call 24/7. Her infant charge was only a slight nightmare – frisbeeing breakfast bowls at her head, claiming he had bought her at an auction, for instance – and all the first-class tickets and fancy dinners in the world couldn't replace a friendly face and someone to talk to. Drew finding happiness with someone else – when he really should still be pining after her – just about put the cherry on top.

'I've been swerving your calls because I didn't want to worry you. Plus ...'

'What? Plus what?!' I wanted to climb through the screen and shake her.

'Jim. I couldn't get a word in. It was Romeo this and fucking Twitter fame that. I didn't want to spoil it for you and, to be honest, you didn't really seem like a sympathetic ear.'

I cringed at my own insensitivity. 'I'm so sorry. I should've been here for you. I've failed you.'

'Yes, you have, frankly. But I'll have to forgive you because I've got nobody else, and I'm coming home.'

It was a much less harsh drubbing than I deserved.

'How can I make it up to you?'

Bella wiped away the very last tear and blinked into the lens. 'You can ditch Oliver immediately, stop worrying about a load of strangers who don't like you and call Finn. Stop being proud, stop being stupid, stop being *you*. Call Finn.'

I had thought about it, but somehow all my Romeo confidence

drained away from me when it came to Finn. Not knowing of Nate, Silvie often asked me what happened to the 'hot guy at the party', and I would pretend not to know who she meant until she described him in great detail. Whenever I reached for my phone to call, I imagined his phone ringing out, my name flashing up on the screen, unanswered unanswered unanswered.

What if he had had a change of heart? What if he was with a bunch of mates – he looked like the kind of guy who would have a large coterie of equally good-looking and charming pals; the beautiful are seldom alone – and they all started asking who this 'James' was, and he'd have to tell them, and as he described me maybe he'd realise he wasn't into me at all, his voice slowing to a drone as he got to the part where I had grey hair. Would he even have me down as 'James' in his phone? Had he called me Jim? I couldn't remember. Would it say 'bloke from party'? Or 'older guy who hated Antony'? Or something awful, that young people think is a compliment, like 'silver fox' – do me a sodding favour. Barely a word spoken between us and already Finn was bad for my health.

As I saw Oliver approach, late, my heart leapt, but not in the way I'd hoped. His eyes seemed smaller, his expression more pinched. His eyes darted round the bar, no doubt looking for a better table for us to move to, as he had on our first date, then he kissed me on the cheek, twice. Kinda French. I pretended I kinda liked it.

He took his seat and motioned to the waiter he was ready to order his drink. 'Aren't you a little warm in that jumper?'

I looked down at my sweater. 'No, not really. It's *February*.'

'It's not February inside. You're making me feel warm just looking at you.'

I raised an eyebrow. 'Well that's a good sign ... '

The joke flatlined. 'Seriously though; it's sweltering in here.'

I tossed the sweater aside while Oliver ordered a bottle of wine. A whole bottle to himself? Wow. The waiter turned to me. I was about to order when Oliver asked for two glasses and sent him away.

'Cheaper if we both drink the wine.' Oliver eyed my beer glass. 'And anyway, you don't want to feel bloated.'

I shivered a little.

Oliver was talking about the benefits of booking train tickets in advance when I happened to catch sight of a familiar face across the bar. It couldn't be. Could it? I must've spent too long squinting over because Oliver noticed and his eyes followed my gaze. 'Am I keeping you?'

I shook out of my trance. 'No, sorry, I know that guy but can't think how.' Oh, I knew all right.

'One of your *celebs*, perhaps?' He said the word like he was too cool and important to care about famous people.

'No, I don't think that's it.'

'One of your other dates, maybe?'

I jolted in my seat. Noticeably, because it made Oliver spring back. 'What?'

'Other dates?'

'Off Soulseekers or, you know, the *apps*. I see random guys I went on dates with all the time.'

Phew. I engaged deflection mode. 'You jealous?'

'Oh, I don't do jealousy,' he roared. 'It's a waste of time.' I'd heard that one before. He signalled for the waiter again. 'I'm not really feeling it here. Not somewhere I'd have chosen. I think we should go.' While Oliver was tapping in his PIN, I braved another quick glance over at the guy – Finn, by the way, did you guess? – and saw, to my horror, he was looking back with more than a flicker of familiarity. He was alone, nursing a pint. Oh no, I thought, please don't come over, not now.

Oliver didn't notice. 'I think we should go somewhere *gay*

next.' He sounded like a toddler trying not to blurt out a secret. 'Get to know each other better.'

I knew what that meant, as would regular Romeo readers – somewhere safe, where we could kiss without offending anyone's sensibilities. Well, except other jealous men, of course. I'd engineered similar scenarios enough times. But I didn't think I wanted to get to know Oliver any better. I knew enough. The wine, the jumper, getting the bill without asking me. The micro criticisms. I looked down at the way I was sitting, my hands in my lap, subservient, waiting to be told what to do. Romeo had left the building. I felt like Adam's boyfriend again. I didn't want that.

Oliver mistook my silence for compliance and said he'd be right back. He sloped off toward the toilet, rearranging the semi in his crotch as he did. My desolation was vast.

Within milliseconds Finn was at my side.

'Have you been trying to work out where you know me from? Have you cracked it yet?'

I laughed. 'I know exactly who you are.'

He leaned on the table. 'Do you really? Because every time I've seen you around, you've blanked me. Cold.' He winked to show me he was joking. 'The only reason I didn't wave at you just now was because I assumed you were on a *date*. Are you?'

I ignored the question; I didn't want to admit it and send him away. 'You said you've seen me? Where?'

'The Vauxhall Tavern at Sweetie. I said hi but you looked kind of out of it.'

Of course.

'And in Boohoo House. I never knew you were so well connected.'

I peeked over at the toilet door. No sign of Oliver yet. Had he fallen down the pan? Was it wrong of me to hope so?

'Well connected?'

226

'You were with Nate Harris. Mate of yours, is he?'

I flinched at the memory of that perfect night.

'Yes, we go way back.' I fixed Finn with a steely glare. 'How's Antony?' I didn't want him to know that I knew.

He looked down at the floor for the briefest of seconds. 'We broke up.' Finn tracked my gaze over to the toilets. 'So *are* you on a date?'

I grimaced.

Finn grabbed at my wrist, just like he had that night at the club.

'Ditch him.'

I gasped. 'Are you mad? I can't do that! What would I say to him?'

Finn grinned. 'Don't say anything! Let's just split.'

I stared at the toilet door. God, he'd been ages. What had he been eating? 'We might bump into him! The loos are right next to the way out.'

'Is that all that's stopping you? You wanna stay here? So you weren't looking over to me hoping to be rescued?'

I sniffed. 'I don't need anyone to rescue me, thanks.'

Finn laughed. 'Come on, let me be a hero.'

'But the door!' I saw it swing open and Oliver coming through it, engrossed in his phone.

Finn looked around the bar. 'I have another way.' He wrenched me out of my seat and pulled me behind him. 'Come on!'

I glanced back just in time to see Oliver looking over, puzzled, as Finn thrust open the fire exit and heaved me outside.

We kept running, almost doubled up in laughter, until we could no longer hear the insistent blaring of the alarm.

17.

'It's about fucking time.'

And it was.

There are things you think will never happen, and in a way, you hope they never do, because you've wished for them so hard, they can only ever be a disappointment when they finally become a reality. Because reality, as anyone can tell you, bites. So you don't dare to dream it will be everything you ever imagined, that the small chink of light that fantasy has allowed you will ever open up to be a huge burning star. However. When I finally got my hands on Finn, I have to say, it certainly lived up to my expectations. Even though we'd spent only a couple of drunken hours in each other's company at Seonaid's party a million moons ago, it was like we'd known each other for years.

We found a quiet, fairly sleazy old man's pub in Fitzrovia and perched on a battered sofa. My teeth chattered with nerves for the full first hour of polite laughter at impolite jokes, peering at his collarbone helpfully exposed by his shirt, pats on the back or knee that lingered a little too long to be brotherly, and a serious amount of eye-fucking. But before I knew it, I felt totally relaxed. So relaxed, in fact, I told him everything.

It fell out of my mouth. I barely paused for breath. Blog, the magazine column, Nate – albeit with no names – and the fallout. My fans, my haters and how it had made me kind of, almost semi-but-not-really-when-you-think-of-it, famous.

He didn't say much, managing a few 'Wow's and 'Cool's. He bit his lip a lot like a teenager trying to be sexy. Flirtation or awkwardness? I couldn't tell.

'I never wrote about a man until I was absolutely sure I'd never see him again.'

'OK.'

'And, well, I was only ever mean about them if they were mean to me.'

He shifted on the sofa and it let out an awkward squeak. 'Right.'

'I always changed a few details to make them less identifiable, and, y'know, I stay anonymous to protect us both, really.'

'Cool.'

'I mean, I'm allowed to document things that happen in my life, right?' It was an autobiography, I told myself; the men said the things I said they'd said and did the things I said they'd done. Anyone who had a problem with it might want to go after people with much higher profiles who pulled no punches in their own life stories. Why wait until I was dead, for someone else to tell my story?

His mouth twisted in amusement as he listened to my spiel. 'You finished?'

'I think so.'

'What would you say if I told you ... I already knew all this?'

What?

'That I was, uh, a reader?'

What?

'It's brilliant. You're, like, a legend. Reading about your dates inspired me, and terrified me, to be honest. But mainly inspired me. Made me realise I *could* go it alone.'

I tried to keep my cool. 'How long have you been reading?' Had he seen the blog that I'd written all about him? Was he about to list all the inconsistencies and minor fibs? He eyed me over the top of his glass. 'A *while*. It doesn't bother me.'

I dared myself to exhale, and ignored the fact this didn't give me any indication. 'Good.'

'But why did you tell me? I assume you don't blab this to just anyone?'

'Because it's important to be honest. Now we're getting to know each other.'

Finn raised his eyebrow. Again. He knew how good he looked doing that. Rotten bastard. 'Well, I'll drink to that.'

And we certainly did drink to that, over and over until my blinking slowed and focusing was hard. While Finn was in the loo – 'Don't go escaping through the fire exit' – I texted Bella to let her know what was happening. Despite it being 5 a.m. in Moscow, she replied immediately.

> OMG OMG I am trying to feed the baby and he's ill
> and it is coming out of BOTH ENDS but YES YES
> YES to this news!!! Have a wedding date SET by the
> time I come back to London otherwise I'm going
> to make you marry ME. Or I'll make FINN marry
> me. YEEEEEEEESSSSSSSSSSS.

She signed off with exactly thirty-five aubergine emojis. One for every year of my age. I counted.

As the bar closed up, we stepped into the street and pulled up our collars against the cold, walking a little way round the corner away from the hubbub.

A streetlamp shone above us and we moved just out of reach of its fuzzy orange beam.

I pulled him closer and cleared my throat. I wanted to make sure I got this next line out in one go. 'I'm ready for our first kiss now, by the way.'

Finn laughed and obliged.

It was tempting to wait, to play hard to get, to say, once the kiss was over, 'let's not spoil it' and go home separately, arrange another date, maybe. But I didn't think I'd be able to deal with the anticipation, the excitement. And how long would I have to wait? He'd spent a good while telling me how swamped he was at work, and we'd even drunk to our hangovers at work the next day, clinking the final shot glasses that would be our undoing. I couldn't risk cold feet. I had to go for it, while the scent of him was still on me.

I broke away from him but kept a hold of his hand. 'Do you want to come back to mine?'

Our fingers stayed interlocked right up until I had to release him so I could pull my front door key from my pocket. He didn't let go again until we fell asleep. After.

I woke in the morning just in time to see him slipping his underwear over his backside. I stopped myself saying something cheesy and regrettable. He turned and smiled brightly, sitting on the end of the bed to put his socks on.

'Going so soon?' Desperate. Too keen? No, no such thing. Not anymore. Last night had shown me that. No more games. I didn't spend all these months with the wrong men just to start getting shy when I'd met the right one – especially after all I'd done to put him off before.

''Fraid so. I'm going in a bit late but have stuff to do first.'

I sat up, looking down at myself to make sure my belly wasn't hanging out over the duvet. Nope, all good, it looked fine. Seventy-five out of a hundred, maybe. Not quite Finn's definite ninety-nine, but he had a few years on me. God, the comparing, the endless impostor syndrome with every man I met. I was so excited at the prospect of that fruitless hunt being over, of waking up next to the same body for, well, who knew how many years? For ever, maybe. I was just about to see if I could tempt him back between the sheets with a cup of tea, when he stood up and spoke again.

'So, Romeo, are you going to write about me again?'

My mouth went dry. Maybe he was joking, or trying to catch me out, to make sure I wasn't as big an idiot as I'd claimed to be last night.

'What? Um, noooo, I don't think so. Why would I do that?'

He pulled his shirt over his beautiful head – his smooth, bare flesh disappeared before my eyes. I felt a great sense of loss.

'Aren't you? Why not? Come on, imagine how popular a sequel to your last post would be!'

I didn't write about any man until I was sure I'd never see them again. He knew that. I'd told him so. 'Sequels always have diminishing returns.' I scratched my head. 'Um, why would you want me to do that?'

Finn shrugged, still smiling all the way. 'Well, it's up to you. I don't want to censor you. It's your autobiography, isn't it, like you said. It might be a laugh.' I felt the air get heavy. A laugh? But this was serious. *We* were serious. No? He looked round the room until his eyes settled on the door. 'As a big fan of yours – sorry, of Romeo – I'd take it as a massive compliment.'

A fan. Is that why he'd texted me? The reason he'd dragged me away from a legitimate date? To play a supporting role? I remembered all the lecherous messages I used to get from 'fans' – 'I could really give you something to write about' – and I felt sick. He was just like all the rest. Only interested in Romeo, not me.

He had his coat on now. 'Let's catch up soon.'

Catch up? My ears rang. He was still talking; I suddenly tuned back in. 'Even if you don't write about me again, I'll definitely carry on reading you. I love the column. I've been following all your dating tips now I'm single.'

My head suddenly banged, and it wasn't the tequila. I thought I might cry, so swallowed hard.

He leaned over and kissed me very lightly, expertly snuffing out the candle of last night's fervour.

I tried to speak, but he was leaning on the duvet and crushing my balls. In every way possible.

'You're so cool. I hope your blog gets the happy ending it deserves.'

But I'm not your happy ending, he was saying. Not today, not now, not ever. I was just a tonight, not a forever. He'd wanted to try me out; I was a stepping stone to help him on his voyage of self-discovery. So this was how it felt.

He pulled on his gloves. They were bright red. 'Look, I know plenty of places looking for freelancers if you fancy kicking *Snap!* into the gutter where it belongs, or want Romeo to go fall off a balcony.'

I felt violated. I wanted to tell him to get the fuck out, but my lips felt threaded together, as I watched a sure thing turn into a nothing, and close my bedroom door behind him.

In case you were wondering, yes, my medicine tasted just as sour as you'd expect.

The Edamame Romeo

pre-date rating: 5/10. I didn't really want to go, but he was persistent and I was out of better ideas — and offers
age: That's a very good question
stats: 5'9"; brown eyes; greying hair
where: A pub far too near my flat

A good rule of thumb when browsing profiles is: if someone makes very bold personality claims, they usually mean the opposite.

'No hang-ups, no dramas, I'm just me', for instance means you're about to meet a one-man soap opera, commissioned for all eternity and eighteen hours per episode.

And yet here I am with Hugh, who also tells me he is 'very easy-going'.

If I have to sit in and listen to my fridge's rasping compressor teeter between life and that great big scrapyard in the sky for one more night, I'll lose my mind, so despite my alarm bells, I take Hugh up on his offer. His profile hasn't wowed me, to be honest. A little negative. Blurry photos. But he might have a kind face in person and I need to look into the eyes of another human.

Hugh's eyes are human all right, sludge brown, and hidden behind spectacles with severely smeared lenses. I have a friend who, upon seeing someone else's dirty specs or sunnies, can't help but reach over, yank them off their unfortunate owner's head and give them a spit and polish. She once leaned over to do it to an American tourist and I had to step in and say she hadn't been allowed out for over a decade and was socially inexperienced.

The first thing to come out of Hugh's mouth is a moan that the bar is too busy and we'll never get a seat. I smile wider than a final contraction and effortlessly guide him to the free table I spotted as I walked in.

One nil.

Once we're settled with our drinks – vodka and tonic for him, pint for me – the second thing he says is he forgot to mention a small detail when we'd been messaging. I secretly hope his big announcement is the revelation he has to be somewhere else in twenty minutes. I pull my very best interested face and gesture him to continue.

'I'm not thirty-eight.' His voice as melodic as a cow coughing into a harmonica. 'I'm forty-two.'

'Oh,' I reply. 'Well, no big deal.' Though it kind of is, isn't it? I mean, not three years older than me, but seven.

I go on: 'Why would you knock four years off your age?'

Now I look at him in the pub's jaundiced light, he does look much older than those hazy candid shots suggested. Shaving four years off was quite brave.

He sips his drink. 'It's an old trick to outwit the algorithms. It means I show up in the search results.' He shows no embarrassment. 'Gay men can be very ageist. Nobody searches for people over forty, so I thought I'd improve my chances.'

I doubt age has been the only barrier to Hugh's dating success, but I agree dating can be difficult once you pass the magic age of, well, whatever it happens to be at the moment – usually whichever number I'm two years on the wrong side of.

I'm here by fraud, but it's time to make the best of it; I've still got three-quarters of my drink left, after all. I smile breezily. 'Age doesn't matter anyway. You like who you like.' Hugh could be the same age as me and covered in honey and I'd still be unmoved, though.

'I'm glad you said that,' he mumbles from behind his glass. 'I'm actually forty-four.'

Stone the fucking crows.

'What?'

'I'm actually forty-four.' He begins to blurt it all out. 'I just said forty-two to see your reaction. You seemed OK with it, so I thought I'd tell the truth.'

I search for the words. 'Um, is this the actual truth? Definitely forty-four?'

He thinks, swirling his vodka in its glass. And, then: 'I'm forty-five soon.'

'How soon?'

'Three months ago.'

Christ.

'I don't have a hang-up about my age,' he lies. 'But people judge. It's not fair.'

I agree. 'Aren't you better off being honest and getting it out of the way, or, well, lying a bit longer so the age thing doesn't take over the entire conversation on the first date?'

He arches his eyebrow. 'Do you think it's taken over the first date?'

'Well, what else have we talked about since we arrived?'

'We mentioned how busy it is and how we'd never get a seat.' He gestures around the room. Fucking hell, how is it possible to be having so little fun a mere twelve minutes in?

'That was just you.' I smile. 'It's only a conversation if I reply.'

A waiter – a haircut in a greasy apron – appears and hovers menacingly.

'Do you want to order some food?' he says, plonking two dog-eared, laminated menus on the table.

Without checking whether I want to eat, Hugh orders a curry. This cheers me, in a way. No one in their right mind would expect a snog after being on the business end of a chicken jalfrezi.

But I don't want to have a meal with him. I don't want to do anything with him. If his social skills are this warped, what the hell are his table manners going to be like? Less than impeccable, I imagine. But I don't want to give him the satisfaction of walking out, and I don't want to appear rude by admitting I'd rather have my head torn off by a combine harvester than spend another five minutes here, so I glare at the uninspiring menu while the waiter wriggles awkwardly like he's shoogling a python down his trouser-leg.

I can feel Hugh's smudged specs trained on me, so I select some fried rice and hand the grubby menu back to the waiter.

But he's not going anywhere. 'Any nibbles while you wait?'

Nibbles. Like we'd really want to prolong this absolute disaster. Hugh still has his menu. He points at something. 'Some of those, please.'

I am not let into this secret. I hope he hasn't ordered oysters.

Once the waiter leaves, Hugh leans in. 'So.' Chin on hands. 'Does my age bother you?'

What's the right answer? Am I annoyed he's older, or merely that he lied? Both? I could go into all manner of tirades about being truthful on dates, how important trust is. I could, perhaps, offer him sympathy, acknowledge the shallowness of the gay dating scene, and how we're all too hung up on ageing and increasingly narrow criteria. Alternatively, I could say he's full of shit, that his compulsive lying and advanced years are only part of his problem, and I could micdrop my way out of here, jump on a 176 and be back home in time for *Holby*. But I was brought up better than that. Even though he's been less than scintillating company, I don't want to hurt his feelings.

'Let's talk about something else.' Hugh pushes his spectacles back up his nose.

The waiter returns with a huge black tray, in desperate need of a dishcloth's attention. Here we go, the secret starter. No oysters or champagne or, well, much of anything. Instead, in the very middle of the tray is a tiny dish of edamame. Soya beans. That's the big mystery, the secret ingredient that's going to plug that hole in this Titanic of an evening. I smile politely as the waiter places them on the table with a flourish.

So far this date has been a rollercoaster, with enough sharp turns to give me whiplash. I'm trapped in a runaway car and, now, like the rest of the evening, it's about to hurtle off a cliff.

Hugh was not expecting edamame to look like this. He peers at them with suspicion and concern. I put my hand out to take one. As I do, Hugh suddenly nudges my hand out of the way, grabs two bean pods, and pops one – the whole pod – into his mouth and starts to chew.

Well. What to say?

It's very rare to find a man who will admit that he is wrong. I've been on enough dates to know stepping back and realising you fucked up is hard enough; actually saying it out loud is virtually impossible.

And as for an apology? Not until Satan finally opens that ice rink in Hades.

If only men knew how charming, how attractive it is to admit fault. To say they fudged it, to confess they don't know something, to be willing to learn. It's hot, refreshing. It cancels out bumpy noses, comical voices, belly button-picking, bad music taste and the inability to wear a belt with jeans – it is all-powerful. But men must come to this conclusion themselves – they can't be told. They don't like to be told.

I watch Hugh struggle through his soya beans with the finesse of a snake trying to digest a three-bedroomed house. Maybe I should eat one myself – teach him through demonstration? Minutes crawl by. Silence, except for chewing. And more chewing. Finally, my inner sadist begs for mercy; I can take no more.

'You all right?' I ask.

He nods and smiles. I briefly spy green threads of pod between his teeth.

I point at the dish. 'You're not supposed to eat the pod.'

He stares back, replying just a beat too late. 'I know. I just like it.' He has the good grace to redden at this obvious lie.

I smile sympathetically. 'You don't seem to be getting very far.'

The night isn't irrevocable. It can be saved, despite the ageing weirdness and, well, this. If he spits out the edamame, admits defeat, we could laugh, clink glasses, move on.

Instead, he licks his teeth and swallows the remains of the edamame. Victory at last, a mere hour in the making. His eyes turn hard and expressionless. 'Would you say you were a bit of a know-it-all?'

I laugh nervously. 'Errr, I don't know!' I quip. His stare is impenetrable.

His tongue flicks across his teeth again. 'Cos I think you are.'

Our main courses arrive. I feel like I've been here centuries. I pick at my rice. Hugh devours his curry, like he can't wait to finish it and go. I am thankful. We do not speak at all.

The edamame remains between us; we do not look at it. Or each other.

When he's finished, and I am barely halfway through my food, I catch the waiter's eye – no mean feat with that mass of hair halfway down to his chin – and ask for the bill.

'Oh, I see.' Hugh looks up from his empty plate.

'I knew the age would be a problem. Younger men always know best. Little snowflakes who don't live in the real world.'

There's lots I could say. What's the point? Leave it to some other unfortunate soul to play therapist over the edamame. I don't reply.

The bill arrives and the waiter hands me the card machine and I punch in my PIN. But I pay only half – this is not my treat. Or anyone's. When it's his turn to tap in his numbers, he looks back to me. 'I think you're making a big mistake.'

I push the dish of edamame over to him. 'Here,' I say, in as gentle a voice as I can muster. 'Don't forget to eat your beans.'

Out of sheer spite, he reaches for another pod, puts the whole damn lot in his mouth and chews away. And I don't mind, because I know I won't still be sitting here to see him try to swallow it.

This little snowflake is off into a blizzard of better men. We are done.

post-date rating: –1. Minus mark for that second go at the pod. I mean, come on.

18.

'Soooooooo, Romeo, what we'd be looking for you to do is come into the studio and talk about what it's like to be an anonymous blogger. Little bit to camera, little bit of chat with the presenter, that kind of thing. Sound good?'

I hopped from one foot to another, keeping one eye on the lifts in case they opened suddenly, and the other on Roland's desk in case he noticed I wasn't at mine. I switched the phone to my other ear. 'How would that work? I'm anonymous. I can't be on camera.'

'Riiiiight.' I heard gum-chewing. 'I'm sure we can sort something out. Maybe, uh, something fun, like a paper bag with a little moustache drawn on it or something.'

'A bag? Over my head?' The glamour of celebrity was fading like a cheap T-shirt drying on a clothes line in the midday sun. 'I don't have a moustache anyway.'

The researcher tapped his teeth with his pen. The line crackled in sympathy. 'Yeah. Over your bonce, as it were. And it doesn't matter that you don't have a moustache – bit of an exclusive reveal that you don't have one, thanks for that – the moustache is to signify that you're a man. You are a man, aren't you? Voice threw me a bit there, tee-bee-aitch.'

Wow, it was like being back at school all over again. I pitched my voice a quantum lower. 'Yes. Man. Speaking of my voice, people might recognise it, mightn't they?'

'Um, well, maybe we could give you some helium beforehand.' He laughed. 'Or we could use a distorter or something. I don't really get involved in the production side, to be honest. I just, y'know, make sure you get there.'

I sighed heavily. I saw Roland peering over his partition. 'I'm not going on telly with a bag over my head and talking like Mini-Me or Cher during the verses on "Believe".'

'Sorry, I don't know who that is. What about a mask? Like a really fun one? Maybe a fox, or Princess Fiona from *Shrek*. Whichever you think represents you best.'

'No, I don't think it's for me. No matter how much you pay me.'

The researcher coughed awkwardly. 'Um, well, actually it wouldn't be paid. But think of the exposure!'

The one thing I didn't need. I hung up. TV stardom would have to wait.

I was heading back to my seat when my phone pinged. Nicole.

> I'm in the cafe near your office. You free?

I immediately began trembling. Real life. Dealing with things. It sounded too much like hard work.

> Why aren't you at work?

I sat down and tried to look busy while I waited for her reply.

> Day off, I'm taking Haydn to the dentist. Meet
> us. And don't bring Haydn any sweets, for
> God's sake.

Roland rolled his eyes as I approached his desk.

'Have you done any work today?'

I tried to think pale, ashen, unwell thoughts and hoped they would radiate from my face.

'Do not fucking say to me that you're not well. What's wrong?'

I smiled weakly. 'I can't say.'

Roland rubbed his eyes. 'Jim, we're short-staffed with Alicha on holiday.'

We both looked over at Hurley, who was sitting with his head in his hands, a screen full of Tim Prentice photos.

'Looks like your king of breaking news has got it covered, Ro.'

Small-talk is always hard when you know there is much bigger talk to come. Nicole stirred her cappuccino for the billionth time as we tried to piece together each other's recent history through social media updates we'd seen.

'I see you were back in Derry for your cousin's wedding.'

'Aye. That wedding dress, though ... so plain, and she was far too skinny. It looked like a napkin wrapped round a knife and fork.'

Dead air hung between us, so I told her about Finn.

'I think it was just an infatuation, Jim. Convenient. A good story. Eyes across a crowded room and all that.'

I decided to share the funny story about the researcher and how I'd been asked to be on primetime TV. 'Looks like I'm finally famous.'

Nicole looked unimpressed. 'You'd have got there and there'd have been no mask, you know. And they'd have talked you into doing it without anyway, because ... well, you'd have gone all that way and you wouldn't want to let them down.'

'I wouldn't!'

'You would, Jim. It's in your nature.' She glanced at Haydn. 'Or it used to be. And that would've been it, all over. They don't care about your anonymity as long as you fill the gap in their schedule. Tick a box. Make the show. The only person who cares about it is you.'

That was harsh. But I knew she was right. Nicole had worked in TV a long time. The silence was broken by Haydn noisily opening the bag of Skittles I'd brought him.

'I wanted to give him the sugariest thing I could find.'

Nicole's phone went off. It was Silvie, FaceTiming in. I was relieved. There was safety in numbers. Her initial broad smile dropped for a second when Nicole told her I was there too, but she quickly painted it back on.

'We were just talking about Romeo's fairytale ending,' drawled Nicole, even though we'd been doing no such thing. 'Who do you think it will be?'

Silvie sighed. She was slumped at her desk with a massive hangover. 'It seems to me the blog is stopping you from finding your Romeo, not helping you. And when you do meet someone, you'll never be able to share this with him, in case it scares him off.'

All this crazy stuff that had happened to me, the big search, the weird 'fame' – I'd have to keep it a secret. He'd be a main character in a story he knew nothing about. His very own *Truman Show*.

Nicole chimed in. 'Either that or he'd be a superfan, like your man Finn.'

Silvie breathed hard, a mixture of pity and vodka. 'As long as you've got *One More Romeo* in the back of your mind ... well. It's work, not fun.'

Nicole nodded. 'She's right.'

Silvie started to turn green before my very eyes. 'I need to go. I'm going to throw up.'

I stifled a laugh. 'Where were you last night, anyway?'

Suddenly Silvie looked awkward. Haydn looked up from his drawing. 'Mummy's birthday.'

Nicole gave a weak smile. What? When the hell was Nicole's birthday?

'It's today, Jim.'

I looked back at the screen – Silvie had taken this opportunity to bow out.

'Oh my God, Nic, of course it is. I'm so sorry.' What had I been thinking? And why hadn't I been invited?

'You've been busy,' Nicole shrugged. 'I sent text after text telling you. I even messaged Romeo on Twitter. I know you always check *that* inbox.'

I explained I'd been missing messages, about all the haters, and what happened with Luca. My excuses and apologies turned to dust as soon as I said them. Nicole waved them away.

'I feel we've had this conversation about Romeo, and then you, for most Sundays for the last year. We're not going anywhere. Only thing that's changing is you feel worse and me and Richie feel more useless.' She shook her head and signalled to the waiter for more drinks.

'I've got some bridges to build, I know that. And I am so, so sorry about what happened to Haydn. You know how much I love you lot.'

'I don't give a fuck about you forgetting my birthday, Jim. And Haydn is absolutely fine, despite your totally blasé attitude to his wellbeing.' Right on cue, Haydn jabbed at the tiny scar on his chin and gave me serious puppy-dog eyes. 'No, it's none of that. It's this really gross and weird thing you have of not seeming like you care about anyone. It just isn't you. And I'm a bit pissed off you think you're the only one in the world with problems.'

I started to play with a napkin out of sheer awkwardness. 'I thought you'd been enjoying the drama!'

'You talk about this fame stuff and the trolls and fans and whatever but . . . I mean this isn't a relatable problem. Who fucking cares? A few tube trains' worth of people know who you are. You're not Madonna. You said no to the TV thing today – they'll just get someone else. There is always someone else.'

Sure, my problems were fairly weird and specific to what I did, but that didn't mean they weren't authentic, right?

'OK, I'll level with you,' I said. Nicole eyed me suspiciously. 'For too long I felt ignored, worthless, surplus to my own existence. But now I'm Romeo I don't know what I'm going to be doing in the next ten minutes, let alone the rest of the week, and it's exciting.' I slurped my coffee. 'Romeo is clever! He's interesting! People look forward to seeing what he'll do next – in fact *I'm* one of those people!'

Nicole rubbed her eyes, regretting her earlier candour, maybe. And then it came pouring out. 'It's not that we don't care. But I don't get in until ten at night, most nights. If the kids are still up, they shouldn't be, so I end up shouting at them. The fucking supermums waiting to catch me out at every event – why do children have so many activities by the way? Why do they need social lives all of a sudden? I don't have one. The mums and the dads I meet make it look so easy. Like, I'm a mum by default, because I had kids, but these arseholes are, like, professionals.'

'I had no idea.'

The waiter slammed down two more coffees. 'We talk about it all the time. Your head is somewhere else.' My phone pinged. Nicole's eyes tracked over, but I turned it over without peeking.

'Is parenting really that bad? It can't be, can it? Nobody would ever do it.'

'Imagine worrying about someone else the whole time. And this person is never allowed to find out just how worried you are. You've never had to do that.'

'OK so I'm not a parent, I get it. I'll never understand. Does Richie feel the same?'

Nicole nabbed a handful of Haydn's sweets. He took her biscotti in retaliation. 'Last night Richie said to me that all he wanted to do was go and live in a huge white room with nothing in it. Just a bed. And a TV. No people. No one.'

I laughed but Nicole's face stayed frozen.

'I mean, surely all parents feel the same.'

She snorted. 'But *nobody* says! It's like some secret fucking club, or an endurance test, to see who can crumble first and say "I am shit at this". You think dating bloggers are bad. Holy fuck, try parenting bloggers.'

She sat back in her chair and tipped her head back. Haydn took the opportunity to replace the half-eaten biscotti on her saucer. 'Sid is a teenager soon and all I can think of is he'll be bringing home some stupid babywoman I have to pretend to like for the sake of it and my life becomes a *different* kind of over. *I'm* still a baby. But *I* don't get to act like one.'

I sensed a dig. 'Oh come on! That's not fair.'

Nicole laughed. 'You've been off having this big adventure and all you can do is *moan* about it. You always used to say how you hated famous people banging on about how tough it is to be a celebrity. Physician, heal thyself. You can pretty much stop this now, today, if you want, by never writing another word of the blog.'

'Oi!'

'Well. I love you but come on. And for the record, it's *Jim* who is clever, and *Jim* who is interesting, and I look forward to seeing what *Jim* will do next.'

'OK, point taken. No more dramas brought to your door.'

My phone pinged again.

Nicole picked up the phone and handed it to me. 'Go on, check it.'

I glanced at it quickly, as I saw Nicole's mouth draw in tightly.

But then I had to glance again, and again – in horror, fascination, trepidation and excitement – until the notification blinked off and the screen went dark again. It couldn't be.

'Just fucking read it. It's fine.'

I swiped and clicked slowly, deliberately. Yep, it was him. Just seven words. I put the phone back down. Nicole's eyes searched mine. 'Well?'

I took a deep breath. 'Okaaaaaaay, well. Uh. What would you say if I told you I'd been secretly dating an Olympic triathlete ... and, um, that I wrote about him and ...' Nicole's expression became more aghast with every syllable. 'Yeah, *that* one, the one I wrote about, and anyway so what if I said that, by the looks of things, he just found out about the blog and the Romeo *thing* and now he wants me to go over so he can very possibly kick the shit out of me?'

Nicole tried to speak but no sound came out. I pressed on. 'And what if I said that I'd kind of been in love with him, actually, now I think about it, and I'm kind of hoping when he's finished kicking my head in that he forgives me. And then asks me out again. Would you tell me you didn't want to hear all my dramas then?' Nicole was frozen in time. Her hand was in mid-air, like she had been hexed by a demon halfway to her cup. She slowly opened and closed her mouth again. 'I would say you'd literally do *anything* to get attention back to yourself. And that going over there was a bad idea.'

I gave an awkward thumbs up. 'Oh well! What's one more, eh? I'm going anyway!'

Nicole watched as I buttoned up my coat. 'Look, Jim, one thing to remember: women have got better things to do than wait around for gay men to tell them all their problems, you know.'

'Next time I come see you I won't talk about myself once. Not once. All you.'

Nicole sighed. 'You bastard. You know I'll never let you get through the door without finding out how this goes.'

I kissed Nicole and Haydn goodbye, and grabbed my bag. 'I'm sorry, I really am. I love you. I'll make it up to you.'

'Go. Go make your mistakes.'

'So you think I'm making a mistake?'

Nicole shooed me away. 'Don't ask questions you already know the answers to. Go. Go on.'

Outside, before I put my gloves on, I had to read it one more time, just to be sure. The thrill of seeing his name in my inbox was tempered with the fear the walls were finally caving in on me. Swipe. Tap. Open.

What. Have. You. Done? Get here NOW.

19.

As I travelled over to Nate's flat on the DLR, I gave the infamous blog another once-over. It felt like it was written by another person, in another century altogether. The faux wide-eyed innocence, the slightly smug knowingness made me shiver in embarrassment – but there was still heat. Time hadn't dulled the thrill. It was also much less discreet than I remembered. There were direct quotes, many details left unchanged; I was about as subtle as wearing a wedding dress to a speed-dating night. How could anyone have thought for a second this sophisticated, charming and humble prince had been that awful show-pony Tim Prentice? I guessed people had just wanted to believe it. Surely Curtis wasn't the only one to see through it? Anyway, this data was raw and unedited – he was going to be so mad. I could feel it.

The weird thing, though? I wasn't scared. A bit nervous, yes, but I'd seen Nate mad before. I was more sad. Sad I'd let him down, that now he knew for sure he'd been right about me – about us – all along. He'd trusted the untrustable. When you're a child and you've messed up, you dread the telling-off, but in a way you also can't wait for it to come. You may get a smacked arse, and a slew of eviscerating takedowns – my mum was not to be messed with and I pushed my luck daily – but once it was done, it was *done*. You could move on. The bit in between, the actual shouting match, or the 'talking to' or, worst of all, 'is there a reason you're behaving like this?' was always the most painful part. Explaining yourself. Taking the shame. My life now, however, was this middle part in perpetuity. It never seemed to go away.

I thought back to Finn – he'd *loved* being written about. Vain dog. It still stung that we weren't going any further, but at least I'd got away with my crime. Nate's reaction – whatever it was going to be – was probably the one I really deserved, the one I knew had been coming all along. They would all find out now, wouldn't they? Nate would be the first domino to tip over; one by one every Romeo would seek me out, and message me in fury. I'd spend the rest of my life on trains like this, weighed down by thoughts like this, on my way to make amends, or preparing for war. And yet I didn't quite feel beaten. I was tired, but ready for a fight. I wasn't *over*. This was my autobiography. I had to keep control. Bring it on.

As I left the station, there was a sudden, ominous hailstorm. I took shelter in a doorway while the previously bright and busy street took a battering and totally emptied. Once it was over, the street looked shell-shocked. Sodden awnings dripped pathetically and bedraggled pedestrians shook out their umbrellas, while car drivers got back to tooting impatiently now the spectacle was over. How quickly things could change. The perfect scenario here would be for a giant hailstone to descend and flatten me, but as much as I willed it out of the sky, it didn't happen and before long I was pressing Nate's buzzer. He let me in without a word. With all the enthusiasm of Marie Antoinette being dragged to the guillotine, I rode in what the sales brochure for these grotesque apartments had no doubt called a 'luxury elevator'. Gold buttons. Mood lighting. Was the air scented? Yes. And mirrors everywhere. I didn't need to look in any of them, though – for a change I knew exactly who I was today.

As I was about to rap at the door, it opened and Nate's face appeared. He looked different. It had been a while. Leaner, maybe. Fewer freckles than I remembered. A new, dramatic haircut. He stepped aside and I sauntered in with as much confidence as I could muster. The apartment was as I remembered it: devoid of personality, or clues about how he was. Just as he liked it. I looked around for signs anyone else had been here, but saw only wall to wall, immaculate carpets. No dark corners, and no surprises. My voice cracked as I said my first hello, but that would be last time I'd show vulnerability.

'Have you got anything to drink?'

He wandered off to the kitchen and brought back a stingy measure of whisky. And then he finally said it. 'Hello, James.' His voice. It nearly destroyed me.

There was so much I wanted to know, but this wasn't a catch-up, it was a confessional. I didn't play dumb. 'How long have you known? What I mean is . . . how come you didn't know before now?'

'I never read *anything* gay online, in case my internet history gets out there.' He swept his hand dismissively. 'The press or whatever.' I had forgotten his extreme paranoia and hyper-vigilance of his heterosexuality. It seemed even more toxic and ridiculous to me now, with a few months of distance. 'Someone showed it to me. Wondered if it could be me. I knew straight away it was. And that Romeo was you.'

'*Someone?*'

'Yeah.' He saw my glass was empty and took it from me.

I followed him into the kitchen. 'Are you angry? What was it like reading it back? What did you think of it?'

His whisky measures were bigger this time. 'I vomited, James. It made me feel ill.' Nate glowered at me. 'And I'm not giving you *feedback*, like one of your fans. It was hard to read. To see how absurd my life is.' He glanced aside, blinking away a tear. I'd made an angel cry.

'I'm sorry.'

'It made me feel quite . . . disgusting, I'd say, to know that all the time we were together, you knew you had done that, written all that down, and kept it from me.'

'Another secret to add to our pile,' I sighed, walking back to the lounge. 'It was like a time bomb in my pocket. I couldn't have told you. I didn't want to spoil everything. Can I sit down?' We both lowered ourselves into the opposing sofas in perfect symmetry. 'I got a lot of shit for it, if it makes you feel any better. Creepy messages and haters online. Tim Prentice fans baying for my blood. It went quite badly for me.'

Nate shook his head. 'Pfffft. Not badly enough for you to stop. I read the whole thing. Way back. You still posted about dates while we were together. That's pretty cold. Were you seeing other men?'

I didn't bother explaining that they were old dates rehashed. 'I wasn't even supposed to be seeing *you*!'

Nate stared into his glass. 'How could you do it? And how could you do it to *me*?'

My mouth turned to sand. Only honesty would hydrate it, and I owed Nate that much. 'You've read the rest of the blog. My life isn't that interesting. You were a highlight. I didn't dare hope you'd want to see me again. By the time you did, it was out there.' I paused for a moment, for effect, and stuck a pin in him. 'Unlike you.'

Nate leapt up from his seat, angered. 'This was always the thing with you. You don't get to fucking decide why someone should be in or out of the closet!' he railed. 'For you, it was a breeze, I'm sure.' His eyes were wild; he started to redden. 'You knew what you were getting into with me, and you're sure doing some *great* work with *your* liberation!' he sneered. 'Setting a great example!'

I stood up too, in case things got physical. I mean, he was an Olympic athlete who looked like he'd been raised in a kingdom whose currency was protein shakes and gym memberships, by two parents who were actually a set of dumbbells and a cross-trainer, so he'd probably pulverise me. I didn't want to give him any more of an advantage.

'Oh come on!' I shouted back. 'I had no idea what I was getting into. I thought I could handle it! I wanted to handle it!' I jabbed at him. 'And, by the way, you don't know how hard it was for me, or *anyone* else, to come out. You're in a fucking *bubble*, Nate. Are you telling me that being frightened nobody's going to want to buy your range of *shampoo* is the same as a fifteen-year-old guy who's gonna get chucked out of his family home for being gay?'

Nate looked startled. 'Is that what happened to you?'

I wiped my whisky mouth. I sat down again, exhausted from the effort. To my relief, he did too. 'No, it isn't, but it happens a lot, to men and women with much less to lose than you.'

Nate had his head in his hands.

'Look, Nate, I'm not saying this has been a piece of cake for you … but you will always have a home and you will always have your career. It is not 1955. Companies will be queuing up to throw their pink budgets at you.'

'That's not what this is about.'

I stared blankly at the wall. 'People would be surprised you were gay. And that makes you powerful, desirable. Straight media will lap it up. "The acceptable face of gay." And gay media will make you a god.'

'Like I said, that's not what this is about. I didn't want anyone poking into my life. Tabloids hounding me.'

255

Oh, please. 'I doubt the tabloids would be very interested in you,' I replied, acerbically. 'Not beyond your big reveal, anyway.' He looked almost disappointed. 'You're just an athlete, Nate, not a Hollywood A-lister.'

Nate stared up at the ceiling. 'Well, that's me told. And here was me expecting a humble apology from you.'

I jumped off the sofa and sat on the floor at his feet. I expected him to spring back. He didn't.

'I *am* sorry. I will always, always be sorry I hurt you. And I don't want you to think I'm taking this lightly, what it means for you. But . . . ' I rested my chin on his knee. 'You cut me off in a flash when things started to get real. I can't even imagine why you'd want me anywhere near you now. I'm not sure we're getting anywhere. Or ever will.' I looked down at my empty glass. 'Seriously, this whisky is awful. You're gay – how can you not even have any vodka in the house?'

'Do you feel bad about the others?' Nate slurred, two large vodkas and a family-size bag of popcorn later. 'All those guys?' By now, we were lying on our backs on the carpet, staring up at the ceiling. I closed my eyes and tried to forget how woozy I felt.

'Honestly? I do. I got carried away. Being adored, it's . . . ' I rolled over and leaned on my elbows to look at him. 'It's a bit addictive. I didn't really think about what it would do to anybody else.' This was a lie. I wasn't a sociopath. Nate raised his eyebrows and I corrected myself. 'OK. I did, yeah, I did. But I didn't think hard *enough*.'

Nate clanged my empty glass with his. 'Well, I'll drink to that.'

I had to know. 'You said someone showed you. *Someone*. Who?'

Nate leaned up on his hands. 'Actually, this is why I asked you here. Not to shout at you, believe it or not. I need a favour and

I figure you owe me.' He gave a sheepish grin and I knew what was coming next. I wanted time to stop, a plane to crash into the flat, anything – anything at all that would keep him from saying what he was about to say. 'I've met someone.'

I didn't shout no. I didn't scream. My eyes stayed dry. 'Someone.' Again. 'The same someone?'

'Yeah. Someone special. And ... I'm ready to come out. Tell the world I'm gay.'

This couldn't be happening. Whatever happened to 'I don't think I'll ever be ready'? A few months ago, Nate was barricaded firmly in the closet. Now, his head was full of springtime romance and he was giving up his borderline Masonic secrecy because of this mysterious 'someone'? Why hadn't it been me? Rowing on the lake! Holding hands on the sofa! Shopping for my favourite jam! What had tipped him over, made him see this other person as a someone when we'd had so much together?

His eyes were joyful and glassy at the thought of whoever it was. 'He might not even be the *one*. But he made me realise I can't live a lie anymore. No more silent taxis.'

I wondered how he'd managed that. He must've been very persuasive. The rage and regret burned in my chest. I couldn't say it. It would be throwing away my dignity. I couldn't. No. I had to, though. 'Why him? Not me? Why wasn't I worth coming out for?' Oh, pride. How could you abandon me now?

Nate reached for my hand. 'You taught me so much. But it had to be someone who understood my life, who knew what it meant to me.'

'I knew.'

'Well,' he grimaced. 'The blog would kinda suggest you didn't. It had to be someone my mum and dad could relate to. It was never gonna be—'

I should've told him it didn't matter, bade him to stop. I couldn't resist goading him. 'Never gonna be someone like me?'

Nate took his hand away. 'No. Someone like a celebrity journalist. The very type of guy I'd been hiding all this from. My family don't get fame, and showbusiness. They wouldn't have *got* you.'

I sat up and leaned against the sofa and poured a really large vodka. 'They don't even get *you*, do they?'

Nate joined me. 'They do, actually, now. And ... well, you were right. It didn't matter to them. They're getting over it, slowly.'

I was right. But not right enough. 'You are lucky. And so is your someone. So when are you doing it? And how? When's your big announcement?'

Nate explained that his agent had tried to persuade him to negotiate a huge deal with a magazine. Reclining on soft furnishings in pastel-coloured knitwear, wearing a grin that would stretch from Kansas to Kentucky and flashing his veneers. Perhaps with a dog – his sister had a labradoodle who liked to wear a shiny ruby-red collar and would look great on camera.

'But I don't want to make money out of this,' Nate said, in a childlike voice.

I butted in. 'I told you. You'll make money from it as soon as you open your mouth.'

'Yeah, OK, Mr Media Gay. But I'm not selling my story.' He looked right at me.

I didn't get it. How was he going to pull this off?

He breathed out gently. 'I want *you* to tell it. I want Romeo to write about me again. The real me.'

'What?' I started to tremble.

'Interview me. Reveal everything on *One More Romeo*. Say it was me all along. Let me tell them all who I am. What I am.'

My head was swimming. I tried to stand up but flopped down again on the floor.

'I can't do all this again, Nate. It's so much more than just a few words on the screen. It's life-changing stuff.'

Nate groaned. 'Come oooooooon. It won't be like last time. You can redeem yourself. And you get to write it. Spin it any way you like.'

I felt dizzy. 'Why me?'

Nate leaned on one elbow and looked at me. I melted a little. 'Because, despite everything, I think you know how important it is that I get it right and, weirdly, I trust you to help me make sure I do. And I figure you owe me that much.'

I began to think practically. This could take care of more than a few bills if I pitched it right. I could take this to a national newspaper.

Nate shook his head. 'Nope. That's the catch. You don't profit from it either. Not directly. It has to be a proper sequel. On your blog. If we do it on *One More Romeo* then we both have control, and we're not cashing in.'

I held out my glass for a refill. 'Nate, this is big. Like *really* big. Bigger than me *or* Romeo. Once it comes out who you really are, that we dated, I might be attacked even more.'

As the vodka glugged, Nate smiled. 'It might sound nuts, given that I don't necessarily like you that much right now, but I have faith in you. And I still ... care about you.' The hiss of a tonic bottle opening. 'I'll protect you. I'll never say who you really are. Please just do this for me.'

Tears sprang to my eyes. But it wasn't Nate's protection I wanted. Nor did I deserve it. I took a swig. If this were a romantic comedy, Nate and I would have tender goodbye sex right here on this floor. I checked for cameras. Nope. Not a movie. Still disappointing old real life. 'No.'

'No?' Nate looked hurt.

'No, not that. I mean, yes. I'll do it, of course, if that's what you want. But you can't protect me; I won't need it.'

'What do you mean?'

'It's time to take my punishment. Wrap things up.' I raised my glass for Nate to clink. Bewildered, he complied. The chime rang out. 'If you're coming out, so am I. Let's have a double-reveal. It's time for Romeo to show himself.'

20.

The place was looking tired. How many launches and events had I been to at this sticky-carpeted dump, dripping in faded glamour it never had and rocking upholstery trends that went out of date two years before it opened. The club belonged to the night-time, dark and full of B-list drunks swirling free fizz around their porcelain teeth and grinding to generic dance music. Instead it was lit to NASA specifications – which was playing havoc with the acne and hurriedly applied make-up of half the room – and packed with people barely on their first cocktail all pretending not to notice that the place smelled of paninis and stale beer. Everybody knew the drill: turn up, neck as many free glasses as you can lay your hands on, steer clear of the nibbles unless you knew the chef, and applaud in all the right places until it's time to go home.

I couldn't see anybody I knew so I stood as inconspicuously as I could and checked my messages. Bella had sent her flight times.

> Bring champagne and a huge bag of Seabrook
> crisps to the airport please and do NOT expect me to
> share. xoxoxo

Feeling closure imminent, I'd sent messages to Luca. No reply, despite all my apologies and pleas for him to get back in touch. I looked at the last one. *Read 18.33* was underneath.

I looked up to see Curtis walking in. He gave a desultory stare at the buffet – a sea of beige and carbohydrate – and marched over to me.

'Oh Jim.' Air kiss. 'Can you believe we've trailed all the way to this den of iniquity for *this*? I wouldn't be surprised if we found used condoms or old wraps of cocaine behind every chair.'

'Hello, Curtis.'

'Where are all the tray trolls?' Curtis peered about the room in search of a glass of something carbonated and lethal.

I spied Roland making his entrance with Alicha, the pair of them immediately swooping on the champagne.

'Over there.' I motioned to the food. 'Shouldn't that all be a bit healthier, considering we're in the presence of an Olympic athlete?'

Curtis sighed. 'Well I guess when you train as hard as they do, you can eat what you want.'

'Not partaking?'

Curtis shivered exaggeratedly. 'No I am *not*. You don't know how long the cling film's been off.'

He was in a bad mood and it didn't take long for him to tell me why. He'd been fired yet again. 'I'm always the first to go when the budgets get cut. I'm too expensive.'

That was absolutely not the reason. 'What are you going to do?'

Curtis craned his neck around the room. 'Schmooze like my life depends on it, because it does.'

I felt a jolt at my elbow as someone bumped into me. I spun round to face whoever it was and was stunned into silence when confronted by Toby, the editor of *HIM*. My editor. I was about to say a huge hello but stopped myself just in time – realising he'd have absolutely no idea who I was, even though we spoke over email every week when I handed in my column. He patted my hand and apologised for the shove. 'I'm so sorry, darling, but nothing gets between me and a silver tray of anything teriyaki.' He raised his bright blue eyes skyward. 'Thanks to this horrendous lighting I didn't see you there in your, uh, muted colours. Did I maim you?'

I laughed and assured him I was fine; he nodded serenely before gliding on. He'd know me soon enough, wouldn't he? Everyone would.

Roland and Alicha walked over. I wasn't surprised to see Roland and Curtis knew each other, but I briefly wondered how – and just how *well*.

Suddenly the star of the show himself took his spot on the stage at the front of the room. With his sparkly suit and rictus grin – which looked winched into place – Tim Prentice looked more like a bingo caller than the author of his first autobiography. *Author*. Ha.

Curtis leaned in. 'He must've spent that supposedly huge advance on sequins for that *divine* jacket.' I laughed nervously. I still felt uneasy whenever Tim Prentice was in my eyeline.

Alicha nudged me. 'He wrote this book pretty quickly, didn't he? It's *almost* like he had it ready to go before the big announcement.'

No comment.

'Where's Hurley?'

Alicha grimaced. 'Not coming. Breaking news and all that. He's covering in case anyone dies while we're stuck in here. In fact, I need to chat to you about that.'

'Poor Hurley. And him Tim's biggest fan, too.'

A woman with a big handbag who I recognised from a rival magazine turned round to us and said, 'This is ridiculous. I knew he was gay all along, you know. *Years* ago. We *all* knew.'

Curtis reached for a canapé from a passing waiter – a ball of something hot and greasy, covered in breadcrumbs – and handed it to her. 'This is for you.'

She took it from him and squinted down at it. 'What is it? What's that for?'

'It's your prize,' Curtis whispered viciously. 'You get it for being so clever, so perceptive, and spotting Tim was gay. I hope there's room for it on your CV.'

She scowled and turned to face front.

'Well,' said Curtis breezily. 'I'm definitely sacked now.' The four of us laughed way too loud until other eyes in the room turned to us and gave us the 'shush' face and Tim's speech began.

It was all very beautiful and he said the right things. Nate had told me the real reason Tim had decided to come out was that his sponsors were looking for more 'diverse' spokesmodels and Tim was scared he'd miss the boat if he didn't fess up. I wasn't buying that, though. Rather it looked to me that his secret boy-friend – a scrawny youth with an angular face like the figurehead of a Viking ship, standing just to the left of the stage pretending to be fascinated by what was under his fingernail – clearly wasn't planning on being a secret for ever. And I certainly knew how that felt.

Once Tim's speech wrapped up, Curtis drifted away, and I signalled to Alicha to get networking – I had business to attend to. It was time to tell Roland what I was planning to do. I'd booked the next few days off work to deal with the fallout, but I didn't want him hearing about it second-hand. He wasn't a bad sort, really.

I'd weighed up the pros and cons of what Nicole and Richie called 'exposing myself'. No more anonymity, no more freedom to write what I liked, nowhere to hide, the possibility of being criticised for my looks, my hair – oh God, what if they say horrible things about my beautiful, beautiful hair?!

Was I ready to be potentially *properly* famous and not just anonymously semi-famous to the few people who cared enough to look? Even worse: what if nobody cared at all? I wondered how Roland would feel about it all. I reckoned any actual, proper 'James Brodie did this' fame would be short-lived. And surely it would be good for *Snap!*, because the few people that *were* interested would come to the website to read more stuff I'd written. Just like Hurley and his ridiculous videos. Or so I told myself. I did worry my credibility among Romeo fans might nosedive when they saw I wrote about reality TV stars falling out of taxis. Blogging didn't pay the rent, however, and I was sure most of them were guilty of a quick scroll down *Snap!*'s sidebar of sadness in their lunch break. 'But I have forty zillion followers' wasn't valid currency when it came to paying the bills. That didn't mean I was glad it was ending this way. Sure, I was tired, and had aged considerably in the last year or so, but I'd kind of hoped it would be me calling the shots at the very end. This felt like being dragged into the spotlight rather than stepping confidently onto the stage and having it shine upon me.

Roland showed no emotion while he listened intently to why I was doing it, why my 'mystery sportsman' wanted it to be me, and why he wasn't approaching any of the magazines with the story. I thought Roland might try to convince me not to do it, or at least be excited for me.

'Why aren't you telling him to bring this to us?' I started again to explain Nate's moral position, about not making money off it.

Roland waved this away. 'So? We won't pay him, then. Donate to charity. Orphans. Rhinos. Homeless. Anything. Whatever he's into.'

I shook my head. Roland breathed deeply and closed his eyes. I couldn't read him. Was he angry? Did he get it?

Oh. Angry. Because: 'Fucking hell, James. Do you know what this'll look like when it comes out? You, sitting on this scoop all along? Do you know how hard it is to get a proper exclusive?'

'I know times have been hard.'

'Hard?! Gossip is dead. If those attack dogs on the top floor find out the guy behind Twinky Twonky Tim's coming-out, and now this other guy, whoever the fuck he is, was a reporter sitting *right there* on their very own news desk, they will go nuts. And I'll be fucked because I let it happen. You HAVE to give this to us!' His eyes were wide with anger and he was gripping my arm tight. 'To *me*.'

'I'm sorry, Ro, I promised. It's the right thing to do.'

Roland released me and grabbed another glass of champagne off a passing tray. He didn't get one for me.

'James, if you go ahead and do this, I'll have to let you go.'

No, not this. I needed this job.

He folded his arms. 'Your blog is small, but it's the opposition, and you've been sitting writing it on company time, when you should have been working for us.' He leaned in closer, his voice a low growl. 'Who the *fuck* do you think you are? You're our employee. This story belongs to us.'

Now hang on a minute! I pleaded my case desperately, hoping Roland would change his mind. I was self-employed, a freelancer; they'd never had the budget to give me a proper contract. And I'd gone on every single date in my own time – none of those drinks or half-hearted blowjobs had been claimed back on expenses.

Roland listened to my speech and cracked his knuckles. 'What*ever*. I'm serious, James. Blog this, and I will sack you.'

I struggled to catch my breath. 'Why would you do that?'

'Because, James, you're being entitled and disloyal. As usual.'

266

As usual?! I was about to protest again when I spotted Nate across the room. What the hell was he doing here? Nate certainly knew a lot of gossip about Tim, but did all Olympians hang out together in their spare time? Either way, this was risky, being seen at something so *gay*, so close to his own news about his coming-out, erm, coming out. Maybe he didn't care anymore. He was talking to Tim's boyfriend. Quite closely, actually. Surely that wasn't the someone Nate had been talking about? No. Oh whatever. I didn't know what was down and what was up anymore. He caught my eye and raised his glass.

I felt someone else grip my arm. I was going to be covered in bruises by sundown at this rate. I turned to see Finn, wearing his usual adorable grin. The ghosts of Christmas past, present and future were all turning up at the same time by mistake. In March. 'James! What are YOU doing here?'

I turned to Roland to see he'd huffed off across the room. Back to Finn: 'Everybody has to be somewhere. I'm *journalising*. What about you?'

Finn laughed. 'Oh, I wrote Tim's book. So glad it finally found a publisher. All thanks to you, of course.'

Oh for fuck's sake. 'I should've known he couldn't manage it himself,' I groaned. 'He looks like he wouldn't be able to connect to wifi, let alone write a book.'

Finn raised that bloody eyebrow. 'He's a nice guy. You shouldn't be so judgey.'

'He nearly ruined my life. Nice guy?!'

'He is! And I seem to remember you nearly ruining *his* life first.' Finn chuckled as I scowled back, too tired to protest that I did no such thing. 'Look, what he's good at, he's really good at. Who am I to criticise? And he paid well.'

I would've loved to stay and chat and swap pointless flirtations with someone who not only wasn't interested in me but also had

267

a better job and was considerably better looking – I had a career to go save.

'Look, I'm sorry, I've got a bit of a situation I need to fix. I'll have to go.'

Finn winked. 'No problem. I do want to talk to you about something, though. Can we meet for a chat soon?'

A chat. Like I was short of those.

I shrugged impatiently. 'Oh, Jesus, just text me. You've got the right number *now*.'

Finn gave a sharp intake of breath. 'Oof! The trouble with playing hard to get, Jim, is that people stop chasing eventually.'

I saw Roland and Curtis deep in conversation across the room – the last thing I needed was Curtis getting hold of this story. Before I could reach them, Nate put himself in my way. 'Hello, Romeo.' Why me?

'Ssssh!' My eyes darted around the room in a paranoid frenzy. 'Don't call me that!'

Nate grinned conspiratorially and took a swig of orange juice from the champagne flute in his hand. Bloody sportsmen. 'Why? In a few days *everyone* will know, won't they?'

It was true, they would. I nodded disappointedly and felt ... what was that? A tear in my eye. A tear of mourning for Romeo. Pathetic.

'Look ... ' Nate put his arm round my back, and I saw Roland look over, the vol au vent in his hand halting suddenly en route to his mouth. 'I've been thinking about that.'

I didn't take my eyes off Roland. He carried on staring right at us, his eyes flicking from my face to Nate's hand on my shoulder. I shook it off. 'What about it?'

'I've changed my mind.' Well, great, it was too late for that now. He sensed my breathing getting slightly panicked. 'No, not about me, about coming out, but about you.'

'What do you mean?' I wasn't really concentrating. If looks

268

could kill, Roland would be doing life for double murder right now. I saw him lean over and whisper in Curtis's ear. Shit.

Nate pulled me closer, and smiled. 'How can I bitch about you forcing people out of the closet when it's exactly what I'm doing to you?'

'It's not the same, Nate. That's a . . . a false equivalence.'

He'd clearly never heard that term before. He bit his lip. 'Right, yes, maybe, but I'd feel bad. Plus . . . er, if I'm honest, my agent thinks it would take the shine off me.'

I finally looked away from Roland to glare at Nate. 'Your agent?'

'Yeah, he's mercenary. He saw 12,000 comments under a picture of me in trunks on MailOnline and is using it to negotiate a new swimwear range.'

'Tim won't be happy.'

Nate laughed. 'Fuck Tim.'

I raised an eyebrow. 'Your agent. You were saying?'

'Oh. Yeah. He wants to keep the focus on me. He thinks you should get your own coming-out story, complete your own mission. This is about me, not you.'

'You need a new agent. He sounds like a bastard. But are you sure?'

'I am.'

Was I relieved or disappointed? I was only postponing the inevitable, after all. From the look on Roland's face, I couldn't rely on him to sit on my secret for long. I went to rest my hand on Nate's but remembered where I was and pulled it away. 'Thank you.' This was the reprieve I needed right now. One crisis at a time. I really needed to fix things, so told Nate I'd catch up with him in a minute – killing what he'd considered a big moment, I could tell – and made my way over to Roland. Alicha slid right into my path like she was on rails. Foiled again.

'Jim.'

'Oh, hang on a minute, hun. Roland is threatening to *sack* me if I don't let him reveal who my mystery celebrity blog was about, so I am *kinda* busy.'

Alicha took a few seconds to process the information. 'Right. God. Erm. OK, well this might help you hang on to your job. I know who's been sending you those awful messages. It was someone at work.'

I knew the answer before she even said it. 'Hurley. Of course. How did you find out?'

'Roisin in IT hooked me up.' I raised my eyebrows, and Alicha winked in return. 'We're close personal friends. She's a honey.'

'And breaking company rules.'

'Yeah, but I only asked her because I saw him screen-grabbing something off your Twitter and mailing it off. I just had to be sure.'

Right. This was it. Finally I'd get rid of useless Hurley, and Roland would see who the real villain of the piece was here and hopefully look more kindly upon me as a result. I hugged Alicha and stomped over to Roland.

Curtis scuttled off, blowing me a kiss as he made his exit.

'Roland—'

He waved me away. 'Oh, I'm not interested.'

'I think you will be.' I filled him in on what Hurley had been up to – a breach of company rules, surely.

Roland sighed. 'Do you know, Hurley came to me about you, James, a long, long time ago and told me what you were doing.'

I was gobsmacked. 'What?'

'He told me you were Romeo. He found out when you left yourself logged in one day. You know how obsessed he is with sitting in your chair. He said I should fire you for working on company time. Because I liked you, I didn't.'

'He tried to get me fired?!' I was an idiot. My nemesis had

been hiding in plain sight. He hadn't even been concealing his loathing for me that well. 'But why would he do that to me?'

'You *are* an idiot, James. Why *wouldn't* he? You've never treated him with anything other than disdain or contempt.'

I felt my eyes throb. 'He started it!'

'Are you sure? It's his first job, James. Imagine how it feels to watch you waltz into work hungover every day, saying, "Oh I don't know anything about celebrities," treating his career like it doesn't even matter.'

This wasn't true, was it? He'd been rude to me since the first day, right? And he'd been reporting back to Roland. My heart started to sink.

My voice was small in reply. 'I ... It still doesn't explain why he hated me on sight. It doesn't excuse him doing *this* to me.'

'Well, no, of course not, but really you did all this to *yourself*, internet celebrity, but I was totally willing to defend you because ... I liked the blog, and I figured you would tell me yourself eventually. We've known each other a long time. I care about you.'

I reached for another glass of champagne and knocked it back. 'Oh, really? You care? I've been working for you for nearly four years and you never made me a permanent member of staff, never gave me any responsibility.'

Roland stared back in disbelief. 'You know why, Jim? You know why you got passed over time and time again, despite being the most capable writer on the team?'

I was drunk. It was too early to be drunk. 'Oh, let me guess. Because you wanted to bang me and were too afraid to say?'

The look on Roland's face told me I had lost him for ever. 'No, Jim. No. You flatter yourself. Romeo has gone to your head. Your trouble is, you're good at it, but you're winging it. Imagine how brilliant you *could* be if you took your head out of your arse and stopped thinking you were above everything. You could

271

have had *my* job. Or better. Why do you think we haven't made you permanent?'

I shook my head. Roland continued. 'Because your heart isn't in it. You just don't *deserve* it. Hurley and Alicha are pretty much beginners, but they're worth ten of you. They *want* it, they *breathe* it. You're just phoning it in, day after day, on a very bad line. And now I'm hanging up. There's people who would kill for your job. It's time you stepped aside for them.'

I strained to speak. 'You just said you cared about me.'

'I do. I *did*. Not that you make it very easy. But now you tell me you're coming out all by yourself anyway. And . . . ' he glared over at Nate, who was chatting to Alicha. 'Now I know who for.'

'What do you mean?'

He jerked his head in Nate's direction. 'It's him, isn't it? Nate bastarding Harris. I saw you two were thick as thieves. You fucking him?'

I tried to calm him down. 'Look, OK, it is him, *was* him but—'

'Great,' spat Roland. 'That's all I needed to know.' He reached for his phone.

'What are you doing?'

'Calling Hurley. Thank God there is one man I can rely on.'

'Why?! What has he got to do with it?'

'He's my breaking news star, isn't he? Looks like I've got my exclusive after all.'

'What?!' My chest tightened. 'What do you mean?' I felt like I was trying to put a fire out by squeezing a lime at it.

'I don't need you. Nobody cares about you; it's Harris I want. Now I know what I'm looking for, Hurley can get digging. Someone, some bit of fluff, someone who wouldn't mind lunch at the top of the Shard, will come forward by the end of the day; you know how it works once the whispers are out there.'

I reached for his arm as he walked away. 'You can't!'

272

'I can and I *am*. I'll have someone send your precious pens on to you. Your pass will be deactivated within the hour.'

'Roland! Please.'

Roland put his face right in mine. 'Goodnight, Romeo.'

'What is it? What's wrong?' Nate rushed after me as I stumbled outside. 'Are you ill?'

I started to sway as my breathing quickened. My champagne headache began to travel the length and breadth of my body. Two Olympians in jaunty tracksuits pushed past me to make their way in, shooting Nate a quizzical look.

I caught my breath. 'Are you absolutely sure about going public?'

'Yeah, sure, why?'

'And that I can leave my real name off it?'

'Yep, of course.'

'Then we should get you home and wait for your agent to call.'

'Why?'

I raced out onto the street and flagged a cab, my legs jelly. 'Get in. This is the last silent taxi journey you'll ever have.'

We flopped onto the seats. I wrenched my phone from my pocket – I was way too old to be wearing skinny jeans – and stabbed at the screen, typing furiously.

'What's going on, James? You're freaking me out.'

I looked at the screen one last time, closed my eyes and hit the Publish button. 'It's happening now, right now. It's over. You're out, Nate. You're coming out.'

21.

Adam and I always used to say nostalgia was for the lonely and the loveless. We used to feel a kind of sad, patronising pity for people on social media who harked back to the past. You know the ones: posting old dance tunes, sharing news stories about rough nightclubs in university towns they'd long abandoned, looking back on selfies from decades past – fresh-faced and hopeful, with cut-glass jaw lines and shining eyes, youth's exuberance undimmed by time, reality, cultural redundancy and sexual dysfunction.

'Imagine how bad their life must be going for them in the present that they need to retreat back *there*, back to poverty, Pot Noodles, and wanking,' Adam used to laugh. It seemed blunt and cruel of him at times, but I'd join in, of course, because *we* were all about looking to the future – a future which never actually arrived, as it turned out. 'I wish I could be someone again. Instead of just anyone,' all these lost souls seemed to be saying with every backward-looking post, finding solace in conversations with ghosts. But now, waiting at the airport for Bella, amid tearful reunions, slobbery kisses and cute toddlers getting their hair mussed by overjoyed grandparents, I understood. Now I longed for my own good old days. I didn't yearn for Adam again, or my dishwasher, or my childhood storybooks – I just wanted it to be 'before' again. Before Romeo.

Within seconds of heaving open the door to my flat, Bella threw open her suitcase and unrolled a bottle of premium-grade vodka from layer upon layer of sports socks, a kind of budget matryoshka to keep everything intact during the flight.

'Have you smuggled that in?'

'You can stick to water if you prefer, you virgin.'

She was soon castigating me and dispensing sage advice, but as she opened bottle number two, before the room really started to rock, she turned to me with a very serious face.

'I'm not going to ask you this now, but I will ask you eventually. Two weeks tops. In fact . . . ' she reached for her phone. 'I'm setting an alarm. Two weeks from today, I'm going to ask you.'

The question I dreaded the most. Of course. 'What are you going to do now?'

'And you'd better have an answer.'

I poured the vodka into shot glasses, held my nose and downed the first one, euphoric that I had a whole fourteen days to come up with a plan.

But Bella wasn't done yet. Tired of my ceaseless notifications and the insistent ping of messages, not to mention my distressed face every time one came through, Bella was confiscating my phone.

She grabbed at it, snapping her fingers like pincers as I wavered. 'You can have it back once a day, but you're to stay off social media and only keep in touch with people you actually *know* and have met in real life more than three times. No Seizer, no sexting, no dick pics, no *blogging*, no tweeting, no anything – not even posting pictures of your ultrasound if you find out you're pregnant.' We both guffawed. 'But most of all: No. Internet. Weirdos.'

'So what are we supposed to do for two weeks? I can't just sit here overthinking,' I asked, putting my life in someone else's hands for the first time since ... well, Adam.

Bella lined up more shots. 'Well, for the first time in our lives, one of us is loaded with oligarch millions – that's me, by the way – so I propose we have a fucking ball.'

As I'd predicted, things had calmed down for Romeo pretty quickly. Nate's agent was right to cut me out of the deal – it was Nate they were interested in. He quite quickly became the role model he swore he didn't want to be; I felt a little like a proud parent. The swimming-trunks deal was going through, but he'd turned down all additional endorsements in favour of staying loyal to his core sponsors, and no doubt Tim Prentice was silently fuming that his thunder had been well and truly stolen by someone nicer, fitter and with a slightly more impressive smattering of body hair. These things mattered, apparently. I imagined how his taxi journeys would be from now on: joyous and noisy, maybe packed with snogging, frotting and all kinds of confidences blurted out. He'd been silent so long, his freedom was long overdue. He kept his promise to me, too, which was more than I deserved. All he said when asked about Romeo was that I – sorry, *he* – was 'very, very handsome'. It made me laugh the first time I heard it on daytime TV, but gradually it made me feel a great sense of loss. Occasionally he'd text me, usually after an interview or on his way to training, just the odd 'thank you' or 'I've never felt so free'. One day:

You're my favourite trash journalist. Nx

Sometimes even a drunken:

Miss you Romeo. Nxxx

It wasn't all plain sailing for him – there were accusations on social media, and in boring newspaper columns, that he'd lied about his sexuality to make money from endorsements and calendars. I advised him how to handle it as best I could, reassured him that every coming-out was different and up to the individual how they handled it, and he was fine. The attack dogs retreated eventually, once it became clear that there was overwhelming support for him. Nate's coming-out was an inspiration to others. For better or worse, I had made that happen. Despite everything – being a massive bitch, slating men behind their backs after dates and generally having zero thought or care for anyone's feelings – I'd managed to do some good in the world. Just a little too late for me and him, sadly, but I wished him and the Someone all the best.

Nicole, Richie and Silvie sent me an emoji a day to let me know they were thinking of me, and photos of the Sunday Club roasts I was missing.

> Come back soon. Bring your sanity and your will to live
> with you and we'll do our best to relieve you of both. We
> love you Jimeo.

Alicha's messages were full of crying emojis and 'xoxoxoxoxo', but also genuine empowering advice.

> Make this work for you! You are brilliant. Pay
> those bitches dust. Come on, DADDY, you can do
> it. xoxoxoxoxoxox

A few days into my exile, Bella handed me my phone with an awkward smile. There was a message from Adam.

> Nate Harris, eh? You lucky bastard. Hope you're OK,
> Boo. x

I didn't know how he knew and I thought it best, for my sanity, not to ask. The thaw between us, however tiny, felt good, and I smiled with relief as I replied. It was an act of kindness that had once seemed beyond both of us, but it was good to finally feel we might be able to stand in the same room one day without shooting death rays at each other.

Toby sent me a copy of *HIM*, with Nate on the cover – in those swimming trunks – plus a bottle of champagne and some trashy novels.

> Drink this, read these and everything will seem better. And then write your next column. I still want your weekly wittering and that half a page is still yours if you want it – and so is the other half. Don't keep us waiting, the world wants you.

I wasn't sure whether I should carry on. Online, in my absence, Toby had been rerunning old blogs with added commentary from other gay writers and fans. It was weird to see my work, my life, picked over by people who'd never met me. It amazed and frightened me how passionate they were about it. What would it all mean if it stopped now? Would anyone care?

A few offers of work came in, but most of them wanted to unmask Romeo. 'It would make a great feature, and if it's successful, we can maybe do some more,' they said, but maybe not enough to sell Romeo out. Like Alicha said, I had to make it work. But I was realistic: I knew the longer I stayed hidden, the more opportunities would pass me by. Once being Romeo had protected me; now it felt like a prison and I was languishing in it, even though the cell door was open. Whatever happened next, I needed it to be big. And the rent needed paying.

*

After a week of decadent dining, boozing and lazing in my own personal exile, I had a sudden urge to go out alone. I left Bella snoozing on my now infamous red sofa, and slipped out. I found myself on a bus to Kensington, and somehow sleepwalking my way to my old office, where I'd spent the last four years of my life. I had no phone, nobody knew where I was – a spectre in search of a feast. I scrabbled together some coins to buy a coffee from the miserable guy at the stand outside the office and hovered across the road a while, watching people come and go. The once-familiar revolving doors continued to spin. Knowing I couldn't go in was weird, like I was grieving at the death of an enemy.

I idly wondered what was happening up there. I'd forgotten my watch but guessed it was half-five or so. Everyone would be killing time before the end of their shift – the night-time free-lancers would be sloping to their desks, clutching antibacterial spray to wash the stench and the germs of the day staffers off their keyboards. I'd looked at *Snap!* once since my showdown with Roland, checking up on what they'd managed to dig up about Nate. Amazingly, all his friends and former flames had closed ranks, so there was no scandal to be had. His only 'exclusive' material was cribbed from *One More Romeo*, which meant I got a credit and a link, and lots of their visitors.

I was surprised Roland hadn't outed me – the temptation must have been strong – but it seemed he'd found one last shred of decency. Whatever had spurred him to keep quiet, I knew I couldn't count on it for ever; if times got tougher, as they tended to do, he'd use it. He'd have no choice. Hurley wouldn't stay silent – it wasn't in his nature. Ah, Hurley. I couldn't decide whether I was disappointed to be denied my big moment with him. Huge confrontations never panned out how you imagined, and Hurley definitely had more power than me. For now, anyway. Was this why I was here, to hand over my pound of flesh to him? To look him in the eyes? Or maybe scratch them out?

All of a sudden, like I'd summoned him with my daydreaming, there he was, clomping through the door in a huge pair of trainers, swinging his ID pass, without a care in the world. I felt a rush of unease and I shuddered, shrinking back into a doorway so he wouldn't see. Right behind came Roland, calling after him as he hurriedly threw his scarf round his neck. Hurley stopped and waited for Roland to catch up, and when he did, he kissed him lightly on the mouth, before turning his head in my direction.

What.

The.

Fuck.

Roland's keenness to keep Hurley on, and overlook his ineptitude; Hurley's hysterical reaction every time Roland called me in for a meeting. They'd been *at it* all this time.

I was too stunned to move, but Hurley didn't see me at all, even as he checked out his reflection in the window right next to where I was standing. I buried my face in my scarf, staying rooted to the spot as I watched them leave arm in arm, engrossed in chatter. As they disappeared off down the high street, clouds of their breath in the cold air seemed to rise up in enchantment and spell out 'WE WON'.

I wanted to shout after them, but the frost got my tongue. That was how real life worked.

I was frozen to the bone and my coffee was long cold. I was about to head off when I heard excited footsteps running toward me from the *Snap!* offices.

'Jim! Back to see if it's crumbled to the ground without you? Still here, I'm afraid.'

Curtis. Who else? We brushed cheeks. His was unsettlingly warm against mine. 'What about you, Curtis? Jumping in my grave?'

Curtis gasped lightly, as if burning his finger on a match.

'Oh, you heard then? Well, when you moved on and Roland was looking . . . I couldn't say no.'

I'd heard nothing of the sort but now was no time to argue. We began to walk down Kensington High Street. Curtis patted my back. 'If it makes you feel better, whenever your name is mentioned, Roly goes drip-white, then green, then purple.'

Roly. It all sounded very cosy. 'I assume you know all about it, then.'

Curtis shook his head. 'He won't say what happened between you two. Everyone just assumed it was sexual. It usually is. But if you're asking me whether I know about Romeo, then, yes, I do.'

I nodded slowly. 'OK.'

Curtis pulled his mouth in tight. 'Don't you want to know how I worked it out?!'

I sighed and nudged him lightly. 'Not as much as you want to tell me.' I paused at my bus stop.

'This is me.' Curtis looked furious not to have his little moment. Detectives always love to show everyone how they worked it out, but I had no intention of being Curtis's captive audience while he played Poirot. I hugged him warmly. 'Best of luck with it all, Curtis. I hope you can keep my secret a little while longer.'

'You know me. I'm the soul of discretion.' He pulled away from me and looked at me seriously. 'No hard feelings, I hope, Jim. A job's a job.' He tilted his head to one side like someone comforting a child. 'But what about you? What will you do next?'

I hopped onto the 345. 'By my calculations, I've got another week to work that one out.' I gave him a half-hearted salute. Curtis barely waited for the bus to pull away before he got out his phone and began to type. I wondered if he'd give me that long.

*

Despite Bella's orders, I did sneak a few glances at the internet. I managed to distract her by asking if she fancied making some almond milk – it turned out she missed playing earth mother to her little charge, so she was happy to oblige. I saw the targeted nasty messages and bitchy comments had stopped – Roland exerting his influence over his new lover, I supposed – and now I only had to contend with the more easily digestible, general menaces from all four corners of the internet's dank basement.

The usual: 'delete yr account', 'this is a garbage opinion gyac', 'u carn't write'. Nothing controversial, just the internet being the internet. And the fans stayed with me, even though I hadn't posted a word since Nate's announcement. I managed to read about one message in a hundred, but I made sure I looked at the ones from the people who'd been there since the beginning. All the regulars still left comments, and likes. They *were* friends, I realised, even though I'd never met them. Friends had your back when times got rough, even if they didn't know what you looked like. Luca didn't send me any messages, and never commented, which made me feel sad, but he did like tweets that praised me and even stepped in to defend me a few times. He hadn't forgotten. I wondered if he knew I was watching.

I would spend my brief window with the phone replying to pals, ignoring only one person in particular.

'Look, I don't want to tell you what to do,' said Bella, who was just about to tell me what to do. 'But you need to talk to Finn.'

I spent a lot of time dodging his texts and calls – Bella practically had to sit on her hands to stop herself answering on my behalf. It seemed strange that just a few weeks ago I'd have killed to have him calling me and now I was blanking him.

'He's not the one.'

'Fuck the one. He only wants to meet for a drink.'

'How do you know?'

'Um,' she turned away and pretended to be very busy stirring

282

some pasta. 'I may or may not have read his texts. Please. For me. I looked at his Facebook. Forgive me. He's soooooooo pretty.'

He'd already ordered me a G&T. He must've been there a while; the ice had melted. I tapped the glass to signal my arrival. 'I stopped drinking gin after that awful parody blog took the piss out of my habit of playing with the stirrer.'

Finn chuckled. 'Aw, I loved the Homeo guy. Really captured your essence . . . ' He leapt up and shook my hand. 'Thanks for coming. You're a hard man to get hold of.'

The jokes wrote themselves, but I didn't bite.

We sat, and Finn leaned over the table and cupped his chin in his hands. What a beautiful chin. A dimple in it. Nice hands, too. God, did I ever have a day off?

'So.'

I instinctively moved forward. 'So?' My voice was low.

'I have an opportunity for you.'

Oh. My knees snapped together like a bulldog clip, my imagination buttoned its nightie all the way up to the top. 'Go on.'

He was heading up a huge new project, the British launch of a new online magazine and content juggernaut already doing big business over in the States. I didn't want to dare think he might want to involve me in some way – Finn had a track record of dashing my hopes. I played it icy.

'I've heard of it. I do the quizzes in my break sometimes – well, I used to, when I actually had a job to take a break from. My editor at *HIM* says it's only a magazine if you can roll it up and hit someone over the head with it.'

'Good point. But this is your actual genuine publishing phenomenon. It's making stars of its staff. They've got book deals and TV appearances coming out of every orifice. And I'm heading up the UK launch. It's all mine.'

I smiled. So fucking unusual for beautiful young men to get

a break like this. I looked forward to reading all about it in his autobiography. 'Shall I order some champagne?'

He shifted in his chair. 'You're being dim and kind of unpleasant, James. I don't think for a minute you're as dumb as you're pretending to be right now. I want you, you know that.'

My heart nipped into the express elevator and rocketed right up to my throat for a brief second. I considered undoing that top button. But he was still talking.

'I want you in there, at the beginning, with me.'

He did? 'You do? Why? Why me?'

Finn laughed. 'Seriously. You're a phenomenon all of your own. Romeo is big. He could be bigger. *You* could. I want big names, with talent, and—'

'A big following.'

Finn did gun-fingers at me. Ironically, I hoped.

'Right.'

I played with my stirrer before realising I was a parody of myself. 'I'm not interested in a book deal or being on TV.'

'*Aren't* you? Then you're an idiot, because people are interested in *you*.'

'In Romeo. Not me.'

'Without you, there is no Romeo. Look, James, you win: we spotted you, you got noticed. I mean, isn't that why you told me about the blog that night just after Christmas? You were looking for work, no? That's what we talked about.'

I suddenly felt epically sad. He hadn't got it at all. Just thought I was schmoozing, angling for a job, rather than confessing my sins to start with a clean slate in the hope of it going somewhere.

'This could change your life, James.'

I looked away, my cheeks burning. 'My life has changed quite enough as it is. And I don't want to write about celebrities anymore.'

Finn laughed. 'I wouldn't have you doing that – you weren't

that good at it, to be honest.' Ouch. Come *on*. 'I'm looking for people who are passionate about their work, not someone just clocking on.'

I thought of Alicha – she'd be perfect for this job. The least I could do was rescue her from *Snap!* Finn took her number. 'Great, I'll call her. Tomorrow. But what about you? You've got at least 60,000 people out there wanting to say hello to you. Isn't it time?'

'Sixty thousand people you want reading your website.'

'You're damn fucking right. And when they're there, I want them to be reading your stuff. Your lists, your quizzes, your features, your long reads. The contents of your head, all there. Don't *you* want that? Don't you want to have fun at work?'

Of course I did. But I'd been around long enough to know dreams didn't come true for everyone. Not without chucking a few principles under the bus. And I was scared.

'But I'd have to show myself, right? I wouldn't be Romeo anymore?'

Finn shifted awkwardly in his seat. 'Look, I'll be honest, for this job, the US will want to see someone with status, profile. You can't stay anonymous – you'd have to go public. Isn't this worth it? What will be worth it?'

Finally a question I knew the answer to, after all this time. 'Look, this is amazing . . . fantastic, and I . . . never dreamed . . .' I could hardly believe what I was about to say. 'But this isn't how I said it would end. I promised. I haven't found the last Romeo yet.'

When it became clear he wasn't getting the answer he was looking for tonight, Finn pulled on his sweater. 'Will you at least think about it? I can wait . . . a little. You need to get in there. This doesn't happen every day. And . . . you're not getting any younger.'

I slurped noisily as my straw fruitlessly searched for gin at the bottom of my glass. He laughed.

'You know what I mean. When you're ready not to be Romeo anymore, I want to be the first to know.'

I shook my head. 'I can't promise that, I'm sorry. The last Romeo ... he'll be first. But I'll make sure you're the second.'

It was time. Bella hauled one of the last bottles of vodka out of the freezer, picked a few stray frozen peas off the bottle, lined up two shot glasses alongside two tumblers, and readied ice, limes and tonic water.

We both sat on the floor. Bella tipped a bag of Bombay mix into my least-scratched melamine bowl. 'We live like kings.' We did a shot. And another. I watched as she poured us two large vodka and tonics. It was serious, ceremonial.

I couldn't keep a straight face. 'I love how dramatic we are.'

Bella's solemn expression gave way too. 'I know! I don't even think I was this hysterical when I was a teenager.'

'But back to business.'

Bella composed herself again. 'Yes. So, I've given you some time. But this self-pitying shit isn't very you. It isn't even very *Romeo*. So ... ' We clinked glasses. 'What are you going to do?'

'I am going to be a better friend.'

'Thank fuck.'

'I don't want to stop being Romeo just for a job. It's not about money. It's the principle.' Brave words indeed from someone who'd spent the last few weeks burning through their savings.

'You can't eat principles.' Bella tutted but let me carry on.

'I mean, what about my readers? It has to *mean* something. I can't go back to being myself again.'

Bella put her hand on my shoulder. Freezing cold hands, as usual. 'You are *not* saying no to this opportunity. How can you not get this? There is no "going back to being myself". This is who you are now. It already has *meaning*.'

'But the last Romeo ... '

Bella sighed dramatically and threw her head back against the sofa. Suddenly, from the bottom of Bella's bag, my phone pinged. She scrabbled for it. Glancing at the screen, a hint of a smile on her face.

'Well, here you go, I reckon this is the message you've been waiting for.' She handed me the phone. What was she talking about? I looked down. Bella yawned and stretched out to ruffle my hair. 'But, remember, Jim, the last Romeo isn't out *there* waiting – you've found him. He's right here. Mission accomplished. The least you can do is enjoy it. *Own* it.'

Everything I'd done. The men, the mistakes, the fans, the haters, the writing – they'd all brought me here. I'd changed so much, some of it for the worse, but I'd come out the other side. She was right. Romeo had been the latest in a long line of aliases. Before that, Adam's boyfriend, the guy who never spoke up, or the man who pretended to be something he wasn't because he didn't even know who he was half the time. I'd actually been looking for myself all this time. And, finally, with nowhere else to turn, I was out of all options – except one.

I said it out loud, the revelation feeling natural, obvious. 'It's me.'

Bella handed me another shot. 'At last. His lordship finally gets it. The last Romeo is you, you moron. It's *you*.'

I unlocked my phone and read the message. I began to type.

[Draft]

It feels important to arrive first. I know, I know. Don't think I'm losing my mind. Yes, usually I hang back so I can be sure of making my entrance, but for once I am not trying to impress, or dazzle, or wow – I'm trying on something new. The cloak of humility. It is a tight fit.

The bar is just busy enough. I have never been here before. A thousand new brooms are sweeping clean. The barmaid wrestles with a bottle of ginger ale and the metal top rings out as it hits the bar, but other than that, it's fairly tranquil – just the low hum of conversation. I should be able to hear him when he arrives, and, although the sun is slightly in my eyes, I have a clear view of the door through the crowd. I will not look away, not this time, nor pretend I haven't seen him. I will acknowledge his arrival. Wave, even. Should I wave? No, maybe a nod of the head.

I don't believe in comfort zones, nor coasting along, but this time I'm not at my usual table, not in my cosy shoes. I am starched, formal, not in control. Because today, I have decided – we have decided – is not a date.

Even though I spent a good half-hour on my hair, it is not a date.

I specially selected the trousers I know to be a perfect fit, that hug my arse like it's their firstborn, but it is not a date.

I have spritzed with two different fragrances – deciding the first scent was too heavy and overpowering and that I needed to be a little less 'out there' so scrubbed it off – yet it is not a date.

I went for a run and snuck off to the gym so my T-shirt muscles would pop ever so slightly through my old faithful polo tonight, but this is not a date.

I picked the pub where it all began, but it is not a date.

We are going bowling, and maybe for food, breaking yet another rule, because it is not a date.

Even after I sent the text to say 'Yes' I told myself over and over and over, that it is not a date.

I am done with dates. I am over first impressions. Consigning them to history.

It. Is. Not. A. Date. It is about getting this right.

I should have written it on my arm to remind myself, or the inside of my eyelids. It is ringing in my ears when he arrives, exactly three minutes late – he is a regular reader, after all.

Here he is. He looks different. Not good different or bad different. Just different.

I forget I'd decided to nod, and try to wave, but it ends up a salute. That's OK, though, because it's … yeah, exactly, you get the picture.

He walks toward me and extends his hand. His handshake is just firm enough, his hands soft. Nails immaculately trimmed, I notice, even though I've never picked up on this before, ever, with anyone. But tonight I do. I am taking everything in. It's almost like I know I'll never forget this.

'Hello, Romeo,' he says, smiling. His voice is calm, reassuring. 'It's good to see you.'

I lean in to give him a welcoming kiss on the cheek and remind myself it isn't a date, it really isn't.

'No,' I begin, but my voice cracks, so I pull back and start again, fully taking in Luca's bright, handsome face, making this a moment. 'No, not quite. Romeo couldn't make it tonight.' The smile. 'I'm James. Hello.'

[Publish?]

Acknowledgements

This is even weirder than I thought it would be. At the back of a book that I've actually written, saying my thank-yous like I've just been handed the keys to the city for my services to local pantomime.

I owe many people my thanks for getting to where we are right now. I hope I haven't forgotten anyone. If I have, it means you're my favourite.

I'll kick off with Dominic Wakeford at Little, Brown, for sending me the email I think I'd been waiting for all my life. 'Have you ever thought of writing a novel?' He has never stopped believing in me and the book, and has been kind, patient and brimming with enthusiasm – and an insightful editor who lived the story as much as I did. I really couldn't have done it without you. And thank you to everyone at Little, Brown who's been involved in making this happen. Huge thanks to my agent Becky Thomas at Johnson & Alcock for being as excited about this book as I was and just getting it, and me, instantly; I can't wait to see what we do next! Thanks also to Sophie Hutton-Squire for making it all make sense.

To my mum, Carol, who over the years has perfectly balanced

parental interest with just letting me get on with it. She's never intrusive, but always supportive, and trusted my judgement.

To my dad, Austin, and step-mum Louise, whose support has also been crucial and rock-solid. Dad is a big fan of my work, not just because he feels he should be, and it means a lot.

To my sister Sophy, for lending me one of her names for a brilliant character, and being an undisputed sass queen.

To my partner Paul Lang for his love, patience and support; I know my, errrr, shall we say idiosyncrasies, haven't been easy to live with at the best of times, especially during the writing of *The Last Romeo*.

To Ian Nicholson, for being great and kind, and nothing like the horrible ex in this book. It meant I really had to stretch my imagination, and gave me new places to go.

To the special friends, my most vocal cheerleaders who let me pinch tiny pieces of them, and our conversations: my very best friend Catherine Riordan for over twenty-five years of love, fun, and pinge; the Sunday Club massive, Nichola and Neil Richardson, the boys Luke and Zach, and Claire Tomassini, for two decades of laughing and smut; and Kim Falconer for always leading me astray just when I needed it the most.

To Ilana Fox for ceaseless encouragement and being responsible for so many of my breaks. Jack Dooley, for his brilliant mind. Lily and Mark McIvor, for being such dear, dear, dear, dear friends. Charlotte Andris, for all the coaching and wisdom in the Hoi Polloi. Rob Copsey, for listening in the hospital canteen, and Liv Moss for being a concerned pal when I got dangerously thin. Darren Scott for all the hats, gloves and shoes. Hilary Galloway for all that work way out east and reintroducing me to school dinners. Francesca Serra for always laughing at my snark. Mr Tennant and Mrs St Ruth for being such wonderful teachers.

And also to my brother Sam, my cousin Joanne Birbeck, my Auntie Hilary, Mary Lang, Trevor and Jean Nicholson, Tim

Stileman, Debbie Flatley and Patrick Lappin, Laura Stokes, Daniel Scroggins, Mel Jarron and Dominic Ibbotson for giving it laldy, Neil Saunders and Robbie Williams (no not that one – but *maybe* it's that one), Stephen and Rowan McLeod, Manuel Chacon, the warmest woman in media Olivia McLearon, Christie and Glen Staunton, Lauren Kreisler and Jack White, Conrad Quilty-Harper, Matthew Jones, Becky Lucas and all at *GQ*, Sean Rowley, Martin Doyle, Adam Kay, May Fang, Laura Davis and International Business Times, Melissa Denes and Ruth Lewy at *Guardian Weekend*, Padraig Reidy and Caroline Christie at *Little Atoms*, Hester and Nic Stefanuti, Dan Williamson, Benoît Aublé, Athanasia Price, Hayley Rogers, Emily Jordan, Morwenna Ferrier, Mark Wood and Duckie, Marina O'Loughlin, Roz Wilkinson, Alice Beverton-Palmer, Jaimie Horne and every motherfucking last one of you who said I should do this.

Nearly at the end now, don't panic: to everyone on social media who has read me, talked to me, encouraged me and debated with me – on Twitter, especially. Twitter gets a bashing from those who either don't understand it or wish they didn't understand it quite so well, but it changed my life, bringing some wonderful people into it, and I will never, ever grow tired of talking to you – and clicking on your threads. A thousand thank-yous. I could not, and would not, have done it without you.

And to everyone who's read this book – thank you for making a dream come true.

Afterword

We're never truly ourselves, are we? No matter how much we claim, 'this is the real me', we can't always be sure, we all fake it at some point.

Compare your behaviour down the pub against having tea with your gran and, unless you have no filter or sense of decorum, you'll play a role in at least one of those scenarios. We're shapeshifters, different versions of ourselves adapting to whoever we're with.

As a shameless play-actor and assimilator myself – I never give my real name in Starbucks and I've learned how to read a room, finally – this usually harmless duplicity fascinates me, and that's why it's one of the predominant themes of *The Last Romeo*. I wanted Jim to be quite oblivious to this too – he assumes Romeo is the other side of his coin, but he's a tiny dot on the side of a dodecahedron. At work, Jim thinks himself super-efficient, gets sassy with Roland, and is cutting and dismissive with Hurley. He's anxious to keep Alicha onside, however, so acts avuncular and out of touch, while also regressing to his youth to match hers. With Adam, he spend years in subservience, and Nate has him playing a calm, romantic, idealistic version of himself, all the while trying to control his internal fears he'll be unmasked as Romeo and the relationship will implode. He's a clever guy, but his only admission he's changing comes when he notices Romeo 'allows' him to do things he wouldn't normally do – following someone into a changing room on the promise of a phone number to name one – but as he realises much later, Romeo is the latest in a long line of disguises.

We're all more conscious of the duality of our daily lives thanks to social media – few present online as they are in real life. We're all complicit too: we know those beaming couples on sun-kissed beaches can't possibly be happy 24/7, but we buy into it, encourage them. It's a comfort. Plus, we can slate them behind their back. To Romeo's readers, he lives a thrilling life: dashing to dates, boozing, kissing and telling. James's real life, however, is routine and lonely, aside from his friends – although you may notice most of his socialising is done at birthday parties and other planned events, rather than casual catchups, adding fuel to James's suspicion that he's 'out of sight, out of mind' and everyone is too busy for him. His only thrill, then, is the validation of those who assume he's much more exciting than he actually is.

Years ago, when I started my own dating blog, while I was always honest about what happened, I'd leave out certain thoughts and feelings, and I declined to meet anyone who followed me, because I knew the fantasy was much more compelling than the reality; I'd spoil it if I gave too much away. While some parts of the book are based on real-life events – I must stress Adam is a gruesome invention; my own ex-boyfriend is much, much nicer – James and I are not particularly alike, but I did feed this looming uncertainty into his character. What really frightens him about being exposed? The attention? His dates finding out? No, his real fear is once fans get a look at him, hear him talk, and attach a live human to the words, his power and popularity would be diminished. He'd be just some guy. Basic, even. At the end, when James works out what his search for his Last Romeo has all been about, he acts like now he can truly be himself. We know different, of course: we're all in a permanent state of evolution, every experience altering us irrevocably; with each blink of the eye, we're someone else all over again. Perhaps we should settle for that rather than trying to 'find ourselves' – the truth lives far away at the end of a rainbow.

Book Group Questions

1) What was your favourite part of *The Last Romeo*, and why?

2) If you were James's best friend, what advice would you have given him? What could he have done differently?

3) Which character did you most identify with, and why?

4) Who would you like to see play James/Bella/Luca/Nate in a future screen adaptation?

5) Where do you think the main characters will be in five years' time?

6) Have you ever shared anything online that you regretted?

7) In your opinion, has internet dating made finding love easier or harder, and why?

8) Is internet anonymity a blessing or a curse?

9) Do you think there's a difference between online/IRL friendships?

10) Imagine you're writing an online dating profile – describe yourself in three words.